THE GIRL FROM VENICE

A heart-breaking page-turner, based on
actual events in Italy during World War II

SIOBHAN DAIKO

ASOLANDO BOOKS

Published by ASOLANDO BOOKS
First Edition 2021
The English used in this publication follows the spelling and idiomatic
conventions of the United Kingdom.
The moral right of the author has been asserted.

All enquiries to asolandobooks@gmail.com
Edited by John Hudspith
Content editing by Trenda Lundin
Cover design by J D Smith
Photo of girl on cover by Richard Jenkins Photography
Painting of Venice by Clodagh Norton

Prologue

Lidia, 1938

Lidia drew back her bedroom curtains and opened the shutters. The humid morning air caressed her face, and she tucked a wayward curl of dark brown hair behind her ear. She smoothed her hands over the cool marble windowsill and gazed out across the lagoon. The pearly pink façade of the Doge's Palace shimmered in the early autumn sunshine, its colonnades and balconies bearing witness to the immense power which once resided there.

Her skin prickled and she stepped away from the window. On the fondamenta, the street lining the canal below, two of Mussolini's blackshirts—an armed squad whose job was to bring into line anyone who opposed him —were marching purposefully towards the vaporetto water bus station. It was unusual to see them out on the street like this, and the sight of them set her heart hammering. As far as she knew, the *squadristi* usually kept a low profile, having been warned not to scare the tourists. Tourism was vital to the economy, apparently, and Mussolini had ordered the blackshirts to desist from such practices as openly tying a "troublemaker" to a tree and forcing a litre of castor oil down their throat. Lidia shuddered. Venice boasted few trees, but the blackshirts would find pillars where they secretly carried out this despicable act. She was an ardent anti-Fascist like her sweetheart, Renzo, and her group of university friends; they made it their business to keep tabs on the blackshirts. From a distance. She wouldn't like to get too close to one.

The enticing aroma of coffee brewing filled her nostrils. She made her way down the narrow corridor to the kitchen, a square room at the rear of the palatial apartment. Her papa glanced up from the book he was reading. 'Ready for your first day back?' he asked, adjusting his spectacles on his thin nose.

She helped herself from the moka pot on the stove, then dragged a chair out from under the table. 'I've been looking forward to it for weeks.' *And to seeing more of Renzo.*

She added two teaspoonfuls of sugar to her coffee. The sweet, dark liquid slipped down her throat, and she gave Papa a smile. 'Do you have a lot of patients to visit?' In the mornings, he would make his rounds.

'Too many, *cara mia.* I can't wait for you to be qualified so you can join me in the practice.'

She picked up a piece of bread and spread jam on it. 'Five more years to go. Seems like a lifetime…'

'For you, it does, because you are young. Five years, for me, will pass in a flash.'

After she and Papa had finished their breakfast, she took their dishes to the sink. Rinsing them with hot water, she let her mind wander. How she would have loved her mamma to be here and to see her starting her second year of medicine. Mamma had been an English professor at the university until she lost her battle with cancer six years ago. It was thanks to her that Lidia had learnt to speak fluent English, and it was also thanks to her that she had learnt to value her Jewish heritage. Mamma had enriched their home life with Jewish traditions such as lighting candles on Friday nights, cooking Jewish food and celebrating Jewish holidays. But Lidia and her parents only went to the synagogue for weddings or funerals; they were secular Jews, Italians who celebrated Passover instead of Easter. She swallowed the lump of sadness that had swelled in her throat. She still missed Mamma so much.

She fetched her coat from the cupboard in the hallway and slipped it on. Papa was already opening the front door. They passed their neighbour, Signora Rossi, at the foot of the stairs leading up to the apartments. '*Buongiorno,*' the plump middle-aged woman greeted them, a bag of freshly baked loaves under her arm.

They wished her a good morning in return, then stepped out of their palazzo onto the fondamenta. 'I'll see you this evening, *cara mia,*' Papa said, swinging his physician's bag. 'Enjoy the start of the new term.'

'I will.' She kissed Papa's smooth cheek, inhaling the familiar spicy scent of his aftershave. He was her rock and she loved him unconditionally.

At the Zitelle vaporetto station, they went their separate ways—Lidia taking the waterbus to Zattere, from where she would walk to the university, and Papa heading in the direction of the San Marco district to visit the first of this morning's patients.

Lidia found a seat at the prow, hugging her satchel as the engines went into reverse and the boat pulled away from the pier into the Giudecca Canal. Would Marta get on at the next stop? Marta was her best friend. They'd met at secondary school and had in common their dislike of the cult of Mussolini. Once, they'd been forced to read his biography in class and had sniggered behind their hands when they read about the Duce playing with a lion in its cage at the zoo. Marta's father had told them beforehand that the lion had been toothless.

Soon, the waterbus was tying up at the Redentore stop. Lidia waved as she spotted Marta's fair hair in the crowd of morning commuters. '*Ciao,*' she called out.

Marta jostled to the front of the boat and sat herself down. 'Are you going to be dissecting any more dead bodies this year?' she asked with a grimace.

'No, we leave that to the freshmen,' Lidia grinned. 'I'm looking forward to learning about all the different diseases instead.'

Marta made a gagging sound. 'Rather you than me.' She was studying to be an architect and was far more interested in art than science. 'At least we're both doing something with our brains.' She lowered her voice to a whisper. 'If Mussolini had his way, we'd be wives and mothers by now.'

Lidia glanced at the people sitting close by. It wouldn't be a good idea to give voice to her thoughts in public. She pressed a finger to her lips and winked at her friend.

Fifteen minutes later, she and Marta were strolling arm in arm towards Ca' Foscari. She knew these narrow calli

—what Venetians like her called their pedestrianised streets. She knew the bridges spanning the small canals along the way. She knew the squares, or campi. She knew the dark alleyways, so narrow she could reach out and touch both walls with her outstretched hands. This was her city; she knew it like she knew herself.

Not many universities in the world were housed in a Gothic palace overlooking a waterway as beautiful as Venice's Grand Canal, she marvelled as she and Marta stepped into the courtyard. Her breath caught. There was Renzo, tall and handsome as ever. But what was he doing standing on the steps? He'd mentioned only yesterday that he had an early class in the law faculty and would meet her for lunch in the mensa, the canteen where they always ate during term time.

She unhooked her arm from Marta's. 'I'll go and say *ciao* to Renzo.'

'Run to your *moroso*,' Marta laughed. 'I'll wait for you here…'

But Renzo had seen her and was racing down the steps. They met each other in the centre of the courtyard. Her heart skipped a beat as she took in his serious expression. 'What's wrong?'

He glanced from one end of the patio to the other before his eyes met hers.

Eyes filled with wretchedness.

'All Jews have been expelled from the university,' he said without preamble.

She gasped. 'What do you mean, "expelled from the university"?'

'I went to register, and they shoved a piece of paper at me. There's been a Royal Decree excluding Jews from public office and higher education.' Renzo's deep baritone voice seemed to have gone up an octave.

Lidia shook her head. 'There must be a misunderstanding. They can't do this to us.'

'We're Jews and that's a good enough reason for them.'

She pressed her lips together. 'Well, I still think there has been a mistake. This is Italy, not Germany…'

'We are becoming more like Germany every day.'

'I hope not.' She glanced around for Marta, who must have been wondering why she was lingering.

Marta had already started walking towards them. She came up and touched her hand to Lidia's. 'We'd better go and register,' she said.

'I can't.'

'Whyever not?'

Lidia explained, and Marta's cheeks reddened. 'I'm so sorry. This makes me ashamed to be Italian.'

'Renzo and I are Italians too,' Lidia said. 'There must be something we can do…'

'Be careful, *cara*.' Renzo put his arm around her shoulder. 'People are staring at us.'

'Renzo is right. Don't call attention to yourselves,' Marta advised. 'There are blackshirts posing as students, you know.'

Lidia nodded. She set her jaw, determined not to let the tears of anger and frustration spill from her eyes.

'We'd better go home.' Renzo's hold on her shoulder tightened. 'Let me walk with you to the vaporetto station.'

'I'll catch up with you later, Lidia,' Marta's eyes searched her face. 'After you've told your papa.'

O, Dio, Papa. I wonder if he has heard.

'This will be the final straw for my parents,' Renzo muttered. 'They've been considering leaving Italy for a while now.' He squeezed Lidia's arm. 'I hope you and your father will come with us…'

Her chest tightened. *Leave Venice? Would Papa consider it?* And, more to the point, would she? She loved this city and always felt bereft when she left it.

She spent the rest of the morning moping about the apartment. Renzo phoned her in the afternoon, and they talked for over an hour—trying to devise ways of continuing their studies. Perhaps they could study privately? But the cost of lessons would be prohibitive, and they needed to sit exams to gain qualifications.

At five past six, the sound of a key being turned in the lock alerted her to Papa's arrival. 'How was your day, *cara mia*?' he called out, dropping his physician's bag in the hallway and shrugging off his jacket. 'Did you learn anything new?'

'No, I didn't.' Haltingly, she went on to explain about the Royal Decree.

For a moment, Papa's face darkened. Then, he reimposed his habitual sunny expression. 'I'm sure the situation is only temporary. In a few weeks, the decree will be reversed.'

Papa always looks on the bright side.

'I can't help feeling upset.' Her voice wavered. 'How can Mussolini make the King do this? It's so unfair.'

'There, there.' Papa patted her arm as they went to sit on the sitting room sofa. 'I'm sure it's just a political game on Mussolini's part to cosy up to Hitler.'

She dragged her hands through her hair. 'I don't understand how you can be so calm about it...'

Papa peered over his spectacles. 'There's no point in behaving otherwise.'

He appeared on the verge of adding to his statement when the ring of the telephone interrupted him. He answered the call and Lidia left him to speak to whoever it was—a patient, probably.

In the kitchen, she poured herself a glass of water. Papa's stoic attitude was his way of coping. *You should try and be more like him, Lidia.*

She spun around as Papa came through the door. 'That was Giacomo Zevi on the phone. He and Eva have invited us for dinner.' Papa rubbed his belly. 'Their maid is cooking grilled sea bass with pine nuts and raisins.'

Giacomo and Eva were Renzo's parents. Lidia chewed her lip, remembering what Renzo had said about leaving Venice.

'Isn't it a little late to be going out?'

'We'll take a *motoscafo* to save time,' Papa suggested. 'There's bound to be one at the vaporetto station.'

'Just give me a minute to freshen up,' she sighed.

A sour taste filled her mouth and turned her stomach. How could she be more like Papa? She was about to lose everything she had always imagined to be her future.

In her room, she changed into a clean blouse and

brushed her lips with deep red lipstick. The *fascisti* disapproved of women wearing lipstick, but she was in a defiant mood. After a quick glance in the mirror, she combed out the tangles in her unruly hair.

Papa met her in the hallway and half an hour later they were alighting at the San Toma jetty on the Grand Canal. From there, they walked to the Zevi's apartment in the Calle del Forno.

Giacomo had made his money selling expensive jewellery to tourists in his shop in Saint Mark's Square and the Zevi apartment reflected that wealth. Chandeliers hung from the ceilings and velvet curtains adorned the windows.

Renzo greeted Lidia and Papa at the door and led them through to the dining room. She caught the resignation in Renzo's eyes, and her heart ached for him.

'Let's enjoy our dinner first and then we can discuss the situation afterwards,' Giacomo suggested, pouring everyone a glass of white wine.

Lidia had always liked Renzo's parents. They'd been a part of her life for as long as she could remember. The Jewish community in Venice was small and they and her parents had known each other since they were children, just like she and Renzo had known each other. How could the Zevis even think of moving away from their roots? She hoped against hope that would not happen.

But her hopes were dashed as soon as the meal was over, and everyone went through to the opulent living room.

Eva patted the sofa, and Lidia sat next to her on the plush cushion. Renzo perched himself on the other side, while Papa and Giacomo took the armchairs opposite.

'These racial laws are insulting,' Giacomo came right out and said, making a steeple with his fingers.

Papa nodded. 'I agree, but it will surely be only a temporary annoyance…'

'I disagree.' Giacomo shook his head vehemently. 'All the newspapers now speak with one voice, and that voice is raised against us Jews. The movement has been building steadily for years. A newspaper editorial here, an official memorandum there. It's as if this is all a carefully planned campaign.'

'You are exaggerating, my friend,' Papa huffed out a breath. 'Didn't you and I fight with our countrymen against the Austrians during the Great War? Our military service is proof of our allegiance to Italy.'

'What do you make of the *Manifesto of the Scientists*, Dottor De Angelis?' Renzo asked Papa. The article had been published a month ago in *Il Giornale d'Italia*, saying Italian Jews weren't true Italians, but a foreign race.

'Just propaganda. There is no anti-Semitism in Italy— even the Duce says so.' Papa wagged his finger. 'We are a small minority, deeply integrated into Italian culture and society. We've been here since Roman times. It isn't like elsewhere in Europe. Mussolini himself has criticised the racism of Nazi Germany. He once had a Jewish mistress, didn't he?'

'Then why has he made the King decree this horrible law?' Lidia tilted her head towards Papa.

'I told you, *cara mia*. Mussolini wants to ally Italy with Germany. This is all for show and won't lead to anything.'

'You have too much faith in the regime,' Eva inter-jected. 'Giacomo and I have been thinking of moving to

Switzerland for months now. We've had an offer for the business. What happened today made us decide the time has come for us to accept it and depart.'

Lidia slumped into her seat. She knew what Giacomo would say next, and, sure enough, he said it. 'Why don't you and Lidia come with us? We'll help you settle until you can set up a new practice in Lugano.'

Papa stiffened. 'Thank you, but I couldn't accept your charity. Besides, I won't leave. Lidia and I have done nothing wrong. Our life is here. My patients need me, and Lidia has her studies to think about. Things will get back to normal soon enough.'

Normal? How could life ever be normal without Renzo? Lidia twisted her fingers in her lap. She remembered their first kiss. They'd only been six years old at the time, walking through Piazza San Marco behind Renzo's English nanny. He'd taken her hand and had pecked her on the cheek. 'Will you be my *morosa?*' he'd asked. Her heart had filled with happiness and she'd agreed to be his sweetheart. They'd been inseparable ever since.

But, if he genuinely loved me, he would move heaven and earth to stay in Venice.

The thought had come unbidden, and try as she did to suppress it, the notion gained force as the evening wore on and the arguments between Papa and the Zevis became mere background noise to the sickening feeling of dismay that had invaded her soul.

Chapter 1

Charlotte, 2010

I hefted the bag of exercise books through the open doors of the lift and dragged them down the hallway to my apartment. With a sigh, I retrieved the keys from my handbag. Another day over at Tower High. Another day battling the indiscipline of the kids. Another day wading through ridiculous amounts of paperwork. I yawned, so tired I could have fallen asleep on my feet.

I staggered into the open-plan living area, dropped the bag on the sofa, and kicked off my heels. I'd been struggling with my marking, because of visiting Gran in the hospice every afternoon for the past month. *Dear Gran.* My heart grew heavy with sadness. She'd always been there for me, ever since I'd started boarding school at the age of eleven.

I'd suffered from terrible homesickness when I'd first

arrived in the UK after growing up a pampered expatriate kid in Hong Kong. My long weekends and short holidays from school in Herefordshire spent with Gran had been a welcome respite from missing my old friends and had forged a strong bond between us. A bond that had grown when I'd moved to London after qualifying as a history teacher. Gran had been widowed shortly before I'd arrived in England, and I hoped I'd helped her through the grieving as much as she'd helped me settle into my new circumstances. I dug for a tissue in my pocket and wiped at my eyes. Gran was dying, and I didn't know how I would cope without her. Ninety-one was a good age, but the pancreatic cancer had snuck up on her, dooming her before she had any inkling something was wrong. Why should she have to suffer? *Life could be so unfair.*

I made myself a cup of tea, then changed out of my work clothes into a pair of jeans and a jumper. I was used to coming home to an empty flat. Even when Gary had lived here with me, I would always be back before him. What I wasn't used to, though, was the loneliness of the nights without him. I'd kicked him out after discovering he'd had a one-night stand with my best friend Mel, while I'd been on a school trip to the Normandy landing beaches during half term. The earring left on the bedside table, such a cliché—I'd recognised the pearl studs immediately as I'd given them to Mel on her last birthday.

It was Gran's shoulder I'd cried on. Boarding school had distanced me from my parents — not that we were ever close. They led an active social life in Hong Kong, where Dad was a bigshot in the Far East Bank, and the evenings when they would abandon me at home with our Filipino maids stood out more in my memory than any time spent together as a family. Gran's death would be hard to bear. *So very hard.*

I stared at the bag of books on the sofa. *I'd better deal with them.* On a long exhale, I carried them to the desk in the corner of the room. Last night, when I'd visited Gran, she'd been heavily sedated and had slept most of the time. I divided the pile into two and put half back in the bag. I'd take it with me to the hospice; Gran would probably still be out for the count.

The O2 Arena across the Thames filled the periphery of my vision as I stepped onto the pavement outside the block of flats. A strong breeze whipped a strand of dark brown hair across my face; I took an elastic band from my pocket and tied my unruly mane into a ponytail. Being blown to bits outdoors was the downside of living here in Docklands so close to the river. Not that I was complaining—the apartment belonged to my parents and I only paid a token rent.

It was a five-minute walk to the DLR station, and I didn't need to wait long for the train. After two changes—one at Canning Town, and the next at Stratford, I arrived at Hackney Central. The hospice was housed in a modern building nearby.

I signed the visitors' book in reception and went up to the ward. The sight of Gran's pale face, white as the pillow on which she was resting, made my chest tighten. *How can my feisty Gran be lying there so still and defenceless?* Only a couple of months ago she'd been hitting the shops with me in Oxford Street and going to the theatre in the West End.

I put down the bag of books, bent and kissed her parchment-dry cheek. Her breathing was slow and even.

With a sigh, I reached for her hand. It lay limp and warm in my palm. 'It's me, Lottie,' I whispered. *Could she hear me through the morphine fuzz?*

There was no response.

Just like yesterday.

The day before, she'd been hallucinating, calling out the word, 'Sant'Illaria'. She'd opened her jaundiced eyes and had fixed them on me. 'We're running out of ammunition,' she'd said as clear as a bell. 'We've got to hide…' Then she'd dropped off to sleep again.

I'd had no idea what she'd been on about. Some film she'd watched, maybe?

A young, male nurse bustled up to check her drip, oxygen levels and heart monitor.

'How is she?' I asked as I drew up a chair.

'As comfortable as can be expected.' He took her temperature and wrote in her notes. 'We've given her extra opiates for the pain.'

After the nurse had left us, I took an exercise book from the sack by my feet and a pen from my handbag.

My Year 9 class's homework, interviewing someone who remembered World War II or researching from the internet, had been completed to varying levels of proficiency. I needed to make suggestions for improvement in practically every book I marked, and it was slow going, especially as I was multitasking, chatting to Gran about my day and filling her in on the latest shenanigans in her favourite TV soap opera, *Coronation Street.* I didn't know if she heard or even understood what I was saying, but it felt right.

The nurse returned. 'Doctor would like a word with you,' he said, giving me a sympathetic glance.

My heart pounded. *Oh, shit...*

Gran's doctor was waiting for me in the family room. Middle-aged with steel-grey hair cut in a severe bob, but her smile was kind and so were her eyes. 'Please, take a seat,' she said.

Her words made my insides quiver, and I swallowed hard.

She sat in the chair facing me. 'You need to prepare yourself, my dear. Your grandmother doesn't have long.' She paused. 'Is there anyone else who should be here?'

'Mum.' She should have come days ago. *What daughter would wait until her mother's dying breath before visiting?* 'I'll ring her right away.'

The doctor left me alone, and I pulled my mobile phone from my pocket. It was the middle of the night in Hong Kong, but Mum had said to call when Gran's death was imminent. I pressed *Mum* in my contacts and waited for her to pick up.

'Lottie?' her voice sounded groggy.

'It's time,' I said, my voice trembling. 'You need to get on the next flight if you want to say goodbye...'

Two days later, Mum and I were sitting next to each other by Gran's bed. My heart was breaking, and I committed every feature of her dear face to memory, counting every breath she took—breaths that were coming slower as the evening wore on. Gran was lying so still, so deathly still, it was if she had already left us.

I sent Mum a quick glance from under my lashes. Stony-faced as usual. She was the archetypal ice maiden. Did passion seethe and boil beneath her frosty exterior, or was it completely absent? Impossible to tell; she'd never once cracked in my presence. How she'd ever melted enough to fall in love with Dad was a mystery to me. Gran had said Mum was her father's daughter and took after Grandad not only in looks but in personality. I barely remembered him... just that he'd been tall, distinguished looking, and always seemed to have his nose in a book.

I tensed.

Gran's breathing had changed.

She inhaled a rasping breath.

Nothing.

My heart pounded.

Then, I gasped with relief. She'd finally exhaled that breath.

But a couple of minutes later, tears blurred my vision and furrowed my cheeks. Gran passed quietly, peacefully, inhaling one more rasping breath, then exhaling and never taking another.

The heart monitor flatlined and beeped, alerting the nurse who approached to check her pulse. He shook his head when he couldn't find one. 'I'm sorry,' he said.

I kissed Gran's forehead, surprised to feel it had already lost its warmth. 'Goodbye, Gran. I love you.' Stepping back, I waited for Mum to do the same. *Surely, she wanted to?*

Except, she simply stood by the side of the bed, looking slightly put out.

It was as if, by dying, Gran was causing her an inconvenience.

Finally, she patted Gran's leg. 'Rest in peace, Mother. If you see Father on the other side, please give him my love.'

I wanted Mum to wrap her arms around me and comfort me so I could comfort her in return. Instead, I followed her out of the ward, my shoulders heaving as I wept.

At the entrance to the hospice, Mum whirled around. 'Stop blubbing. You're making a spectacle of yourself.'

I sniffed and wiped away the snot with the back of my hand. 'Your mother has just died. Don't you care?' I spat the words at her.

'Of course I care.' She gave me an exasperated look. 'I come from a different world to you, that's all. It seems that, after Princess Diana died, no one has any self-control anymore.'

She hailed a passing taxi and we climbed in. 'We'll call your father when we get back to the flat. He'll want to be at the funeral.'

'If he's not too busy.' He was always too busy; he'd been too busy to come to my graduation.

'He was fond of your grandmother and will want to be there, I'm sure.' Mum pursed her lips.

I stared out the window at the London skyline. Hearing Gran being referred to in the past tense had brought a painful lump to my throat.

'I'll start making the arrangements in the morning.' Mum gave a yawn. 'After I've spoken to your father I'll go straight to bed. This jetlag is exhausting.'

'Yeah, whatever,' I said ungraciously. I was already

missing Gran so much. If it had been Mum who'd passed away and not her, Gran would have held me tight as if she'd never wanted to let me go. How could she have produced such a cold daughter? I gave Mum a sidelong glance. The times when I'd seen her and Gran together had been few and far between. Had there been a rift between them? If so, what had caused it? And why had neither of them mentioned it?

I lifted my chin, determined to find out.

Chapter 2

Lidia, 1943

At the desk by the window in her bedroom, Lidia held the pages of Renzo's latest letter up to her nose and tried to identify his once familiar smell. But all she could discern was the scent of ink and paper. Silly of her to expect otherwise. A deep sigh rose from her chest — it had been nearly five years since he'd left for Switzerland with his parents. Five years of writing to him. Five years of missing him. She smoothed the crumpled sheets and closed her eyes, remembering their farewell kisses as they'd said goodbye.

They'd gone for a walk the night before he departed and had found a quiet place under a bridge where they hugged and ran their hands up and down each other's body, as if, by doing so, they could commit the shape of each other to memory. They'd never gone further than those innocent explorations—they'd been so young and fearful of the consequences.

Her heart pined with a recurrent concern. Had Renzo met a girl in Switzerland whose body he was exploring? His letters, at first so full of love and longing for her, were now more about day-to-day life. And, to make matters worse, she hadn't heard from him in over three months.

She blinked open her eyes, trying to picture him. There'd been photographs, in the beginning. Images of him and his parents standing by Lake Lugano. About a year ago he'd sent one of himself on the steps in front of the University of Zurich, looking as tall and handsome as she remembered. Jealousy had burned her insides at the time; he'd been able to continue his studies while hers had been put on hold. And now he'd completed his Bachelor of Law and was studying for his master's degree.

A feeling of hopelessness spread through her. Her dreams of qualifying as a doctor had shattered like broken glass. Not only were there the racial laws to contend with, but also this never-ending war.

Six months after she'd bid Renzo that tearful goodbye, while she was helping Papa as his unofficial assistant on his rounds, Mussolini had annexed Albania, justifying his actions by proclaiming the ethnic affinity of Albanians and Italians. Everyone knew he'd made the move as a reaction to Hitler's annexation of Austria and occupation of Czechoslovakia; Mussolini had wanted to show his strength.

What a relief when, at first, Italy had stayed out of Germany's conflict with Great Britain and France. But, in the spring of 1940, when it had looked as if France was about to fall and the fighting might have been coming to

an end, Mussolini had joined in on Germany's side —
almost certainly hoping for territorial spoils.

She recalled how the Franco-German armistice had cut
short Italy's initial attack on the French Alps in June 1940.
The real war for her country only began that October—
when Mussolini attacked Greece from Albania. It was a
disastrous campaign that obliged the Germans to rescue
the Italian forces and take over Greece themselves.

'Mussolini overstretched Italy by opening multiple
fronts in Africa, the Balkans, Eastern Europe, and the
Mediterranean,' Papa had said, when the decisive second
battle of El-Alamein led to the surrender of our North
African forces four months ago. 'Perhaps all would have
gone well for him, but the entry of the Soviet Union and
the United States into the war put paid to his plans,' Papa
had added.

The worst thing was that a quarter of a million Italian
troops in Russia, sent to help the German invaders, had
suffered untold hardships. The epic winter retreat of the
Alpine division had killed thousands. One of whom was
Signora Rossi's son, Osvaldo, from next door. Lidia would
never forget finding the plump woman, collapsed in her
open doorway last February, screaming her agony with a
telegram in her hand, her husband trying to help her to her
feet while begging her to tell him what had happened.

Lidia had run for Papa, who'd given Signora Rossi a
sedative. They'd helped her to bed and had offered to give
her and Signor Rossi all the support they could manage,
shopping for them, cooking for them, and helping with the
laundry until they were up to managing on their own. That
had been over six months ago, and the middle-aged couple
still barely ate, their grief was so intense. Signora Rossi

was no longer plump and Signor Rossi's hair had turned grey almost overnight.

Last spring Lidia had written a special letter to Renzo, telling him about the strikes all over the north of the country. Huge anti-war demonstrations. She'd also told him she wished she could have marched in one herself. Twenty-two years of fascism. The disastrous alliance with Germany. Five years of being treated like a second-class citizen. To go out and join with thousands of others and shout, 'No more!' would have been wonderful. But she hadn't sent the letter, fearful of the censors. More so since the demonstrators had shut the factories down and had almost certainly helped run Mussolini out of power.

In July, there'd been a series of disturbing events that took place in quick succession. On the tenth, a combined Allied invasion of Sicily and, nine days later, the bombing of Rome. On the twenty-fifth, the King, Victor Emmanuel III, ordered Mussolini's arrest and imprisonment, naming Marshal Pietro Badoglio as Head of the Government. The Allies took Sicily at the end of August and, just a week ago, forces of the British Eighth Army had landed in the "toe" of Italy.

Lidia sighed woefully. The killing would continue now on Italian soil. Countless lives lost because of Hitler and Mussolini. She was relieved, in a way, that Renzo was safe in neutral Switzerland. Although, being Jewish, he wouldn't have been called up to fight for Italy.

She slipped his letter back into its envelope and put it with the others in her bedside table drawer. Perhaps she'd write to him tomorrow and ask why he hadn't replied to her last letter. She glanced at her watch; it was time for the evening news; she always listened to it with Papa. Then

she would go to Marta's to meet up with her and their
group of friends.

Lidia perched on the sofa next to her father, who'd already
turned on the radio and had tuned into the public service
broadcaster. She felt him stiffen beside her as a solemn
voice began to read.

'*The Italian government, recognising the impossibility
of continuing the unequal struggle against an over-
whelming enemy force, in order to avoid further and
graver disasters for the Nation, has sought an armistice
from General Eisenhower, commander-in-chief of the
Anglo-American Allied forces. The request has been
granted. Consequently, all acts of hostility against the
Anglo-American force by Italian forces must cease everywhere. But they may react to possible attacks from any
other source.*'

Papa leapt to his feet. 'It's over. The war is over.' His
voice was jubilant.

'Are you sure?' Lidia asked with hope in her heart.
'Badoglio said our forces may react to possible attacks
from any other source.'

'If we are no longer fighting the British and Americans, who else would attack us?'

She didn't want to put a dampener on his spirits, but
she couldn't help it. 'Hitler will be furious that Italy has
switched sides.'

'We aren't switching sides,' Papa argued. 'We've
simply stopped fighting the Allies.'

'If we aren't fighting the Allies, then we must be fighting the Germans.'

'I disagree, *cara mia.* Spain is neutral in the war. Italy can be as well. The country will no longer be subordinate and subjugated by Nazi Germany.' His smile was wide. 'The racial laws will be repealed. You'll be able to go back to the university.'

Papa was being optimistic as ever. 'I hope so,' she said. *No point in arguing.* She got to her feet. 'Do you mind if I go out for a short while? I'm supposed to be meeting Marta and the others.'

It will be interesting to hear their views on the situation.

'Don't be home too late. Our patient list for tomorrow is as long as my arm. We'll need to make an early start.'

'Of course, Papa.' She kissed his stubbled cheek. 'I promise.'

She left him to tune into *Radio Londra* on the BBC and let herself out of the apartment. She walked along the Fondamenta Croce as far as the rio of the same name, a wide canal which cut across the Island of Giudecca, and where a line of small boats, belonging to residents, were bobbing on the water. Papa had never bothered to have a boat of his own, but Marta's father, Signor Pivetta, was the proud owner of a flat-bottomed rowing boat with an outboard engine. Lidia spotted it under the streetlight, tied to a wooden pole. She gazed at it nostalgically. Marta had learned to navigate the channels of the lagoon and, in the heat of the summer months, before life had changed, Lidia and Renzo would go with her. How they used to enjoy diving into the tepid waters to swim and cool off. She so longed for those days to return. Did she still long for

Renzo to be a part of them, though? She sighed to herself. *He might prefer to stay on in Switzerland when the war comes to an end, anyway.*

She rang the doorbell of the Pivetta family home—a simple two-storey building where Marta lived with her parents and younger sister. Her father, a croupier at the Casino of Venice, and her mother, a primary school teacher, were happy for Marta's friends to meet up in their *salotto* away from prying eyes and blackshirt spies. 'At least we know you are safe with us,' they'd told her.

Marta answered the door and led Lidia through to the lounge. 'Have you heard the news?' Her tone was serious and Lidia's heart sank.

She went up to the group seated around the coffee table in the middle of the room, drinking and smoking. '*Ciao*,' she said, smiling at Angelo, Stefano, Giovanna, and Marisa. Both Angelo and Stefano had managed to avoid conscription into the army due to medical conditions. They were among the few male students left at the university. Giovanna and Marisa were their sweethearts.

They greeted her as she drew up a chair. 'Some wine?' Marta offered, lifting the bottle to pour a glass of red.

'*Grazie*.' Lidia took a sip. 'My father thinks the war has ended.'

Angelo barked out a cynical laugh. 'The armed forces have been ordered to resist attacks from "any other source". That can only mean Germany.'

'Hitler will take the armistice as a personal insult, and he'll make Italy pay,' Stefano added, shaking his head.

'We've heard that the Germans have something like a hundred thousand troops on the peninsula,' Giovanna took a drag from her cigarette and exhaled a puff of smoke.

Women smoking was another thing the *fascisti* frowned upon. 'Kesselring managed to get his men out of Sicily onto the mainland last month.' Giovanna tapped off a coil of ash.

'No matter what *Radio Londra* says, the Allies, by letting our troops and the Germans evacuate, didn't achieve what they'd called a "rout".' Marta pulled a cigarette from the pack on the table and leaned forwards while Stefano lit it.

'*O Dio*,' Lidia groaned. 'I was hoping they'd all go back to Germany.'

'No chance of that.' Angelo swigged from his glass. 'By all accounts, Hitler expected Badoglio to switch sides, and he's sent eight more divisions here since July.'

'*O, Dio,*' Lidia said again, unable to keep the consternation from her tone. 'What will happen now?'

'The SS will arrive in Venice, that's what,' Marisa muttered. 'And they don't mess about pouring castor oil down your throat.' She grimaced. 'They kill you instead.'

Lidia's stomach churned. 'What can we do?'

'Fight back. Either that or become a vassal state of Germany.' Marta glanced at Lidia. 'You and your father should leave. Go to Switzerland. Jews won't be safe here when the Germans come.'

Lidia shook her head. 'I'm Italian like you. I won't be forced from my home.'

Stefano leant across the table and touched his hand to hers. 'We've heard of terrible things going on in German occupied territories,' he said quietly. 'Reports of mass deportations of Jews.'

'To where?' Lidia gasped.

'Labour camps,' Marta said. 'Men, women and children. All ages, healthy or not. Arrested and transported. Their homes and possessions seized.'

'Listen to us, Lidia.' Angelo looked her in the eye. 'You have to convince your father to leave. Once the Germans arrive you might not have another chance.'

'I suppose I could try.'

She rubbed a hand through her hair. She would never convince Papa. Her friends meant well, but they had no idea of his stubbornness and belief that all would be well in the end.

Chapter 3

Charlotte, 2010

Rain sheeted against the window of Gran's kitchen. I was shivering—the weather was cold for early April and the heating had been turned off. Wrapping my arms around myself, I glanced at Mum, who was opening and closing the cupboard doors, her forehead creased in a frown. 'Such a motley collection of crockery,' she tutted. 'It will all have to go to a charity shop.'

'Don't you want to keep anything? I mean, there must be something of sentimental value…'

She shook her head. 'What would I do with it? The Docklands apartment is tiny. And I'm not keen on shipping stuff out to Hong Kong.'

I picked up Gran's favourite mug, the last of a set she'd bought from Marks & Spencer years ago. Sudden sadness brought a lump to my throat—she should have been here with Mum and me. Instead, she was lying in a cold grave in Highgate Cemetery, where we'd laid her to rest next to Grandad only a week ago.

I cradled the mug in my hands. 'I'm going to keep this to remind me of Gran.'

'Please don't keep too much, though,' Mum huffed. 'You know Dad and I prefer the minimalist look.'

'Yeah, I know.' *So minimalist there's barely any personality to it.* 'Maybe I can stay here until we find a buyer?' I'd always loved Gran's house. Okay, it was dated —but there was a warm, homely feel to the place.

Mum threw me a crisp nod. 'Good idea. It will give you time to sort through all her rubbish bit by bit and take it to the dump.'

I made a pleading face. 'Do you really have to fly back to Hong Kong so soon?' She was booked on a flight the next morning. 'It would be nice to have some help…'

She shook her head. 'I need to get back and help your father entertain some important clients from Tokyo.'

'Shame he couldn't have stayed longer too.' Dad had managed to get over for a couple of days. He'd combined his visit with a business trip, of course, and departed shortly after we'd listened to Gran's Will being read in her solicitor's office.

Gran had bequeathed Mum and me a half share each in this property, but probate would take at least nine months, apparently, which meant we couldn't put it on the market yet. Even so, Mum had gone ahead and organised an estate agent's valuation, which happened yesterday. Gran's "imposing and substantial Victorian house in the heart of Islington" was "in need of some modernisation but will make a truly stunning family home when done". My mouth had fallen open when the agent recommended an asking price of 1.9 million pounds. 'You'll be able to buy a flat of your own,' Mum had said.

I'd nodded, too stunned to speak.

'What's the matter?' She'd given me a searching look. 'It's unlike you to be at a loss for words.'

London housing was among the most expensive in the world, and Islington's terraces had become highly sought after. But I'd never imagined Gran's old-fashioned home could be worth so much. 'I'm just surprised,' I'd said.

'We can make a start on some clearing out now if you like.' Mum closed the kitchen cupboard door, jolting me back to the present. 'How about we begin with your grand-mother's room?' She picked up the roll of black bin bags we'd brought with us.

Mum went ahead of me up the stairs, past the reception rooms on the first floor, to the master bedroom on the second. My heart felt heavy as I stepped across the carpet towards the cavernous walnut wardrobe. Gran's favourite scent, lily of the valley, wafted towards me, and I breathed it in while I lifted dress after dress, skirt after skirt, and blouse after blouse off their hangers and into the bags.

Mum, in the meantime, was tackling Gran's chest of drawers. We worked quietly, the two of us, lost in our separate thoughts. For me, there were the memories of my hols here. Gran had always made a point of treating me to something special like a West End play or musical when I was let out of school. I remembered how we'd both loved *Mamma Mia* and had strutted our stuff in the sitting room to *Dancing Queen* on Gran's stereo every day during my half term break the summer I'd turned sixteen. I'd spent most of the time revising for my exams, and I'd welcomed those moments of silliness for light relief.

The sound of Mum inhaling a sharp intake of breath made me drop a woollen cardigan onto the floor. 'What's wrong?'

Her face had turned pale, and she crumpled onto the mattress, holding a photograph in her trembling hands. 'Oh my God,' she blurted.

I rushed to the bed and sat next to her.

She passed me the faded black and white image.

I gasped.

It was as if I was staring at myself so strong was the resemblance between me and the girl in the centre of the picture. The same dark hair, the same heart-shaped face, the same determined expression. Our mouths, with cupid's bow lips, were identical. The girl was standing with a group of other young people in front of the iconic Doge's Palace in Venice.

'That's Gran,' I said in awe. Her hair had been grey when I'd first known her, turning to pure white as the years had passed. Wrinkles furrowed her cheeks and her jawline seemed to have melded into her neck. But there was something about the girl in the photo, the tilt of her head and the curve of her smile that identified her as my grandmother.

'It's the only picture I've seen of her before she came to England. It was tucked into the back of the drawer liner,' Mum's voice wavered.

I touched her arm. 'Must have been strange not seeing any photos of Gran when she was young.'

'Yes, it was…'

'Did you ask her for an explanation?'

'Oh yes. Several times.' Mum sighed. 'To no avail. In the end, she made me feel like a part of myself was missing.'

'What do you mean?' I edged closer.

'I wanted her to tell me where she'd come from. I wanted to know who her parents were. I wanted to know her background to help me understand more about myself.'

I couldn't help gawping at Mum. She was the most self-possessed person I knew. *Or thought I knew.* 'Did you fall out with her over it?'

'Not exactly.' Mum pressed her lips together. 'She simply clammed up and repeated, *the past is in the past, and I want it to remain there.*'

'What about Grandad? I mean, he could have told you about her, surely?'

'All he said was that it was for Mother's mental health that we couldn't talk about it.' Mum took the photo back and stared down at it. 'I should have respected that, but I found it incredibly hard. Father tried to make up for it. He made sure I got to know his parents.' She met my gaze. 'Gramps and Grandy in Herefordshire. Do you remember them?'

'Sort of. They died way before I started boarding school. Didn't we spend a couple of weeks with them in that quaint black and white village when I was about five?'

Mum nodded. 'They were extremely kind to Mother when she and Father were first married. But they, too, wanted to know more about her and found not knowing terribly difficult.'

'Grandad should have trusted you enough to tell you…'

'I don't think it was that. The generational gap between

parents and children was very different when I was growing up. It seems that everyone talks about everything nowadays. In those days, it was normal for adults to keep things from children. Many of us had parents who'd suffered horrible experiences in the war and they preferred to forget all about them.'

As a history teacher, I knew that to be true. It was only recently that a few of those who'd gone through the conflict had started to tell their stories for posterity. I wished Gran had been one of them, but clearly her memories had still been too terrible to relive. Even Granny and Grandpa, my father's parents, never spoke about it.

I stared at the photo again. 'I wonder if she came from Venice?'

Mum breathed out a sigh. 'I have no idea.' She shrugged. 'All I know is that she was Italian, although you'd never have known from her accent.'

I recalled once asking Gran where she'd come from in Italy. An Antonio Carluccio cookery programme had come onto the television. Her face had drained of colour and she'd turned the set off. That was when she'd told me categorically that she didn't want to talk about it. 'I'm British now,' she said. 'My name is Helen not Elena. Please don't ask me again, dear.'

And I hadn't. I'd simply followed her wishes. Maybe it had been easier for me as her granddaughter than it had been for Mum. Except now she'd whetted my curiosity. 'I wonder if there are any more clues lying around this house?'

'Hmm.' Mum's expression grew pensive. 'I doubt it. I think this is a one-off. Something that shouldn't have been there.' She glanced at her watch. 'It's getting late, Lottie, and I have an early flight in the morning.'

Mum had reverted to her usual modus operandi, but I didn't mind. She'd been more forthcoming with me than she'd ever been in the past. 'Let's go back to the flat, then,' I said. 'We can order a takeaway and chill in front of the telly.'

'Sounds like a plan,' she smiled.

Three weeks later, I was up in Gran's attic, sitting cross-legged on the floor and going through a stack of cardboard boxes. Thus far, my searches hadn't revealed anything about her past. All the photos that I'd discovered were of Grandad as a boy and young man and the letters I'd found had been addressed to him. I was going through them now and getting side-tracked by those he'd received from his parents while he'd been stationed in the Middle East during the war. They made interesting reading; his father used to play a long-distance game of chess with him and recorded each move, and his mother wrote about rationing, food shortages, and making clothes from old curtains.

I reached for a sealed brown envelope and opened it carefully.

My heart thudded.

Three letters from Italy—I recognised the postage stamps.

Postmarked Sant'Illaria and dated 1974.

I screwed up my face—I'd heard that name before, but where?

The letters had all been addressed to Grandad, but the envelopes hadn't been opened.

I turned one of them over to see if the sender's name was on it.

Rosina Zalunardi.

Who could she be?

With a gasp, I suddenly remembered where I'd heard the name of the place before. Gran had been calling out *Sant'Illaria* in the hospice during one of her opiate-induced episodes. I pulled my phone from my jeans pocket and tapped the Google icon. After entering the name, I read: "*Sant'Illaria is a municipality in the Veneto region of north-eastern Italy*".

The fact that Gran had been photographed in Venice and Grandad had received letters from someone in the Veneto couldn't be a coincidence. She must have come from there. But why hadn't Grandad opened the letters? *How odd.*

I went down to the kitchen to make a sandwich for my lunch, then pressed Mum's name in my contacts. The call to Hong Kong went through, and I told my mother what I'd discovered.

'Did you open the letters?' she asked.

'I wanted to tell you about them first. What if they're private and contain info Grandad wouldn't want us to know?'

'Strange that he never read them…'

'Even stranger that he didn't throw them away.'

'I suspect they are in Italian and neither you nor I can read, let alone speak, the language.'

I chewed on my lip; an idea forming in my mind. 'How

would you feel about a trip to Venice?' I suggested. 'Or even to Sant'Illaria?'

'Whatever for?'

'Remember you said that part of you was missing? If we went there, we might find out enough to fill in the gaps...'

'It would be a wild goose chase, Lottie.'

'Maybe. Maybe not. We could go during my summer holiday from school. I was saving up for the deposit to buy a flat but now I don't need to. I've more than enough money to pay my way.'

'Oh, darling, I can't.' I heard the regret in her voice. 'Your father and I are off to China. There's a trade fair he needs to attend in Chengdu, and then we've booked to go to Lugu Lake in Yunan for a break to escape the heat.'

Should I go on my own? A daunting thought.

'Maybe I could go on my own,' I came right out with it. 'I've always wanted to visit Italy. I'm a quarter Italian. And I couldn't go when Gran was alive as I didn't want to upset her...'

'On your own?' Her tone was sceptical. 'Shame you broke off with Gary. You used to travel every summer together, didn't you?'

'I'll be fine on my own. In fact, I'd prefer it. Gary always took charge, organizing everything and insisting we stuck to his plans. It'll be liberating to do things my way...'

'Fair enough, darling,' she said. 'I just hope you won't be too disappointed when you don't find out anything.'

'It's worth a try, I think.'

I wished Mum goodnight and went back up to the attic. There was one last box I wanted to check through before calling it a day. I lifted the lid to find a stack of documents. Bank statements. Paid invoices. Even shopping lists. Humming to myself, I rifled through them.

Wow, there was my grandparents' wedding certificate. Dated May 1946. They'd married in Hereford and Gran's maiden name was Moretti. Warmth spread through me at finding another clue. Would there be others? I kept on sifting through the box until my fingers encountered a small book.

There was Hebrew writing on the cover, with the words:

Libro di Preghiere. Ebraico-Italiano.

A Jewish-Italian prayer book! Had Gran been Jewish and suffered for her faith? *Oh, God, I hope not.*

Chapter 4

Lidia, 1943

It was Lidia's day off from helping Papa and she was at the Lido Cinema with Marta. They'd crossed the lagoon in Signor Pivetta's boat so they wouldn't have to ride on the *vaporetto*. Venice was crawling with *Kriegsmarine* naval forces, and she tried to have as little contact with them as possible. Sitting next to a blue uniformed sailor or officer on the water bus would have made her flesh crawl.

Upstairs in the dress circle, she and Marta slipped into the back row—which was thankfully devoid of anyone wearing a German uniform. The house lights dimmed, pulleys swept the red velvet curtains aside, and jaunty music filled the air.

A *Film Luce* newsreel flickered.

Lidia stiffened.

German tanks and armoured cars were rolling into Rome through the Saint Paul's Gate.

She'd heard the news over three weeks ago, but her stomach still tightened—seeing the event played out before her eyes brought home the fact that the Wehrmacht had managed to occupy four-fifths of the country.

She sucked in a quick breath—the newsreel had suddenly switched to a shot of Mussolini. Dressed in a dark topcoat and hat and looking slightly bewildered, he was climbing out of a small plane and shaking Hitler's hand. She hissed along with the rest of the audience. Two weeks ago, *il Duce* had been "rescued" (if you were a Fascist) or "snatched" (if you weren't) by SS troopers from the hotel where he'd been imprisoned on Gran Sasso, a remote plateau in the centre of the Apennine mountains. And now he'd become the principal marionette in a puppet government Berlin had named the Republic of Salò.

The report moved on to Naples in the south. After four days of local insurgency against the Nazi-fascists, the Allies had taken control.

Lidia smiled to herself, but her elation was short lived.

'*Coraggio*, countrymen!' the narrator's voice boomed. 'The Reich has come to embattled Italy's aid! The American Fifth Army and the British 56th Division are held on our defensive line at the Volturno! There will be an all-out defence of Rome! The Gustav Line will hold!' Almost as an afterthought, he concluded, 'The Red Army has retaken Smolensk.'

The audience stirred, murmured, and settled in their seats to watch the featured film, "*Obsession*". Lidia had been looking forward to seeing her favourite actor, Massimo Girotti, in the role of Gino, a vagabond.

She tried to focus on the plot, but thoughts flitted through her mind like moths around a flame.

Two weeks ago, Professor Jona, leader of the Jewish Community, had committed suicide after being asked to hand over to the German authorities a list of Jews living in Venice. She remembered the sick feeling in her belly when Papa had told her. She'd only met the kind man once—he'd worked as a physician at the *Ospedale Civile* and had been nicknamed "the doctor of the poor".

'Do you think they will arrest us?' She'd jammed her hands into her armpits to stop them from trembling. She couldn't imagine why else they'd want hers, Papa's, and the rest of the community's names.

'I am not aware that we've done anything to invite arrest, *cara mia*,' Papa had soothed. 'The King himself says Italy has no more exemplary citizens than the Jews.'

Listening to *Radio Londra* was a forbidden activity, but she'd decided not to remind him of the fact. Instead, she shook her head and said, 'But, Papa, the King himself has fled the Germans. Maybe we should too?'

'And just where do you suggest we go?'

'Marta knows people in The National Liberation Committee. They will help us get to a village in the countryside where we can hide.'

'No need, *cara mia*. The Allies promised the King that they'd send fifteen divisions into Rome alone—that's what I've heard. This war will be over before we know it.'

Papa's optimism knows no bounds.

In the cinema, she closed her eyes to the film on the screen and a different movie played out in her mind. The newsreel narrator had said that the Allies were stalled on the German defensive line. Italy's fortress-like mountains straddled the peninsula from tip to toe, steep and impenetrable. The enemy would almost certainly use them to block a British-American advance. They'd do everything they could not to concede the fertile plains of Northern Italy, which were filled with farms and factories. Food for soldiers and civilians. Fabric for uniforms. Planes, trucks, cars, and manpower.

Hitler is NOT going to give all that up without a fight.

The faint echo of church bells carried across the lagoon as Lidia linked arms with Marta after the film had come to an end. It was getting dark, and they needed to return to Giudecca before the night-time curfew. At the jetty, they skipped down the steps and jumped into Signor Pivetta's boat. Lidia untied the lines and Marta started the outboard engine.

No sooner had they set out on the water when a reverberating sound thrummed in the atmosphere. Lidia's skin tingled, and she lifted her gaze to the sky.

Allied bombers passing overhead.

On their way to rain destruction on the northern cities.

Not Venice, thank God. Her architectural and artistic treasures had spared her from bombardment. *So far.*

Lidia lowered her gaze and her heart hammered. 'Watch out,' she yelled.

A German ship had appeared, it seemed, from nowhere, lights blazing and its decks laden with troops.

Marta pulled the tiller sharp left, barely managing to manoeuvre out of the way.

'*Dio buono.*' She pointed at the men leaning over the railings. 'Those are *our* forces!'

Lidia stared at the white naval uniforms. But why were Italian sailors on a German ship? And, more to the point, where were the *tedeschi* taking them?

The ship was steaming past Lidia and Marta now, heading towards the Adriatic Sea.

Lidia grabbed hold of Marta's arm.

A lone figure had launched itself off the side of the vessel and was making a swan dive into the lagoon.

The figure sliced into the water with barely a splash.

'*O, Dio,*' Lidia whimpered. *Any minute now the Nazi guards will shoot at him.*

'There's a rope in the bottom of the boat.' Marta lowered her voice. 'I'll try and get close and you can throw it.'

Lidia squinted in the dusky light, trying to spot the man.

'He's over there,' Marta indicated with her free hand while turning the tiller with the other.

The massive wake left by the ship made their small vessel pitch and plunge, but they battled through it. Lidia threw the rope. The boat rocked dangerously, threatening to capsize as they heaved the man on board.

Finally, with a grunt, he lay sprawled at Marta's feet. Then he looked up at her and said, 'Am I in Paradise? You are so beautiful you must be an angel.'

Hysterical laughter bubbled up at the back of Lidia's throat. It was the last thing she'd expected him to say— and the most extravagant chat-up line she'd ever heard.

Marta stared down at him. Lidia waited for the usual brushoff from her friend, who was nearing the end of her architecture degree course and so focused on her studies she claimed not to be interested in men. But she simply smiled. 'What's your name?' she inquired gently.

'Giorgio. What's yours?'

Marta told him and fluttered her eyelashes. Giorgio bore a distinct resemblance to the swashbuckling movie star Errol Flynn—she must have noticed. She'd even forgotten to introduce Lidia, so Lidia introduced herself.

The swell of the waves lifted and dropped the small boat. Marta seemed to be at a loss as to what to say next. Lidia leaned towards her and asked, 'What are we going to do with him?'

'We'll take him back to my place and then decide.'

Giorgio had started to shiver in the chill of the late September evening, and his teeth were chattering. Lidia slipped off her coat and wrapped it around his shoulders. 'You'd better keep your head down,' she said. 'Two girls won't attract any attention, but if there's a German patrol out in the canal and they spot you, they'll make a beeline for us.'

Marta's parents said Giorgio could stay the night, but he must leave tomorrow or risk putting the family in danger. They took him upstairs to the attic, gave him dry clothes, some food and a chamber pot, and then left him to his own devices.

Marta went with Lidia to the door. 'I'll send a message to the National Liberation Committee at daybreak,' she said. 'They'll know what to do.'

The Committee was the organisation representing the

Resistance movement, which had come into existence after the armistice, Lidia recalled.

In different circumstances, she would have teased Marta about the way Giorgio was looking at her and the way she'd responded to him, but now was not the time.

'Take care.' Lidia kissed her on both cheeks. 'Shame I have to get home to beat the curfew.'

'Will I see you tomorrow?' Marta asked.

'I'll try…'

Lidia made her way quickly along the fondamenta and let herself into the apartment, calling out, 'Papa I'm home.' She'd decided not to tell him about Giorgio—it wasn't something he needed to be aware of, just like she kept him in the dark about the pamphlets she, Marta, and their friends had recently started clandestinely posting through letter boxes. Leaflets in which they relayed to Venetians the news their group gleaned from *Radio Londra* to counteract the Nazi-fascist propaganda in *Il Gazzettino* and other mainstream papers.

'How was the film?' Papa asked later at dinner, twirling spaghetti onto his fork.

'Not as good as we thought it would be,' she sighed. She debated with herself whether to tell him about the troop ship—leaving out all mention of Giorgio—but thought better of it. Papa was adamant the Allies would defeat the Germans any day now, and, until his hopes had been proved otherwise, she didn't want to cause him any dismay.

They spent the rest of the meal chatting about Papa's patients, after which Lidia went to her room. She gave him the excuse that she wanted to write to Renzo, but her heart wasn't in it. She sat at her desk and gazed at the photo he'd sent her, taken on the steps of Zurich University—she took it out from time to time to remind herself what he looked like.

They'd been apart so long now and she'd kept herself for him the entire time. Her gut instinct told her he'd met someone else, and, although she'd resolved to press him about his silence, if the truth were to be told she no longer cared enough to worry about it.

Her thoughts turned to the man she and Marta had rescued from the lagoon. Who was he and what had made him risk his life by diving off that ship? Those questions and what she'd seen on the newsreel went round and round in her head, making her sleep badly. Papa took one look at her bleary eyes at breakfast and gave her another day off.

Feeling somewhat guilty, she shrugged on her coat as soon as he'd left for his rounds. Within minutes she'd arrived at the Pivettas' front door. She was about to knock when she was joined by Stefano. 'Marisa has taken Marta's message to the Committee,' he said. 'Marta crept out under cover of darkness to see her last night. Marisa phoned me and asked me to meet her here…'

Marta let them in and took them through to the lounge, where Giorgio was sitting at the coffee table.

Stefano took the seat next to him and fixed him with a steely stare. 'How do we know you're not a spy?'

'I swear on my mother's life that I'm not,'

Lidia knew that if an Italian male swore something on his mother's life, then he was probably telling the truth. But how could she be 100 per cent sure?

'Can you explain why you were on that ship?' she asked, pulling up a chair.

'I was with the *Decima Mas*, the Tenth Assault Vehicle

Flotilla, in the commando frogman unit. After the Germans disarmed us, most of my comrades decided to enlist and fight for Mussolini's republic.' Giorgio rubbed a hand across his brow. 'But I refused. I hate the *tedeschi.* That ship was taking me and other dissenters to the south. The bastards said they wanted us to reinforce a defensive line north of Naples to stop the Allied advance on Rome. I would rather die than fight for those miserable, *figli di puttane.* Those sons of whores.'

Lidia leaned back in her seat. Dread spread through her. She remembered Professor Jona's suicide. She remembered the newsreel images of the German tanks and armoured vehicles occupying Rome. She remembered Mussolini stepping out of the plane and shaking Hitler's hand. Papa's prediction that the war would be over before they knew it was never going to be a reality. The Allies had been stalled.

Worst of all, for her and Papa, the Gestapo were already hunting Jews in Venice. They had no list, but they wouldn't let that stop them.

With a thud, the door to the Pivettas' lounge crashed open.

Caterina, Marta's younger sister, burst into the room. 'They've come for you,' she said.

Chapter 5

Charlotte, 2010

I gazed out the window of the Airbus 319 as it descended towards Marco Polo airport, barely able to believe I was doing this alone. The city below lay surrounded by water —the canals, squares, and church spires; it was almost as if I could reach out and touch them. Was this where Gran had spent her childhood and youth? She'd been ninety-one when she'd passed away—only twenty-four, my age, when Italy had switched sides and joined the Allies. I wished she'd felt she could have shared about her life with Mum and me. *A painful past still too raw to relive.* I shivered to myself—I owed it to her memory and to Mum's peace of mind to find out what had happened to Gran in those turbulent times.

An hour later, after going through immigration and collecting my luggage, I followed the signs to the waterbus, wheeling my suitcase along the covered walkway towards the Venetian Lagoon. A light wind had sprung up, refreshingly cooling in the late July heat. *I'm finally in Italy*, I kept repeating to myself. Would I discover anything? Or would it be like looking for a needle in a haystack?

At the pier, the rumble of the waterbus's engine almost drowned out the chatter of a group of Chinese tourists who'd gathered behind me. The breeze blew my hair back from my face as I took a seat at the prow. I breathed in the salty air and hugged myself. I was about to arrive in Venice, and I couldn't stop smiling I was so excited— albeit nervous at the same time.

The boat's engines rumbled, and a passageway of coloured wooden markers guided us into a wide channel. After we'd passed a church, its stern brick frontage stretching up into the sky, tall buildings began to rise out of the water, then palaces with low entrances—only a few steps separating them from the sea. I gazed up at pointed-arched windows and fretted stone like lacework. *Venice is even more beautiful than I'd imagined.*

The hotel I'd booked was in the San Marco district, and I enjoyed every minute of the waterbus's journey down the Grand Canal. We passed under the Rialto Bridge, and I spotted my first gondola. *At 80 Euros, a ride on one would be far too expensive, and an extravagance for me on my own.*

For a moment, just a tiny moment, I regretted that Gary wasn't here with me in the most romantic city in the world. He'd phoned yesterday, out of the blue, to say he'd only just heard my grandmother had died and wanted to offer his condolences. I'd been nice to him, maybe too nice, when I'd thanked him. To my surprise, he'd gone on to say that he missed me and would like us to get back together again, that he was sorry for what had happened with Mel and that he'd make it up to me. 'It's too late,' I'd said firmly. 'I've moved on.' And I had; the initial outrage I'd felt at his betrayal seemed a distant memory.

But Gary clearly misunderstood what I'd meant by "moving on". 'Are you with someone else?' he'd asked, and I'd heard the petulance in his tone.

I'd almost lied and said that I was—to bring home to him how little I cared— but I'm a bad liar, and he'd have sussed out my lie straight away.

'No,' I'd responded, short and sharp. To tell the truth, our break-up had put me off men—I was better off on my own.

'Let's meet up,' he'd suggested. 'For old time's sake. No strings, I promise.'

I'd pictured his face breaking into a smile of eagerness, his golden blond hair flopping across his forehead—I was always brushing it out of his light-blue eyes. He was a "pretty boy", I supposed was how best to describe him. A foil to my olive skin and dark hair. 'I can't,' I'd said. 'I'm leaving for Venice tomorrow.'

'Why?' *Blunt as that.*

'To trace my roots.' I'd regretted those words the instant I'd said them. He'd given me the third degree and I'd found myself going into long explanations about my motivations.

'You're insane,' he'd told me. 'The chances of you finding out anything are several million to one.'

'I won't know unless I try.'

'Take care,' he'd said. 'Watch out for those Italian stallions.'

'You're stereotyping them,' I'd retorted. 'I'd better get on with my packing, Gary. Thanks for the call and take care too.'

I'd fumed at his crass remark about Italian men. And the way he'd tried to put me off coming here.

But Venice shimmered in the sunshine, her beauty beguiling me, and I decided to forget all about Gary and focus on the task at hand.

I stepped onto the pontoon at the Santa Maria del Giglio stop and wheeled my suitcase down a quiet alley to my hotel, where I checked in and went up to a single room overlooking a narrow canal. After a quick freshen-up I ventured out again, through streets thronging with tourists who were browsing the small shops selling souvenirs and carnival masks.

Almost immediately, I was caught up in the horde surging in the direction of Piazza San Marco—it was sign-posted on every corner—and I was in awe as the crowd spat me out into the iconic square. Of course, I'd seen pictures of it before, but seeing it "in the flesh" took my breath. The cathedral's columns and domes shone in the afternoon sunlight. I stood immobile, gazing at the magnif-icence, then made my way over to the Doge's Palace and placed my feet on the very spot where Gran had posed with that group of young people all those years ago. Mum had scanned me a copy of it, and my breathing slowed as I looked at it now in my phone gallery. I could picture them standing here, just as I was now, and it sent chills through me. *Was this photo taken before or after the war?*

I headed towards the waterfront. The sky had faded to

a smoky blue and the sun was casting golden hues over the buildings. Gondolas bobbed on the waves in front of me, tethered to their moorings. I strolled past them, snapping pictures, staring in wonderment at an island on the other side of the lagoon. A church campanile, like an enormous pencil, was pointing skywards as if about to write a message. I followed the crowd crossing a narrow canal and caught a glimpse of the famous Bridge of Sighs.

The aroma of grilled fish from a restaurant up ahead sent a pang of hunger to my stomach, so I stopped for a bite to eat before heading back to my hotel. I took a shower, then flopped on my bed. Should I open the letters sent to Grandad from Italy in 1974? I'd put off doing so until I'd arrived here. They were in my suitcase, but I was so tired that, within seconds, I'd fallen fast asleep.

After a continental breakfast in the hotel dining room— cappuccino, croissants and a juicy peach—I set out on foot for the Jewish ghetto, feeling a lot more confident in myself after a good night's sleep.

I'd read that there was a monument in the square with a list of the Venetian Jews who'd been deported to concentration camps from the city between 1943 and 1944. My skin tingled with nerves; I hoped I wouldn't find Gran's family's name etched onto the memorial.

I deliberately avoided the main tourist route and wandered through the hidden calli and across the small bridges spanning a network of tiny canals. I gazed around me, captivated, and took my phone from my bag to frame a shot of the strings of laundry hanging from a window above. The contrasting bright colours against the pastel walls of the building simply begged for a photo.

I got lost a couple of times, going down darkened alleyways to find myself at a dead end. Finally, I emerged into the sunshine of a campo, where umbrella-shaded tables cried out for me to take a break. I sat and ordered a chocolate ice cream cornetto with a glass of sparkling mineral water to wash it down. The *gelato* arrived, and it was delicious. I took a picture of it and sent it to Mum, with the caption "wish you were here". My phone pinged almost straight away, but it wasn't her responding; it was Gary.

'Let me know how you are getting on,' he messaged.

'On my way to the Ghetto,' I pinged back. 'Catch you later…'

I chewed on my lip, mulling over a niggling thought. Strange that he'd only contacted me after hearing that Gran had died. When he'd lived with me in my parents' flat, we'd both been saving for the deposit to get a mortgage for our future home. Gary was a teacher, like me. Neither of us earned mega salaries. Had Gary put two and two together and deduced that I'd inherited enough from Gran's estate to be able to afford a place of my own? As my partner he'd have all sorts of rights—

Releasing a long, slow breath, I got up from my chair and went to pay the *conto*. I checked my location on Google Maps—thankfully, Venice offered city-wide Wi-Fi for free—then tapped in my destination. It was time to stop wandering about like a lost soul and do what I'd set out to do.

Soon, I found myself crossing the wooden *Ponte di Gheto Novo*, a lump of trepidation in my throat. The bridge led to another of those ubiquitous dark alleyways. I'd read, though, that this one used to have a gate at the end, which was locked at night by Christian gatekeepers after the Ghetto had been established in 1541. It wasn't until Napoleon conquered Venice in 1797 that the practice ceased.

Once again, I stepped into the sunshine of a square. My eyes were drawn immediately to the monument on a red brick wall to my right. With heavy feet, I walked up to it.

A train spilling out its cargo of doomed human beings.

Sculpted in bronze but looking as if it were wood.

The faces and the details of the scene appeared to have been intentionally blurred.

Behind the relief, large boards lined horizontally behind an iron gate, looking just like the wooden slats of cattle trucks.

My stomach fluttered as I read, carved on the surface, the first and last name and the age of each victim, many of them only children. 246 in total. *Todesco, Kuhn, Levi, Polacco, De Angelis, Savini, Gremboni.* Jewish names of old blending with Italian. A fusion of religion and culture. Each name spelt an entire life lost, and my heart wept for them.

I arrived at the final name, relief flooding through me. *Moretti* wasn't there. Gran's family had not suffered the *Shoah.* Or maybe she hadn't been Jewish after all, and the prayer book had nothing to do with her?

Legs trembling, I walked to a public bench in the shade of a leafy tree, where I sat for a short while lost in thought. *What should I do next?*

So many questions leading to doubt. Had Gran come from Venice at all? A sudden idea occurred to me, and I googled how to obtain a birth certificate in Italy. My heart dropped. I couldn't go in person, but would need to write to the town hall and send copies of my I.D. It would probably be weeks before I got the information. I should have thought of it before and made the request before I left England.

Annoyed at myself, I got to my feet and made my way towards the vaporetto stop. The day had turned unbearably hot, and I was thirsty, so I bought a bottle of water from a drinks machine.

Back at the hotel, I laid on my bed, thinking over my options. Gary had pontificated that my chances of finding out about Gran's past would be like looking for a needle in a haystack. Mum had warned it was tantamount to a wild goose chase. Although I was relieved not to have found the name *Moretti* on the memorial, it would have been a significant clue.

I set my jaw; I wouldn't give up at the first hurdle. I swung my legs from my bed and crossed the floor to where my suitcase lay open on the luggage rack. Sighing, I reached for the manila envelope containing the letters written to Granddad. I slid them out and stared at them.

Sant'Illaria.

Rosina Zalunardi.

Carefully, I opened the envelope with the oldest date and pulled out the letter. Written in Italian. Of which I understood only a little. There was always Google Translate, I reminded myself. It would be painstaking on a phone, but I wouldn't let that put me off. I would go to Sant'Illaria and find out if Rosina Zalunardi was still alive. If she was, I would ask why she'd written to my grandfather and if she'd known my gran.

Chapter 6

Lidia, 1943

Lidia paced up and down the fondamenta; she was waiting for Marta to get back from visiting Giorgio on the island of Pallestrina. He was staying with local fishermen until a boat could be found to take him to join the navy in the south.

She wrapped her arms around herself in the cold of the December afternoon, remembering the fright she'd received when Marta's sister had burst into the Pivettas' lounge over two months ago. The newsreel she'd watched at the Lido cinema had made her jumpy. She'd been relieved it was Angelo and a National Liberation Committee's representative arriving to take Giorgio to a safe house on the island—she'd thought that blackshirts had come for her.

Giorgio now spent his time helping mend fishing nets

and being fed hearty seafood stews by the women who lived on Pallestrina—women who'd lost their men to the war and were on the lookout for a replacement, much to Marta's concern. Hence her frequent trips across the lagoon in her father's boat to make sure that the dashing Giorgio didn't succumb to anyone else's charms.

Lidia had told her again and again that Giorgio appeared far too smitten with her to stray. But she lacked confidence, and Lidia didn't blame her. After all, Renzo had been smitten with *her* once. Lidia sighed. She'd finally written to him, asking for an explanation for his silence, but she still hadn't received a reply. Even if he no longer considered himself her sweetheart, it hurt that their friendship didn't seem to matter to him.

She quickened her pacing as worry set in. Marta should have returned by now. It was getting late and, if a German patrol boat caught her out on the water after the night-time curfew, she could be in trouble. Then Lidia shook off her nervousness—Marta was well able to take care of herself. She'd joined the Venetian Resistance and spent her days, when not studying or canoodling with Giorgio, helping her comrades search for weapons—mostly old guns and pistols left behind by the military—to send to the partisans who were forming brigades up in the mountains.

The putt-putt of an outboard engine echoed across the water and, in the gloom, Lidia spotted Marta at the helm of her father's boat. Tonight Lidia was staying at the Pivettas' so she could spend time with Marta before leaving Venice tomorrow. Incredibly, Lidia had managed to persuade her papa at last.

Despite Mussolini declaring Jews to be "enemy aliens" in November, and many of their Jewish friends quietly leaving their homes—vanishing without notice and telling no one where they were going—Papa had held firm in his belief that he and Lidia would come to no harm if they kept their heads down. Even when they'd heard news of a thousand Jews rounded up and deported from the ghetto in Rome, and the same thing happening in Trieste and Genova, Papa had said, 'This is Venice. It won't happen here.'

Two days ago, she'd reported that conversation to Marta, who'd thrown up her hands in despair. 'At this precise moment,' Marta said, 'the SS are compiling the names and addresses of every Jew in the city to give to the police. They had a brief setback when Professor Jona burned all those documents, but your time has run out. Under the November Manifesto, all property owned by Jews can be seized. Your apartment no longer belongs to you, and they will take it any day now.'

'How do you know this is going to happen? How can you be so certain?' Lidia had asked.

'The Resistance has heard what the SS are planning. We've warned as many Jews as we can, but not everyone listens. Your father being one of them.'

'He's an eternal optimist.'

'Which is why it might be impossible to save him. But we can save *you.* There's no time to waste.'

'So I must leave my dear father to the Nazi-fascists? I couldn't…'

'I'm afraid you have no other choice.'

'Would you leave your parents behind?' Lidia's voice had risen.

'It's a terrible choice. But you must make it.'

'Could *you* do it?'

Marta had glanced away. 'I don't know.' She'd paused, apparently lost in thought. 'Perhaps if you tell your papa you'll leave without him, that might make him change his mind.'

'I can't lie to him.'

'Give it a try, Lidia. Turn his love for you to your advantage. His and your future depend on it.'

The seriousness of Marta's warning had made her heart quake. She'd gone home to Papa and had drawn on the acting skills she'd learnt in the after-school club she'd attended when at secondary school. And she'd put on the performance of her life. Papa had argued back, as ever, that he didn't consider them to be in any danger, but she'd stood firm. 'I'm leaving,' she'd said. 'By tomorrow I will have a new identity and the next day I'll be off.'

He'd pulled a dejected face. 'You can't mean that, *cara mia*. You wouldn't desert your dear old papa.'

'I do mean it.' She'd looked him in the eye.

'Where will you go?'

'To the countryside. I'll blend in with the locals, live like one of them. Most Italians are sympathetic to those of us who are Jews. The people I go to will protect me.' She'd hoped what she'd said was true.

'Hmmm.' He'd tilted his head. 'How can you be so sure?'

She'd placed a hand on his shoulder. 'Have faith. I'll find friends.' Even as she said the words, she'd worried Papa might not fall for her ruse. What would she do then? She couldn't possibly go without him.

Papa had gone silent and she gave him what she hoped was a convincing look.

His brows pulled in and he tapped a finger against his lip. 'You are serious?'

She gave him a curt nod, not trusting herself to speak.

Papa had sighed deeply and then said, 'In that case, I will go with you.'

After dinner at the Pivettas', Lidia waited with Marta for someone from the Resistance to bring hers and Papa's forged I.Ds. From tomorrow they would be known as Elena and Alberto Moretti. They'd need to pretend to be relatives of the people they would be staying with and behave as if they were Catholics. Papa had already handed over the cash he kept hidden in the apartment as his contribution to "the cause". He was spending the evening with his precious books—they'd only been allowed to pack what they could carry. She would go to him in the morning, and then they would leave on the train to Treviso.

Lidia accepted the *Nazionali* cigarette Marta offered her. Lidia wasn't a heavy smoker, but she needed one now to calm herself. Had she and Papa left it too late to be setting off into the unknown? The Kingdom of Italy had declared war on Germany. The country was effectively caught up not only in the conflict with the Wehrmacht but also in a civil war between the Fascists and anti-Fascists. And Marta had told her she'd heard that the police in other cities had started to cooperate with the Germans in rounding up Jews, and that soon it would happen in Venice. Every nerve in Lidia's body was on edge.

Suddenly, the shriek of air raid sirens pierced the air.

Her heartbeat racing, Lidia leapt to her feet and hurried outside with Marta.

They found Signor Pivetta on the fondamenta, gazing up at the sky.

Marta ran to him. 'Babbo, is this just a drill?'

'With all these clouds and mist, it's certainly not a night for an air raid,' he yelled above the din. 'A pilot wouldn't be able to see two metres in front of him.' He called out to three men who stood stamping their feet in the cold, their cigarettes glowing. 'Have you heard any news?'

'Nothing on the radio. My wife is calling her sister in Marghera to see if she's seen anything,' the tallest of the three bellowed back.

People were emerging from their homes. Bundled in coats and shawls, they shouted questions over the unceasing racket. Everyone wanted to know what was going on. Venice had never been bombed by the Allies; they'd put it on their list of places to be preserved, but nothing was guaranteed.

A man in a dark overcoat approached. He handed Marta a packet, and said, 'The police and Fascist agents are going door-to-door, arresting Jews.' He stared at Lidia. 'I've brought your new I.D. You must disappear tonight. With these sirens and all the chaos, we'll be able to get you to safety.'

'What about my father?'

'The police might already be at your apartment.'

'I can't leave Papa behind!' She spun around and prepared to run.

'Lidia, wait!' Marta grabbed her and pulled her to a halt.

She squirmed out of Marta's hold.

And she ran.

Oh, how she ran.

She ran as if her life depended upon it. Her feet pounded the paving and her breaths burst in and out. She didn't care if she bumped into a thuggish blackshirt enforcing the curfew—all she cared about was getting to Papa.

The air raid sirens continued their unceasing wails—it was as if the heavens themselves were screaming.

She pelted across the bridge over the canal and raced up the fondamenta.

O, Dio. She stared in horror at a bonfire on the pavement below the palazzo. Flames were licking at a mound of books and papers. *Papa's books and papers.*

'He's gone, Lidia,' Signor Rossi's voice came from the door to the building. 'Your papa has gone.'

'Gone? Where?' Lidia shook her head, uncomprehending. 'What do you mean?'

'The police came with some *fascisti*. I don't know where they took him…'

Lidia brushed past her neighbour and headed up to the apartment, taking two steps at a time. The front door had been splintered and hung open on one hinge. She stepped inside, and her eyes widened. The entire place had been ransacked.

Broken crockery.

Shards of glass.

Clothes strewn everywhere.

A sick feeling in her stomach, she went from room to room, hoping Signor Rossi had been wrong.

'Papa!' she called out.

'Lidia…'

It was Marta; she must have followed her. 'Come with me. You can't stay here. They'll be looking for you and could well return.'

'I need to find out where they've taken Papa.'

'Yes, yes.' Marta soothed. 'But we must leave here before it's too late.'

Chapter 7

Lidia, 1943

Lidia was spending the rest of the night in the Pivettas'
attic, just like Giorgio had done over two months ago.
She'd insisted on coming up here; she didn't want to put
Marta and her family at risk. Giudecca was a small
community and not everyone was anti-Fascist. It would
take only one person to tell the police they'd seen Lidia
leave the palazzo with her friend, and they would easily
work out where she'd gone.

She sat on a lumpy mattress on the cold wooden floor
and knuckled away a tear. What she'd witnessed tonight,
the wilful destruction of hers and Papa's personal property,
had brought home the grim reality of her situation. Obviously, those air raid sirens had been a distraction. People's
eyes had been on the sky and the noise had prevented them
from hearing what was going on. Would they have done

anything, though? She doubted it; they would have been too afraid—

A knock rapped at the attic trapdoor, and Lidia almost jumped out of her skin. Then came two further knocks in quick succession followed, after a beat, by two more. Lidia's knees buckled with relief. It was Marta, using a broom handle to tap their agreed signal—the same code she'd put in place for Giorgio.

Just to be sure, Lidia peered through a crack in the wood.

Marta's dear face was staring up at her.

With trembling hands, Lidia lifted the trapdoor, fetched the ladder resting against the attic wall, and eased it down.

Marta climbed the rungs and pulled the ladder up after herself. She kissed Lidia on both cheeks and inquired how she was feeling.

'Scared,' Lidia breathed.

'I think we got away with it,' Marta said, hugging her. 'If anyone ratted on us, the police would have been here by now. Oh, and I know where they've taken your papa—'

Lidia grabbed hold of her arm. 'Where?'

'The Collegio Mario Foscarini, that private school in the Cannaregio district. Angelo found out that he's there with hundreds of other Jews rounded up by the police.'

'*O, Dio.*' Lidia's chest tightened. 'My poor dear papa. I must go and be with him.'

Marta stiffened. 'You can't mean that—'

Lidia held her in a firm gaze. 'Where he goes, I go too. He would do the same for me.'

'Are you crazy?' Marta shook her head. 'From what I've heard, your papa and the others will soon be transported to a labour camp.'

'He will need me to help him.' Lidia's voice quivered. 'I've always helped him.

'Your papa won't expect this of you. I'm sure he would tell you if he could.'

'I must hand myself in.' Lidia's chin lifted. 'I will go to the police first thing in the morning.'

'Don't do that,' Marta pleaded. '*Ti prego.* I beg of you.' She fell silent momentarily, then said, 'If we can find a way for you to talk to your papa, and tell him what you are planning, would you agree to that?'

Lidia sighed. There was no point in going to see him; she'd made up her mind. She stared at Marta, and Marta stared back at her. Lidia caught the love and concern in her friend's gaze. She owed it to her to go through the motions. 'Alright. I'll talk to him. But how do you propose I do that? I mean, there are probably guards.'

'Some guards are more lenient than others.' Marta gave a wry smile. 'Try and get some sleep, bella.' She hugged Lidia again. '*Ti voglio bene.*'

'I love you too, beautiful,' Lidia said. And she did. *O Dio*, she would miss Marta so much. *So very much.*

Lidia tossed and turned for the rest of the night. Papa's eternal optimism would have him making the best of things, and he'd be helping anyone in need. But she couldn't help worrying about him.

At breakfast time, Marta brought her some bread and milk, as well as a bowl of water, soap, a facecloth and a towel. 'Giovanna came to find out how you are coping.

She'll be back later today with more information about what's going on at that school.'

'I'm serious about handing myself in,' Lidia repeated.

Marta put her arm around her shoulders. 'Be patient, bella.'

She nodded. 'I'll try.'

Throughout the morning, she waited and worried. Marta came up at lunchtime, and said, 'It seems the police aren't looking for you. Come down to the kitchen and eat with us. You can stay in my room tonight.'

'How about we go now, just the two of us, to the Collegio?' Lidia gave her a pleading look.

'I think tomorrow would be more sensible. Better to wait until we know more about what's happening there.'

'*Va bene.*' She would give it one more day. If she couldn't find a way to speak with her papa, she'd hand herself in. It was only for Marta's sake that she'd agreed to talk to Papa anyway.

Giovanna and Marisa dropped by before the night-time curfew. The four girls sat together in the Pivettas' lounge.

'The school has been transformed into a primitive detention centre,' Giovanna said without preamble.

'There aren't any facilities,' Marisa added. 'Even the old and sick are sleeping on benches or on the floor.'

'*O Dio*,' Lidia muttered. 'I hope they are being given food.'

Giovanna tapped the ash from her cigarette. 'I'm afraid not. Some of the neighbours, hearing the children crying with hunger, have been passing bread, fruit and cheese through the windows.'

'That's terrible,' Lidia choked back a sob.

'It is.' Marisa leant towards her. 'But you can use the

situation to your advantage. If you mingled with the people who are helping the detainees, you could ask about your father.'

Lidia wiped her eyes. She would do it. She had nothing to lose. If she was caught, she'd be imprisoned with Papa. And, if she wasn't caught, she'd go directly to the police station anyway. 'I will walk to the Collegio my own,' she said, sending Marta a determined look. 'It will be too dangerous for you to come with me.'

'Absolutely not.' Marta shook her head. 'We'll go in my babbo's boat. The patrols won't take any notice of us. It's as if they consider women not worth worrying about; I've sailed right past them so often—'

'But won't we use a lot of fuel?' Lidia asked. 'The school is on the other side of Venice.'

'We can cut across San Marco via the smaller canals. I know the route from visiting my nonna's grave at San Michele cemetery.'

Lidia decided not to press the argument. When Marta got the bit between her teeth she never gave up. Lidia sat back in her seat and listened to her friends as they talked about the upcoming Christmas celebrations, and how miserable they would be with the Germans infesting the city like a plague. Lidia stared down at her hands. Hanukkah would start on December 22nd this year. What-ever happened, she knew she wouldn't be lighting the menorah candles with Papa. And the realisation made her heart weep.

~

The canals were quiet as they putt-putted through the San Marco and Cannaregio districts the next morning. It was as if the entire city was holding its breath. They moored in the Rio de Santa Caterina and then strolled down Calle Foscarini, eager to catch up with anyone passing food through the windows of the Collegio.

But there was no one about. Lidia sagged against the terracotta brick wall of the building, heavy disappointment weighing her down. She'd hoped against hope she would see Papa and talk to him, even if it was only to tell him about her plan.

Without warning, a voice came through the high window. 'Help us, please. We need food…'

Lidia glanced at Marta. She wished they'd brought some groceries with them. Except, there were hundreds of people inside and they wouldn't have been able to feed them all.

The sound of running footsteps reverberated down the street. A group of about twenty people had arrived with hessian sacks. Before too long, they were passing food to outstretched hands. Lidia and Marta joined in, delving into the sacks and handing over bread, cheese, oranges, apples, pears and grapes. All the while, Lidia's heart pounded. Would the police arrive and arrest them? She didn't mind for herself, but it was the last thing she wanted for Marta.

'Will it be possible to speak to Dottor De Angelis?' she called out eventually. It seemed that whoever was guarding the detainees was turning a blind eye to them being fed. *And rightly too. They should be ashamed of themselves for their treatment of their fellow human beings.*

'Why?' someone asked.

'I'm his daughter.'

'Your father is a wonderful man. He's been tending to the sick. I will get him for you.'

O, Papa. I had no doubt you would be helping people.

She kept on assisting with the food distribution until her papa's gravelly voice called out, 'Lidia, what are you doing here?'

'I came to see you,' she said in a false bright tone.

'It's far too dangerous. What if you are caught?'

'I'm planning on handing myself in. I don't want to be separated from you.'

She heard the sharp intake of his breath. 'Don't do that. Please.'

'But, why? You said we would always be together...'

'Listen to me, *cara mia*. Listen very carefully. If you disobey me, you will disrespect me. And I'll never forgive you.'

She gasped at his stern words. 'Oh, Papa. How can you talk like this?'

'You must do what we'd planned. Stay with people you trust and who will protect you. I realise now we should have left Venice weeks ago. I'm a stubborn old fool and I'm sorry it has come to this.'

'No, Papa. It's not your fault. I didn't want to say goodbye to Venice either. It's the only home I've ever known.'

'You must leave straight away, *cara mia*. Promise me!'

'What about you?'

'We've been told that they will transport us to a labour camp.'

'I want to go with you,' she wept.

'No, daughter. I forbid it.'

Lidia had never disobeyed Papa in her life. 'But, how will you manage?'

'All will be well. It won't be so terrible. I'm not afraid of work, and perhaps my medical skills can be used.' His hand stretched over the high window ledge, and he held out a small, rectangular book. Mamma's *Siddur.* 'I managed to grab this from the pile of books those thugs were throwing out onto the fondamenta below our apartment,' he said. 'Keep it safe until we meet again.'

She stood on tiptoe and took the prayer book. Then she kissed his outstretched hand, bathing it with her tears. 'I will come back and see you tomorrow,' she said.

And so she did. For the next three days, she and Marta came to help with passing food to the prisoners and contributing what they could. Every day, Lidia spoke with Papa, trying to persuade him to let her hand herself in. To no avail—he was adamant.

On the third day, the calle was strangely quiet. She nudged Marta. 'Where is everyone?'

'I don't know,' Marta whispered.

The sudden ricochet of running footsteps ripped the air.

Marta grabbed Lidia and pulled her into a doorway.

Lidia bit back a cry.

Uniformed men in black shirts.

She stared in horror as they stormed into the school.

'We should go,' Marta murmured.

But they stood frozen, transfixed as they watched the men herd families, many with young children, out onto the street. Where was Papa? Lidia swept her eyes over the crowd. Had he managed to slip away? No, there he was, right at the back. *O, Dio!*

The Fascists lined everyone up. 'We're taking you to the train station,' their leader announced.

Lidia's heart sank. So soon. She hadn't even said goodbye to Papa.

She grabbed Marta's hand. 'Let's follow.'

'Only if you don't do anything stupid,' Marta warned.

Darting from doorway to doorway, Lidia followed at a safe distance with Marta at her heel.

The long line of detainees shuffled sluggishly through Cannaregio, crossing bridges and campi, skirting the ghetto, where Lidia used to visit the synagogue from time to time.

Eventually, they arrived at Santa Lucia Station. The guards halted their prisoners in front of the wide steps leading up to the modernist building and started to do a head count.

It was now or never, Lidia thought. She ran up to Papa and threw her arms around him. 'Goodbye,' she sobbed. 'Take care of yourself. I hope we'll be together again soon.'

Papa kissed her, then gently pushed her away. 'Go now, *cara mia*. It isn't safe for you to be seen with me. Oh, and I forgot to mention that I transferred the apartment to Signor Rossi's name last week. He will look after it for us, and we'll be able to live there again after the war.'

Lidia felt Marta's arm around her shoulder, and, tears streaming down her face, she allowed herself to be led to safety by her dearest friend.

Chapter 8

Charlotte, 2010

The late afternoon sun cast a rosy glow over a massive mountain rising like a camel's hump behind Sant'Illaria, as I brought my rented Fiat 500 to a halt in the carpark at the side of the Hotel Villa Corradini. Lines of cypress trees stood like sentinels along the crests of the foothills, olive groves and vineyards covering the lower slopes. Picturesque farmhouses nestled in the dips between the hills, their pastel walls topped by terracotta roof tiles. Would I find the clues I was searching for here amongst all this beauty? *Please, don't let it be another wild goose chase.*

The air was hot, almost too hot, and perspiration beaded my upper lip. I wiped it away with the back of my hand, then opened the car boot to reach for my suitcase. Tiredness seeped through my bones. I'd hit traffic on the road north from Mestre and the drive had taken longer than I planned. My fault for setting off late, I supposed, but I'd wanted to ride the vaporetto out to the Lido this morning and go for a swim off the public beach. If Gran had grown up in Venice, would she have swum there? It had felt reassuring to imagine myself following in her footsteps and visiting the places with which she could have been familiar.

I wheeled my suitcase around to the front of the hotel, looking forward to a refreshing shower and a nice cold drink. *Wow, this place is gorgeous.* Three tall arched windows opened onto balustraded balconies occupying the centre of the cream-coloured edifice on the first and second floors. I swivelled my gaze to the flower-filled garden, tennis courts and swimming pool. The palazzo dated from the 16th Century, apparently, and I was pushing out the boat by staying here—at 150 Euros a night, even with full board, it was way over my budget—but if I found what I was seeking, it would be worth the expense.

After bumping my suitcase up the marble steps, I entered a square lobby with a black and white tiled floor and a reception desk. A man looked up from his computer, his smile welcoming. I took a peek at his name badge, *Alessandro Corradini, Manager.* I'd read online that this was a family-run hotel. Was he the owner? I guessed he was in his early thirties, judging by the laughter lines at the corners of his forest-green eyes, and the fact that the thick chestnut-brown hair at his temples had started to recede slightly. Not a "pretty boy" but classically handsome. *Handsome and married with children, I expect.*

I handed over my passport, and he scanned it into the computer. 'You've booked for three nights, is that correct, signorina?' His voice was deep and melodic, with only a slight Italian accent.

'If I wanted to stay longer, would that be possible?' I wasn't sure how much time I'd need to find Rosina Zalunardi.

The hotel manager nodded. 'We have an annex on the other side of the garden for longer-staying guests. It will become available on Saturday. The price is half what you're paying for a room in the villa, and breakfast is included.'

Hmmm. I was tempted. 'Can I decide tomorrow? Oh, and if you get a booking, don't worry about me...'

'That won't be a problem, signorina. August is a popular month for visitors. We'll get other enquiries.'

His formality seemed at odds with his friendliness. 'Please, call me Lottie,' I said without thinking.

'Lottie?' He cocked his head.

'Short for Charlotte.'

'And I'm Alex. Short for Alessandro.' He held out his hand, and I shook it. 'Dinner is served in the dining room from 7.30 to 9 p.m. And drinks on the terrace from six.' His smile cratered dimples in his cheeks—he was far too good-looking and charming to boot.

Gary was good-looking too, I reminded myself, and could lay on the charm when it suited him. *Don't forget how that ended up.*

I took my key card from Alex and headed towards the lift. From the corner of my eye, I caught sight of a stunning blonde coming out of the door behind the reception desk. *His wife, no doubt.*

∾

My second-floor room was beautiful. I could easily believe this had once been a private country residence it was so un-hotel-like. Exposed ceiling beams, waxed parquet floors, and gorgeous artisan made furniture—described on the Corradini website as being in the Venetian style. My reflection in the elegant gold-painted, wood-framed wall mirror stared back at me. Urgh, I was a mess—my hair had curled even more than usual, and my blouse looked sweaty and crumpled.

I undressed and stepped onto the exquisitely decorated porcelain floor tiles in the bathroom. All blues and greens —I felt cooler straight away, and even more so after my shower. Back in my room, I unpacked and put on my favourite dress—a summery sixties design, floaty white, cinched at the waist and sleeveless, which I paired with killer nude platform sandals. I pinned my hair up and glossed my lips, thankful my thick dark eyelashes didn't need any mascara that would run down my face in the heat. *Thank you, Gran, for passing your genes on to me.*

I grabbed my handbag, left the room and descended the carpeted staircase to go out onto the terrace. Massive pergola umbrellas shaded the tables from the bright evening sunshine, and I pulled out a chair from under one of them. It was the middle of the night in Hong Kong, so I sent Mum and Dad a text telling them I'd arrived safely and would be in touch tomorrow. I smiled to myself. We'd been in contact via Facetime before I'd set off from Venice, and they'd wished me good luck in my quest. I was grateful Mum no longer discouraged me, but I guessed it was because she'd realised that I wouldn't change my mind.

A young waitress approached to take my drinks order.

She suggested a Bellini cocktail, concocted with prosecco and peach juice, and I went with her suggestion. Feeling relaxed, I breathed in the scent of roses and trailing red geraniums tumbling from the urns at the edge of the patio. A bumblebee dipped and darted over a bed filled with lavender, competing with the buzz of conversation from my fellow guests, and sparrows chirped cheerfully as they splashed in the birdbath on the manicured lawn. The waitress returned with my Bellini, and I took a sip, the prosecco bubbles tickling my nose. I sighed with contentment and retrieved the oldest envelope postmarked Sant'Illaria from my handbag.

Painstakingly, I typed the first Italian sentence into Google Translate. *Forgive me for contacting you again,* I read, *but your lack of response is worrying. I hope that Lioness is well.*

Lioness? What on earth? I entered the Italian word, *Leonessa*, again. *Lioness* popped up once more, and I shook my head in exasperation.

'Is everything alright?' a voice came from the left. I glanced up from my phone. Alex had approached without me noticing.

'Yes, lovely, thanks. Your hotel is so beautiful.'

'Glad you like it.' He gave a smile. 'Mind if I sit with you? I'm on a short break before dinner.'

'Go ahead.' I smiled back at him.

'So,' he said, 'what brings you to our part of the Veneto?'

I thought for a moment, then decided to come clean. Alex might know the woman who'd written to Grandad. 'I'm tracing my roots,' I said. 'My grandmother died recently. All we knew was that she was Italian.' I proceeded to tell him the full story, as far I knew it.

Alex tapped his chin with his long index finger. 'I don't know anyone called Rosina Zalunardi in Sant'Illaria. If she's still alive and did, indeed, know your gran, she'd be extremely old by now. So it's probable I haven't met her.'

'Gran was ninety-one when she died. But why has Rosina asked my grandad about a lioness? I'm so confused…'

'You and me both.' He laughed. 'Unless your gran joined a circus…'

I laughed with him. 'Highly unlikely.'

'Sant'Illaria is a small place. I'll ask around.' A cloud passed over his expression. 'Shame my parents are no longer alive—they might have known her—but they were killed in a car crash when I was a kid. My grandfather raised me and my sister. When we inherited the villa from him five years ago, we decided to turn it into a hotel.'

I expressed my sympathy for his loss and we lapsed into silence while I sipped my Bellini. I caught sight of the stunning blonde approaching our table, her face dimpling with a smile. *The same smile as Alex's.*

He smiled back at her. 'Is it time to announce dinner?'

She said that it was and gave me an inquisitive look.

'This is my sister, Francesca,' Alex introduced her. 'Why don't you join us after dinner for a nightcap, Lottie?'

I thanked Alex and shook hands with Francesca, and then the three of us made our way through to the dining room.

～

If anyone had told me a month ago that I'd have been happy to eat on my own in a posh hotel restaurant, I would have thought they were crazy. But I sat at a small, round table in the corner, enjoying every mouthful of a prawn and prosecco risotto, followed by thin slices of grilled fillet steak—*tagliata*—served with roast potatoes and a fresh herb salad. When the waitress asked if I would like some dessert, I patted my tummy and groaned that everything had been delicious but I couldn't manage another bite.

Throughout the meal, I'd watched Alex and Francesca attending to their guests. They were a classy double act, and I was curious to know more about them. I sat and waited until the dining room had emptied, unsure if I should go and find them or if they'd come for me. I needn't have worried—as soon as the last guest had departed, Alex appeared and led me onto the terrace that was now lit up by fairy lights. Francesca was already there, seated at a table with a bottle of red wine and three glasses in front of her.

'We're off duty now,' she said, pouring. 'So we can drink.'

I'd only ordered sparkling mineral water with my dinner and was happy to clink glasses with my new acquaintances. 'Cheers,' I said. 'But what about your own dinner?'

'We grab what we can in between looking after our guests,' Francesca chuckled.

'The risotto was amazing,' I said. 'My grandmother was a great cook, but she didn't make any Italian dishes. She avoided everything to do with Italy.'

Alex leant towards me. 'I hope you don't mind, but I told Francesca about your quest.'

'I don't mind at all…especially if it leads to me finding Rosina Zalunardi.'

'I could take you to the Municipio in the morning,' Francesca suggested. 'The town hall keeps a record of everyone living in Sant'Illaria. We can go and ask them if they're able to help you.'

I'd only just thanked her when my phone started ringing. I checked the caller I.D. *Gary.* Without hesitation, I cancelled the call and turned my phone off.

'We can leave if you want to speak privately,' Alex said, looking me in the eye.

I shook my head. 'It's not important.' I took a sip of wine and swallowed my irritation with Gary. 'Please, tell me more about the history of your villa.'

'It's been in our family for over four hundred years,' Francesca said proudly. 'The Corradini family is one of the oldest in the Veneto. Italy's a republic now, so no one can call themselves a count or countess with any legitimacy. Otherwise, Alex would be Conte Corradini.'

The corners of Alex's eyes crinkled. 'Grandfather was the count—he revelled in the title.'

'What about you, Francesca? Would you have been a countess?' I asked.

'The title only passed through the male line. But when Grandfather married after the war, everyone still called him *Conte* and my grandmother was always known as *Contessa.*'

'I envy you knowing so much about your grandparents,' I said.

'Grandfather was a real character. He pretended to be a Fascist, but he helped the partisans who were fighting up on that mountain in 1944.' Alex indicated towards the moonlit peak towering over the village. 'It was a dark period for Italy.'

'I know.' I blew out a breath. 'I'm a history teacher.'

Alex and Francesca proceeded to ask me more about myself, and I told them about the school where I taught and even about my parents in Hong Kong.

'I used to travel to the Far East often,' Alex said. 'I worked for a company manufacturing leather goods which we exported to China and Japan. But I chucked it in after my son was born so I could spend more time with him as well as run this hotel.'

So, he's married. Or has a partner. I wondered where she was.

'How about you, Francesca?' I asked. 'Have you ever visited the Far East?'

'Never. But I've travelled to London many times. I love your city.'

I thought about what she'd said. Did I love London? Not really. The pace of life, the expense of everything, and the crowds had started to remind me too much of Hong Kong.

'We must get together the next time you visit,' I said, and left it at that.

Alex covered his mouth with his hand as he yawned. 'It's getting late and I have to be up early for a delivery.'

I pushed back my chair. 'Thank you for keeping me company. I enjoyed talking to you both.'

'We enjoyed it too, didn't we Alex?' Francesca's smile lit up her eyes. *Forest green, like her brother's.* 'I must be getting back to Lorenzo. He's my boyfriend. We live together up there.' She pointed to one of the lower hills behind Sant'Illaria. 'I'll be here in the morning to take you to the Municipio.'

'Thanks.'

I waited for Alex to refer to his wife or partner, but he seemed reticent. '*Buonanotte,*' he said. 'See you tomorrow.'

Back in the lobby, Alex went to speak to the night manager while I made my way to the lifts. I kicked off my killer sandals as soon as I'd opened the door to my room. My sheets had been turned down, and there was a heart-shaped box of Baci chocolates on my pillow. Baci meant kisses. *The only kisses I'll be getting tonight.* I picked up my phone. Should I return Gary's call?

I decided not to. Instead, I made myself a cup of herbal tea from the drinks tray and sat by the window to enjoy the night-time view and the chocolates, excited for what tomorrow might bring.

Chapter 9

Lidia, 1943

Lidia stood in front of the floor-to-ceiling window in her apartment, gazing at the panorama of the snow-covered Dolomites that formed a backdrop behind San Marco. It wasn't often the air was limpid enough for the peaks to be discerned so clearly; she held on to the hope that, perhaps, she'd be able to see Venice on a clear day from the village at the foot of those mountains which would be her new home.

Her feet dragged as she walked from room to room. Signor Rossi had tidied up as best he could and had mended the front door, but there were red stains on the sitting room floor from the wine bottles that had been thrown against the wall, and the empty bookshelves were a shocking reminder of what had occurred four days ago. Sudden tears spilled from Lidia's eyes. *Oh, Papa. Where have they taken you? I should have made a bigger fuss at the train station, so the guards would arrest me and deport me too.*

She'd been surprised when they hadn't detained her, but Marta told her last night that she'd heard the police hadn't wanted to imprison any Jews in the first place, and it had only been as a result of coercion from the SS that they'd eventually agreed.

Lidia released a heavy sigh. She'd come to the apartment to collect the bag she'd packed when she'd planned to leave with Papa. She'd stowed it under her bed for the sake of tidiness, and it was there still, miraculously having escaped the gratuitous vandalism unleashed by the Fascists. It had been as if they were possessed by the Devil as well as by the Nazis. *Evil incarnate*. She shuddered. How could they have done what they did?

Marta's secret knock sounded at the front door. One. Two in quick succession. A beat. Then two more. Lidia slid the bolt Signor Rossi had attached.

'Are you ready to go?' Marta asked, kissing Lidia on both cheeks.

'If I have to…'

'You know it's the only solution, bella. There will be more roundups, the SS will insist on it, and soon there won't be a single Jew left in Venice.'

Lidia pulled Marta in for a hug. 'I'll miss you so much.'

'As I will you.'

Lidia took a step back. Marta's eyes were red. Obviously, she'd been crying, and it wasn't just because Lidia was leaving. Giorgio was due to board a trawler this evening, which would drop him off on the Gargano coast behind Allied lines.

How Lidia wished the British and Americans were making better headway against the Wehrmacht, but they'd found the German "Winter Line" impenetrable and were stuck at the Moro river. Bitter saliva filled Lidia's mouth; she despised the Nazis and their Italian Fascist toadies with a hate so palpable she could taste it. She hated them for starting this terrible war. She hated them for what they were doing to her fellow Jews. But she hated them most of all for what they'd done to Papa. And it was that hate which was sustaining her. It gave her a reason to carry on. For, whatever happened between now and the time when she'd be reunited with Papa, she would resist the *nazi-fascisti.*

Boarding the train at Santa Lucia for Treviso, Lidia couldn't help thinking about how Papa must have felt yesterday. Had he been scared? Probably not. His optimism would have surfaced and he'd have been cheering everyone else up, saying the labour camp wouldn't be so bad—just like he'd said to her. She hoped that she would have news of him soon; Marta had promised she'd try and find out where he'd been taken.

The whistle blew, and with a jolt, Lidia's train lurched into motion. She waved at Marta, who was standing on the platform. When would she see her dear friend again? But Marta had other things on her mind and had already turned away to head for Palestrina to bid farewell to Giorgio.

Lidia's heart went out to her as she remembered the sadness of saying goodbye to Renzo.

The third-class carriage was crammed with passengers dozing and coughing. Lidia sat squashed against a chubby nun, who tried to engage her in conversation. She pointed to her throat and whispered that she'd lost her voice. She creased her forehead in a frown; she'd lied blatantly and it wouldn't be for the last time. She'd taken on a new persona—her life would be one enormous lie from now onwards. Would she be able to carry it off? Nerves tied her insides into knots.

The journey to Treviso seemed to take for ever. It was said that Mussolini had managed to get the trains to run on time, but once Lidia's train had departed, it slowed and stopped repeatedly, held up by repairs to the tracks. *Tracks that had been damaged during Allied bombing raids, no doubt.* She stared out of the window at welders, who looked like demons in iron masks as they scattered sparks from a section of twisted rail.

Finally the train arrived at Treviso. Lidia remembered visiting the city on a school trip once; she'd been surprised by the number of canals, which had reminded her of Venice. But this was an entirely different visit, and her heart thudded with fear that she might not get through the checkpoint. But she needn't have worried; she shuffled forward with the crowd, and the guard at the barrier only gave her fake documents a cursory glance before waving her through.

Now came the tricky part of her exodus. She had to find the young woman who'd been sent to meet her. The girl was a redhead, apparently, and she'd be standing with two bicycles by the station exit.

Lidia stepped through the arched door, and her gaze fell on the young woman in question. She went up to her. 'Cousin, dearest, how lovely to see you,' she repeated the words she'd been told to say when meeting the girl.

'*Ciao, cugina,*' the young woman greeted her, kissing her on both cheeks. 'Better we go now if we're to arrive before nightfall.'

Lidia stowed her bag in the basket hanging from the handlebars, then threw a leg over the saddle of the bike. She didn't know the name of the girl she'd just met, nor the name of the village where they were heading. For reasons of security, she hadn't been given the information. The fact that she could have been apprehended and made to divulge those facts had made her tremble the entire way here.

She cycled behind the redhead for kilometre after kilometre through the flat countryside, every muscle in her body aching with the effort. At the entrance to the town of Montebelluna, the redhead said, 'There are German guards here. We must laugh and chat about women's matters so they understand we are defenceless females.'

Which is what they did, giggling about how to draw a straight line with charcoal down the back of their legs in order to make it look like they were wearing nylons. Except a guard with steely blue eyes levelled his gun at them and barked, 'Where are you going?'

Lidia's heart pounded so loudly she was sure he could hear it.

'We need to go to the Asolo hospital,' the redhead said, 'to visit our sick grandmother.'

'*Ach, gut,*' the guard said, lowering his weapon. 'You may pass.'

Lidia had heard of Asolo, one of the most beautiful *borghi* in Italy. However they cycled right past the signpost to the road leading up to it and headed towards a high mountain etched against the deep blue sky. About half an hour later, they'd reached their destination, and not before time as the sun was dipping behind the hills to the west. They'd come to a halt in a farmyard at the top of a steep hill. 'Where are we?' Lidia asked, her legs wobbling as she dismounted.

'My family's home.' The girl rested her bike against the wall of a henhouse. 'You should be safe here. My name is Rosina Zalunardi, by the way.'

'And I am Elena Moretti,' Lidia introduced herself. Would she ever get used to her alias? If the war went on much longer, she would have to.

A middle-aged couple approached—the man sporting a magnificent black handlebar moustache, and the plump woman's greying red hair escaping from a headscarf. Rosina introduced her parents and then her brother, Antonio, a gangly young man who came out of the farmhouse.

'Please come inside,' Signora Zalunardi said, indicating towards the left of the building. The right-hand side of the same structure was composed of a barn with a hay loft above.

Lidia stepped into the gloom of a kitchen lit by ox-fat candles. Plainly, the Zalunardis did not have electricity. There was no running water either, Lidia realised, when she was shown to a basin which she had to fill with water from a pitcher to wash her hands. But the kitchen was warm from the wood burning stove and the aroma of *pasta e fagioli* bean soup made her mouth water. She shrugged off her coat and sat at the table next to Rosina. Signora

Zalunardi handed them each a cup of hot grain coffee and placed a bowl containing some precious sugar in front of them. 'You must be tired, girls. We will eat soon and then you can go up to bed.'

'Thank you so much for taking me in,' Lidia said, stirring a teaspoon of sugar into her drink.

'When we heard what was happening to your community, we had to do something to help.' Signor Zalunardi's voice was gruff. He spread his work-worn hands wide. 'We must speak no more about it. The village people will be curious about you. We have decided to stick as close to the truth as possible, and we will tell them you are the daughter of a distant cousin in Porto Marghera, here to get away from the bombing. Your accent would give you away if we said you came from anywhere else.'

Signor Zalunardi was speaking the local dialect, a variant of Venetian, which Lidia had heard all her life and could speak well enough. She got the gist of what he was saying, even if she didn't understand every word.

She finished her coffee, then suddenly needed to use the bathroom. She crossed her legs and squirmed.

'I'll show you where to go,' Rosina offered, clearly noticing her discomfort.

Lidia's heart dropped when she was led outside into the freezing night air. The toilet occupied an outhouse and the stench made her gag. She relieved herself, then waited, stamping her feet in the cold while Rosina did the same. On their way back up the path to the farmhouse, Rosina lit a cigarette and offered Lidia one, which she accepted gladly to calm her churning stomach. 'I suppose you find us such peasants and our home nothing like what you are used to.' Rosina blew out a puff of smoke.

Lidia shook her head. 'Our apartment in Venice was wrecked by the Fascists. They took my papa away and now I'm alone in the world.' Her voice trembled. 'I'm deeply touched by your kindness. Yours and your family's.'

Rosina patted her arm. 'Oh, my dear, how you must have suffered.'

They finished smoking, then returned to the kitchen, where Signora Zalunardi was ladling the bean soup into earthenware bowls. Rosina went to slice bread from the white loaf on the counter. Signor Zalunardi had sat at the head of the table, and Antonio was pouring everyone a glass of red wine.

Lidia felt the weight of everyone's eyes on her as she spooned the soup into her mouth. Her tummy rumbled in appreciation. 'This is delicious,' she said.

'Here in the countryside, we manage to feed ourselves better than people in the cities,' Signor Zalunardi said proudly. 'We can live off our land.'

Lidia sipped her wine and listened to the Zalunardis' discussion of the upcoming slaughter of their pig to make salami. She was grateful she was one of those Jews who ate pork.

Talk soon turned to the fact that Antonio would reach the age to be conscripted into Mussolini's National Republican Army next year. 'I will not fight for that *stronzo* Fascist shit-head,' Antonio said, his Adam's apple bobbing.

'What will you do?' Lidia gulped. Those who refused the draft were sentenced to death.

'I will go up to the mountain behind us. Monte Grappa. To join with the partisans.'

Lidia remembered learning a song that had been written during the First World War, *Monte Grappa tu sei la mia patria*. Monte Grappa, you are our homeland, you are the star that points the way, you are the glory, the will, the destiny, that brings us back to Italy.

There were trenches up there where, after harsh fighting, the Italians had held back the Austrians in 1918.

'*Viva Italia*,' the words burst from her. 'Long live Italy.'

'*Evviva. Evviva,*' Rosina, Antonio and her parents echoed. Everyone clinked glasses and drank down the rest of their wine.

'Are there many partisans on the mountain?' Lidia asked, accepting a refill of her glass from Antonio.

A smile played across his lips and his eyes glowed in the candlelight. 'More are arriving all the time. It's a place where you can breathe the air of freedom. A place where ex-soldiers have been joined by antifascists, escaped Allied POWs, as well as deserters from Mussolini's republic. The Fascists don't dare set foot up there for fear of being killed.'

Lidia's jaw dropped—it sounded like a utopia.

'The men are spread over a wide area, staying in tents, farms and cowsheds,' Rosina added. 'I work in secret as a *stafetta*, a courier, to take messages to them from my employer, the Conte Corradini, who is in touch with the National Liberation Committee.'

It was the count who'd arranged for Lidia to stay with the Zalunardis, she recalled.

'I'm proud of my daughter,' Signora Zalunardi said, 'but I can't help worrying—'

Rosina patted her mamma's hand. 'There's nothing to

worry about. The Fascists and Germans ignore us couriers as we go about on our bicycles. They believe that women are too weak to be a threat.'

Antonio puffed out his chest. 'I can't wait to fight those bastards.'

'And you will,' Rosina said, her smile warm. 'But first you need to join the partisans.'

Signor Zalunardi, who had been silent during the discussion, leant towards his son. 'Get in some shooting practice with me before you go up there. We can hunt wild boar in the woods.'

'I will take my own shotgun when I join up before my eighteenth birthday…'

'Which won't be until April, thankfully,' Signora Zalunardi said. 'I will have you with me for a few more months.'

Rosina had started to clear the dishes, and Lidia rose to her feet to help. '*A letto*, bedtime,' Rosina said after she and Lidia had done the washing up. 'I hope you don't mind sharing a bed with me, Elena.'

Upstairs, it was freezing, and the windowpanes had frosted up on the inside. Lidia had never shared a bed with anyone in her life, but she was grateful for the warmth of another body. She lay awake for a short while, listening to Rosina's soft snores. Where was Papa? Lidia hoped he was well. And, on that hope, she gave in to her tiredness.

Chapter 10

Charlotte, 2010

I had breakfast on the terrace, helping myself from the ample buffet of succulent fruits, cereals, breads, jams, cheeses, and cold meats. While I ate, the high mountain behind the village drew my gaze, and I decided I would drive up there before I went back to the UK. The view from the summit would be amazing.

I sipped my frothy cappuccino. How strange to find myself interested in visiting a mountain! Having grown up in Hong Kong, where the weekends during the long summer months would be spent escaping the hustle and bustle of the city by heading to one of the outlying islands and snorkelling in the crystal-clear waters, I'd always preferred the sea. I could swim like a fish; at boarding school, I'd been the captain of the swimming team.

The arrival of Francesca interrupted my reverie. She

sat at my table and delved in her handbag for her cigarettes. She offered me one, but I declined. 'Did you sleep well?' she asked.

'Like a log. The bed is really comfortable.'

'Alex said you might be wanting to stay in the annex next week?'

'I told him I'd think about it.' I toyed with my coffee spoon. 'And now that I've thought about it, yes, I'd like to stay on.' And I would. I loved it here, and, even if I hit a brick wall finding out about Gran's past, I could treat myself to a short holiday in this gorgeous place. The past year at Tower High had been gruelling and I needed to recharge my batteries.

I drank my cappuccino while Francesca finished her cigarette. She told me that she and her boyfriend were planning on getting married in September. 'We'll have the reception here at the hotel, of course. I don't suppose you could come?'

I shook my head. 'Thanks, that would be lovely but I need to be back at work on the first. What a shame...'

'In Italy, the schools don't re-start until mid-September. It's too hot, usually, before then.'

I could believe that—the day was already heating up and promised to be a scorcher.

We lapsed into silence, and I scrubbed a hand through my hair, pushing it back from my already damp forehead. I thought about last night and how much I'd enjoyed Francesca and Alex's company. When I'd eventually returned Gary's call after finishing those chocolates, I'd gushed about my new friends in response to his remark that I must be lonely. Had he been hedging for an invitation to tag along with me? *I really hope not.*

Thinking about Alex had stoked my curiosity. 'Your brother said he has a son,' I blurted to Francesca. 'Does his wife work in the hotel too?'

Francesca shook her head. 'Alex and Simonetta are divorced. She's a high-powered businesswoman, working for her family's shoe manufacturing business. Simonetta spends more time travelling than at home with her son and is happy for Alex to look after him when she's away.'

'How old is the boy?'

'Gabriel is six. A great kid...'

I decided to change the subject; I didn't want Francesca to think I was overly interested in Alex. Which I wasn't—I had sworn off men, hadn't I? So I inquired, 'What time should we go to the Municipio?'

Francesca checked her phone. 'We can go now if you like. It will be open by the time we get there.'

'Perfect.'

We pushed back our chairs and left. The walk to the centre of the village took about fifteen minutes down a road hugging the edge of the hillside. A cobbled square opened before us, with a fountain at the centre topped by a statue of the winged lion of Saint Mark—a vestige of the era when Treviso province was part of the Venetian Republic, I remembered reading. A barrel-chested pigeon bobbed down to drink from the water. It flew up to perch on a stone balcony from where purple petunias cascaded in a riot of blooms.

We went up the steps of the solidly built town hall, and Francesca led me through to the registry office, where the clerk listened to her explanation of my quest. He checked his records and confirmed that Rosina Zalunardi was, indeed, a Sant'Illaria resident. 'I can't give you her address for data protection reasons,' he said, and Francesca translated, 'but I will pass on a message to her daughter. It will be up to her if she contacts you or not.'

'*Grazie,*' I thanked him, surprised and thrilled by his offer. '*Molto gentile*. Very kind.' I'd practised the words in advance, having found the pronunciation on YouTube.

After I'd also thanked Francesca for helping me, we stepped out into the bright sunshine, then walked back to the hotel. 'I think I'll go for a swim in the pool,' I said.

'Lucky you. I've got a mountain of paperwork.' She groaned. 'I'm an accountant and do all the bookkeeping. But I might join you for a dip before lunch.'

'Hope to see you later,' I said, waving as I went up to my room to change.

The water was exactly the right temperature to be refreshing, and I swam lengths for about half an hour, working off those breakfast carbs. Then I climbed out and found myself a sun lounger. The pool area was quiet; most of my fellow guests had gone in the Corradini's pullman bus for a daytrip to Venice. I adjusted my bikini and laid back to soak up the rays.

I thought about Rosina Zalunardi and the conundrum of the lioness. The letter was in my bag and it called to me. I tweaked the lounger to sitting position and extracted my phone. But, before I could start inputting the words, the high-pitched sound of a child's voice stopped me in my tracks. A boy with curly dark hair came running towards the pool, followed by Alex, who was dressed in swim shorts, a couple of towels slung over his arm.

With a splash, the boy jumped into the water, calling out, '*Babbo, babbo*,' and other words in Italian.

'*Aspetta un attimo*,' Alex responded. '*Arrivo….*'

He approached me with a smile. 'My son, Gabriel. I've told him to wait, and that I'll be with him shortly.' He dropped the towels on the lounger next to mine. 'Hope we're not disturbing you.'

'Not at all.' I peeled my eyes away from his toned body. 'I was about to carry on trying to work out what Rosina Zalunardi wrote in her letters.'

'I can help you with that if you want.' He smiled. 'After I've had a swim…'

'Thanks. *Molto gentile*,' I said.

He quirked a brow. 'I didn't know you spoke any Italian.'

'Only a few words, but I'd like to learn more.'

'If you're staying longer, you're bound to improve.'

'I told Francesca earlier that I'd like to book the annex.'

'Good. *Bene.*'

I glanced at him from under my lashes. Was he being polite? Or was he genuinely pleased? *Hmmm, his smile looks genuine.*

'*Babbo. Babbo*!' Gabriel jumped up and down in the pool.

'*Arrivo!*' Alex strode into the shallows.

I watched him splashing with his boy. He seemed an attentive father.

'Come and join us,' he beckoned.

'Love to,' I called out. Only to be friendly, I told myself. And because I was feeling hot again.

I dived in at the deep end and swam a slow crawl to

where Alex and Gabriel were throwing a beach ball back and forth. After Alex had introduced me to his son, an idea occurred to me. I recalled a pool game that I used to play in Hong Kong called "Marco Polo". I suggested it, and Alex asked what was involved.

'One player is chosen as "It". The "It" player, with closed eyes, must try to find and tag any one of the other players, relying on hearing to find someone to tag. The player who is "It" shouts "Marco" and the other players must all respond by shouting "Polo", which the "It" player uses to try to find them. If a player is tagged, then that player becomes "It". If "It" suspects that a player has left the pool, they can shout "Fish out of water!" and the player who is out of the pool is the new "It".'

'Sounds like fun,' Alex chuckled before translating the rules into Italian.

'*Voglio essere "It" prima*,' Gabriel squealed, and Alex told me that Gabriel wanted to be "it" first.

We started to play, and. soon Gabriel had tagged Alex, and then, an impossibly short while later, I felt Alex's hand on my shoulder. I wondered if father and son had been cheating, not keeping their eyes fully closed, but didn't give voice to my thoughts.

Alex suggested we leave Gabriel to swim for a while on his own while he took a look at Rosina's letter.

I thanked him and followed him out of the pool.

'How did you and Francesca get on at the Municipio?' he asked as we towelled ourselves dry.

I told him about our successful mission, and handed him a letter, which he read in silence.

'It's mainly about the unveiling of a bronze statue up

on Monte Grappa dedicated to the partisans,' he said. 'Rosina had been invited to attend.'

'Why would she be writing to my grandfather about that?' I wondered.

'There was a terrible massacre in this area during the war. Hundreds of members of the Resistance were killed or deported to death camps by the Nazi-fascists.'

'Oh, God, how awful,' I gasped.

'My grandfather could barely talk about it as he knew some of the people who were involved.' Alex paused, rubbed his chin. 'Maybe Rosina will shed some light on what happened.'

'That's if she agrees to talk to me,' I sighed.

'It's my day off tomorrow. Gabriel loves it up on the Grappa in the summer as it's a lot cooler than down here in the village. We could take a picnic and some bikes. The trails are perfect for cycling. Oh, and we could have a look at the statue, if you like.'

'That would be fab. Thanks.'

Alex leant towards me and touched my arm. 'We'll get to the bottom of the mystery of your grandmother's past. I'm sure of it.'

'I hope so,' I breathed. The touch of his fingers filled my chest with comforting warmth.

'Zia Francesca!' Gabriel suddenly shouted from the pool.

Alex's sister was approaching, her face wreathed in smiles. 'I've had a call from the Municipio. Rosina has agreed for you to visit her tomorrow afternoon.'

'Wow. Just…wow,' I said.

Chapter 11

Lidia, 1944

Lidia opened the farmhouse kitchen door to let in the cool morning air. It had been seven months since she'd arrived in Sant'Illaria—seven long months since she'd stood at the window in the Venice apartment, gazing towards the mountains on that cold December day.

She released a deep sigh; she wished there'd been some news from Marta. Except, Marta hadn't been allowed to contact her; it would have been too dangerous for everyone concerned. Lidia still didn't know where Papa was. She slept with Mamma's prayer book under her pillow, knowing full well it was risky keeping something that would identify her as being Jewish, but clinging nevertheless to the last link with her old life.

Church bells echoed from the village below, clear and bold despite the distance. Signora Zalunardi went to mass every morning to pray for Antonio's safety. She was there now but would be home soon, and Lidia went back to help Rosina with breakfast.

A grunt came from Signor Zalunardi, who was packing his tools for the morning's work. He'd been busy since the start of the summer, making use of the longer days by chopping wood, fixing fences, hoeing vegetables, watering vines, and tending to the olives. Lidia knew the life of a *contadino* farmer was hard, but she'd never imagined how hard. And these days Signor Zalunardi had to toil even harder without Antonio to help him.

Lidia missed Antonio almost as much as his family. He was an accomplished accordion player and would keep them entertained in the evenings with his songs. But everyone was proud of him, proud that he'd joined up with the Italia Libera Campo Croce brigade in April to fight for the freedom of Italy. Only last month they'd carried out an important action, sneaking into the Tombion fort in the valley below Monte Grappa and "removing" twenty-three quintals of explosives. The Germans had planned to use the dynamite in the construction of fortifications for another defence line, apparently. But during the night of the sixth of June, Antonio had gone with a group of partisans to detonate the railway tunnel nearest the fort. They'd blasted a thirty-metre crater in the Valsugana line—a line used by German military convoys.

Lidia smiled to herself, remembering that Radio Londra had praised the protagonists and reported that it had been "the most important act of sabotage at European level carried out thus far by the Italian Resistance". So Conte Corradini had informed Rosina, who'd relayed the praise back to Antonio and his brigade.

The event had coincided with the Allies finally liberating Rome—another piece of information gleaned from Radio Londra. The problem was that the Normandy landings had all but wiped out reporting on the Italian campaign, and the Allies' progress up the boot of Italy was being largely ignored. How Lidia wished she was back in Venice, listening to the news with Papa instead of hearing it second hand from Conte Corradini via Rosina. Lidia had only met the Count once, soon after her arrival in Sant'Illaria. Her first and only impression had been that he seemed rather pompous—he'd spoken Tuscan Italian, not the Venetian dialect, and smoked his cigarette from a holder, his chestnut-brown hair slicked back with pomade and his leather shoes so shiny he could probably see his face in them. The Count kept a house full of servants, and rumour had it that he enjoyed a legion of lady lovers as well.

Lidia stepped across the uneven kitchen floor to where Rosina was heating milk for their grain coffee. 'Remember what we talked about last night?' she whispered to her.

Rosina had explained that the partisans were finding it difficult to communicate with the escaped Allied POWs who had arrived up on the mountain. They had tried involving them in joint sabotage missions—but needed someone who spoke better English than they did in order to coordinate actions with the group. On hearing this, an idea had occurred to Lidia. 'I could be their interpreter,' she'd said.

'I will mention it to the Count,' Rosina whispered back. 'But I'll need to do it in such a way that he won't think I've been betraying secrets.'

'Surely he knows I can be trusted?'

'He keeps telling me not to trust anyone.'

'I could also assist with medical matters,' Lidia murmured. 'Please remind him.' She lifted the pan from the stove. 'And tell him that I can shoot.' Recently, she'd been going out at night with Signor Zalunardi to hunt the wild boar, whose meat supplemented their diet. Signor Zalunardi had taught her to fire a gun and had told her she was a good shot.

If only she could take matters into her own hands and simply climb the mountain, find a brigade of partisans, and ask to join up. Except, she didn't know the terrain or any of the passwords. She might even be mistaken for a spy and executed; Rosina had said that's what happened from time to time. Monte Grappa belonged to the *partigiani,* and they guarded it with ferocity.

Rosina looked her in the eye. 'I will try and speak with *il conte* today, I promise, Elena,' she said.

After breakfast, Rosina left for Villa Corradini. Officially, she worked as a housemaid there and it was only occasionally that she would head up the mountain under cover of darkness with an important message. Sometimes she would stay up on the Grappa for days, acting as a courier between the two Action Party Italia Libera Brigades, the Communist Garibaldi divisions and the Socialist Brigata Matteotti. Other times, she would be back home the next morning. Lidia envied Rosina her involvement with *la resistenza.* She didn't want to say out loud that she was bored. Bored and frustrated by the daily routine of the farm and overwhelmed by the feeling of hopelessness that had built up within her of late. If she didn't do something positive soon, she feared she would lose her mind.

She stared down at her hands, rubbed raw from scrubbing clothes and household linen against a corrugated board in the washing tub, using soap made from pig fat, which had been rendered into tallow and mixed with caustic soda. The water had to be hauled up from the well at the back of the house, then heated in a pail hanging over the fire. In this hot weather, it was sweaty, back-breaking work. Signora Zalunardi had protested at first that Lidia shouldn't put herself out. But Lidia had insisted on helping. It was the least she could do.

She didn't want to seem ungrateful. Didn't want the Zalunardis, who were risking their lives by taking her in, to think she was unappreciative of what they'd done for her. But wouldn't it be safer for them if she wasn't here? The partisans had turned Monte Grappa into a fortress. It would be better for the Zalunardis and better for her if she could be there instead.

She spent the morning helping Signora Zalunardi feed the sow and her piglets, tend to the cows, the rabbits, the pigeons, the quails and the chickens. They gathered up their rich droppings for the dung heap to make manure. Nothing went to waste.

After lunch—a plate of toasted polenta served with salami, accompanied by ripe red tomatoes from the vegetable garden—Lidia sat outside in the shade of a chestnut tree while Signor and Signora Zalunardi went for an afternoon rest.

One of the farm cats perched on an upturned barrel, staring at Lidia while it scratched at its fleas. A wood pigeon cooed in the branches above, and cicadas screeched their mating songs. She brushed a pesky fly away from her face.

Suddenly everything went quiet.

Everything except the sound of a motor engine grinding gears.

The cat jumped off its perch, and Lidia leapt to her feet.

A lorry had pulled up, and five fearsome-looking men were jumping out of it.

Dressed in their signature Black Brigade shirts and caps with skull insignias on the front, they carried submachine guns slung over their shoulders, and ammunition belts hung from their waists.

O, Dio. Lidia's heard thudded. Had they come to arrest her?

'Get Signor Zalunardi for me,' the stocky *squadrista* leading the group barked.

'No need, I'm here,' Signor Zalunardi's voice came from behind. 'What do you want?'

'Supplies.'

'*Mamma, Mamma,*' Signora Zalunardi cried, coming up and standing next to Lidia.

Without another word, the men started helping themselves to the farm animals—the piglets, rabbits, pigeons, quails and chickens. The poor beasts squealed and squawked and bleated as the squad-men threw them into the back of the truck.

Lidia stared open-mouthed. Signora Zalunardi plucked at her apron, whimpering non-stop. Signor Zalunardi planted his feet wide, his moustache bristling.

'Where is your storeroom?' the stocky front man snarled, levelling his gun at Signor Zalunardi.

Lidia wanted the gun to backfire and blow a hole in the despicable Fascist's puffed-up chest.

'Where. Is. Your. Storeroom?' he repeated.

'At... at... at the side of the house,' Signora Zalunardi stuttered.

The *fascista* kept his gun levelled while his squad ran off to plunder. They returned with sacks of flour, boxes of eggs, what was left of the apple harvest from last autumn, the cheese Lidia had helped Signora Zalunardi make, and enough vegetables to show they'd picked the plot clean.

Lidia's breath caught. What if they took the cows? The family would go desperately hungry without their milk.

But they were too big for the lorry, of course.

Without warning, the front man turned his gun from Signor Zalunardi to Lidia. His eyes raked her face and then travelled down her body. He licked his thick lips. 'Who are you?'

'She's our cousin from Porto Marghera, here to escape the Allied bombing,' Signor Zalunardi butted in.

'Let the girl speak for herself!'

Lidia's heart quaked. 'I'm Elena Moretti. As my cousin said, from Porto Marghera.'

'Where are your documents?'

'In the house. I'll get them.'

'I'll come with you.'

Oh God, what if he ransacks the bed and discovers Mamma's prayer book?

Her legs trembling, Lidia hurried up the narrow staircase. She took her fake I.D from the chest of drawers and, heart pounding, showed it to the *squadrista*.

He barely glanced at it. Out of the blue, he pushed her against the wall.

She opened her mouth to scream, but he clapped his pudgy hand over it.

He rubbed his hardened groin into her belly. Making vile groaning sounds, he slobbered his thick lips down the side of her neck and groped at her breasts.

Lidia's stomach heaved. 'Don't,' she pushed her hands against his chest and tried to jerk herself away. 'Please, don't.'

She squirmed, preparing to knee him where it would hurt. *Damn the consequences.*

'Is there a problem?' Signor Zalunardi's voice came from the doorway.

The hateful man stepped back. 'No problem. Just sampling the goods.' He lowered his voice and muttered, 'I will return soon and finish what I started.'

A soft growl came from Signor Zalunardi.

The Fascist turned on his heel and, laughing a cruel-sounding laugh, made his way back down the stairs.

Lidia's legs were shaking so much, she collapsed onto the bed.

'I'll go and get my wife.' Signor Zalunardi patted her on the shoulder.

'I'm fine,' Lidia breathed. 'He didn't do anything.'

'*Grazie a Dio,*' Signor Zalunardi thanked God. 'But I will fetch her all the same.'

After she'd reassured Signora Zalunardi that she was physically unharmed, Lidia spent the rest of the afternoon focusing on doing her chores. Would that Fascist pig have raped her if Signor Zalunardi hadn't come upstairs when he did? The thought of it made her want to throw up, so she avoided thinking about it. She set her heart on Rosina returning soon and telling her the Count had agreed that she should go up the mountain. It was the Count's connections with the National Liberation Committee which had led to Lidia being here, and she owed it to him to get his agreement first.

Rosina came home shortly after six. Lidia met her in the farmyard, worrying about how to tell her about the Black Brigade squad-men and what they'd done. Rosina leant her bike against the empty henhouse and grabbed Lidia's hand. 'I just found out that every farm around Sant'Illaria has been pillaged.' She glanced at Lidia and a frown wrinkled her brow. 'Did any *squadristi* come here?'

Lidia nodded, tongue-tied.

'*Maledetti,*' Rosina swore. 'Curse them to Hell.'

The Zalunardis came out of the house, and Signora Zalunardi took Rosina to one side.

Signor Zalunardi glanced at Lidia, and she glanced back at him, their looks saying more than words ever could.

Within minutes, Rosina had returned. 'I'm so sorry, my dear,' she said to Lidia. 'That man is a *stronzo* shithead for trying to violate you. The Count said you would be safer with my parents, but that is obviously not the case.' Rosina shook her head. 'I will take you up to Antonio and his brigade tonight. There is no time to waste. I will explain everything to the Count when I get back.'

Chapter 12

Lidia, 1944

Darkness was falling as Lidia said goodbye to Signora and Signor Zalunardi She thanked them from the bottom of her heart for their kindness and promised she would try and keep out of harm's way.

'You have become like a second daughter to me.' Signora Zalunardi sniffed back her tears.

Signor Zalunardi patted Lidia's arm. 'I am proud of you, Elena. Like I am proud of Antonio and Rosina.'

Lidia rubbed her hands down the legs of the trousers Rosina had lent her. Wearing *pantaloni* was expected of women who joined a brigade and far more practical than wearing a dress or a skirt. Lidia brushed a kiss to Signora Zalunardi's cheek and shook Signor Zalunardi's hand. '*Arrivederci e grazie ancora.*'

'Let's go.' Rosina swung her leg over the saddle of

her bike and Lidia followed suit. They'd already stowed their rucksacks in their baskets. A mixture of excitement and trepidation made Lidia's heart race. Excitement to finally be doing something positive. Trepidation as to how she would cope. She thought about the prayer book she'd packed in her bag; she so wanted to hold the *Siddur* and feel the comfort of its connection with Mamma and Papa.

After freewheeling down the steep hill, Lidia cycled behind Rosina at a slower pace through the village. She breathed a sigh of relief; no one was about. They passed Villa Corradini, then took the nearest of the several roads leading up the Grappa. The climb was gruelling, and the air had turned heavy, but moonlight shone down between the clouds onto the twenty-nine hair-pin bends and, about two hours after they'd left the farm, Rosina stopped and dismounted. It seemed like the middle of nowhere.

'Why are we stopping?' Lidia asked.

'There's a storm brewing, and this was where we'll spend the rest of the night. We're inside the mountain now,' Rosina said. 'Safe from those Fascist *stronzi.'* She pointed to a dark shape up ahead. 'We'll shelter in that shepherd's hut and go on to Campo Croce in the morning.'

They wheeled their bikes through the open door of the hut, fat drops of rain splattering them. A flash of lightning lit the sky, followed by a loud crack of thunder.

Rosina extracted a water canteen from her bag and took a sip before passing it to Lidia. They huddled together for warmth in the chilly darkness, listening to the storm and sharing confidences. Lidia heard all about Rosina's sweetheart who hadn't come back from the Russian front, and she told Rosina about Renzo. Both of them confided that they'd promised themselves they would never love again.

'What will you do when the war is over?' Rosina asked, yawning.

'Live in Venice with my papa and qualify as a doctor. And you?'

'Look after my parents in their old age and, hopefully, become an auntie to Antonio's future children.'

Lidia knew better than to suggest to Rosina that she would have children of her own one day. She couldn't envisage ever being in that position herself. 'Tell me more about the brigade,' she said.

'The majority are young. Escaping the draft like Antonio. I worry for them, as they have no military experience.'

'Who's in charge?'

'Rocco, Commander of the Matteotti, oversees all the partisans on the Grappa.' Rosina lowered her voice. 'Keep this to yourself, but the Allies have promised to send advisers soon.'

Rosina fell silent. Lidia pondered this development. She was about to ask how the Allied advisers would arrive, but Rosina had dropped off to sleep and was already snoring softly.

The shepherd's hut was made of wooden planks; draughts of air and the occasional raindrop were finding their way through the gaps. A droplet settled on Lidia's eyelids and she wiped it away. What would tomorrow bring? There was no use in worrying about it, she told herself, reaching for the prayer book in her rucksack and clutching it to her chest. *Whatever happens in the future, I will strive to make Papa proud.*

The next morning, after cycling for about half an hour along a narrow road winding through pine woods, Rosina stopped and Lidia halted her bike behind her. A field had opened before them. They'd arrived at one of the ubiquitous Monte Grappa pastures, where in peacetime farmers from the plain would bring their cows to spend the summer. But today, instead of cattle, there were tents and about fifty men spread out in front of a farmhouse with a barn attached. Some of the men were shaving, and others dismantling or assembling an assortment of rusty-looking weapons.

A slightly older man than the rest glanced up from his gun. '*Ciao*, Rosina,' he called out. 'Who's that with you?'

Rosina stepped forward and whispered something to him, which Lidia didn't catch. The man nodded and indicated she should approach. She sucked in a quick breath and did as he'd asked. 'My battle name is Falcon,' he said. 'I'm in charge of this motley crew.' He held her in his dark gaze. 'Rosina vouches for you. She tells me you can speak English. And that you've studied medicine?'

'I'm a good shot as well,' Lidia boasted. Papa had told her never to sell herself short in an interview. And this was surely an interview of sorts.

'Ha,' Falcon laughed, glancing down at his Beretta. 'We don't have any guns to spare. Still waiting for Allied air drops of weapons.'

'I hope they will arrive soon.'

'So do we,' he chuckled wryly, 'so do we.' He slung his Beretta over his shoulder and got to his feet. 'Come and meet the soldiers who used to be our enemies and are now our friends. Let's see how good you are at speaking English.'

They sauntered between the tents and made their way to the edge of the field, where about twenty men were grouped together dunking chunks of bread into bowls of milk for their breakfast. A burly, sandy-haired fellow detached himself from the rest and saluted Falcon.

'This is Captain Smith. Talk to him, Elena. I think I've understood the group are South African POWs who were held in a camp near Padova. Find out as much as you can about them, then report back to me.'

Later, after Lidia had spoken with Captain Smith, Rosina took her to the farmhouse, which was the brigade's H.Q, and sat her down at a refectory table in the dining room, where Falcon was enjoying a cup of coffee.

'How did you get on?' he inquired.

'You are right. They're South Africans.'

Falcon's mouth twisted. 'The *inglesi* can draw on men from their empire in all corners of the world.'

Lidia kept to herself the fact that Mussolini had also tried to create an empire. She wasn't sure how much of a *fascista* Falcon had been before he became an anti-Fascist. So many Italians grew up believing the doctrine.

'The South Africans were captured at Tobruk. A ship brought them to Italy,' she said. 'Imprisoned in a labour camp, they managed to escape after the armistice or they'd have been deported to Germany.'

'Where have they been all this time? The armistice was over ten months ago.'

'They were looked after by farming families down on the plain. Captain Smith spoke highly of them and told me they would forever be grateful.'

'So how did the South Africans get up here?'

'A line of *stafette* conducted them from town to town in small groups. The South Africans plan to make their way to safety in Switzerland, eventually.'

'They all want to go to Switzerland,' Falcon barked a wry laugh. 'Not many make it.'

'Captain Smith said they would be happy to join in with joint sabotage actions against "Jerry".'

'Good. *Bene.* They can earn their keep.'

Lidia gazed longingly at the bread and jam on the table. All that cycling last night had depleted her energy levels.

'Are you hungry, Elena?' Falcon pushed the food towards her. 'Help yourself.' He glanced at Rosina. 'You, too. After you've eaten, take your things to the hayloft. You can both sleep up there.'

'Where's Antonio?' Rosina asked, stuffing bread into her mouth. 'I've been looking for him everywhere.'

'Out on patrol. He'll be back soon.'

Lidia poured herself a glass of milk and drank it down. She spread jam onto a slice of bread then ate it. She could tell that Rosina was worried about her brother. Although the Grappa belonged to the partisans, they fought tooth and nail to keep it that way. Rosina had told her there were constant incursions, and it was up to the patrols to shoot first and ask questions later.

They spent the rest of the morning in a room at the back of the farmhouse, helping with the printing of antifascist leaflets Rosina would take down with her to Sant'Illaria tomorrow. Tommaso, an art student before he became a partisan, had drawn a cartoon strip of the Germans running from the Resistance. 'It will happen,' he smiled. 'I'm sure of it.'

Rosina gave him a brief smile back, but it was obvious her heart wasn't in it.

She looped her arm through Lidia's and they headed to the refectory for lunch—homemade pasta with wild boar ragù. 'Strange Antonio hasn't returned to eat.' She drew her eyebrows together. 'I've never known him miss a meal before.'

'They've probably got held up.' *Stupid, Lidia. It's obvious they've got held up.* 'Try not to worry.'

They went to help do the dishes, Rosina introducing Lidia to Fausto, the cook. 'Your ragù was delicious,' Lidia said.

Fausto beamed with evident pleasure. He said he used to work at a nearby hotel until it closed because of the war.

Suddenly the door crashed open, and a skinny young partisan erupted into the room. 'Falcon sent me to get you.' His breaths burst in and out. 'The patrol has returned and one of them is injured.'

The colour had faded from Rosina's cheeks, and she grabbed hold of Lidia's arm. 'Is it… is it Antonio?' she asked.

'No. Not him,' the skinny partisan said. 'One of the others.'

Fausto shoved a first-aid box into Lidia's hands. 'It's normally me who patches them up. It's good we have someone who's better qualified.'

Lidia ran out of the kitchen with Rosina to find Antonio had arrived in the dining room. After a brief greeting, he took them to his injured comrade, a ginger-haired fellow who was telling everyone not to fuss, that he was fine.

Thankfully, it was only a superficial gash. A bullet had glanced off the side of his face, by the hairline, causing it to bleed profusely.

Lidia cleaned up the injury and taped a gauze dressing to the cut. 'Avoid getting any dirt into the wound, or it will become infected,' she said.

She helped the man to his tent, despite his protests that he didn't want to cause any trouble. But he was obviously exhausted and fell asleep almost immediately.

Antonio said he would stay with his comrade, so Lidia and Rosina kept him company. Whispering, they explained why Lidia had come up to the Grappa.

'Those *stronzi*,' Antonio growled. 'I can't wait to kill a Fascist. But the Black Brigades never come up here. They're cowardly bullies. Too scared to confront us. I've only managed to shoot a couple of Germans.'

Lidia asked him about the camp routine, and he explained it mostly involved waiting around between sabo-tage missions and patrolling. It was hard to keep boredom at bay. 'If we had more ammunition, we could hold target practice. But we can't waste a single bullet.'

'How do you get supplies?'

'H.Q sends up wine, maize, flour and beans. Fausto makes our polenta and pasta. He grows tomatoes and lettuce at the back of the house.' Antonio made a sad face. 'I miss Mamma's cooking.'

He closed his eyes and yawned.

'Are you tired?' Rosina pulled him in for a hug.

'Think I'll take a nap. We were awake well before dawn.'

'We'll leave you to it then,' Rosina said.

After a short rest in the hayloft, Lidia and Rosina washed with water from the pump, then made their way over to the kitchen to lend Fausto a hand. 'Not because we're women,' Rosina said. 'The men have a rota and Falcon will put you on it, Elena, but I'd like to do my bit.'

Supper consisted of bean soup and dark brown bread, washed down with copious amounts of wine. Subsequently, Lidia sat by a campfire with Rosina and the others, singing *Fischia il Vento, The Wind Blows,* the partisans' anthem, while Antonio played his accordion.

If cruel death takes us,
harsh revenge will come from the partisan.
Already certain is the unforgiving fate of the vile
treasonous Fascist.
The wind ceases and the storm grows calm.
The proud partisan returns home.
Blowing in the wind is his red flag.
Victorious, at last we are free.

They sang the final verse, then fell silent. Lidia wrapped her arms around herself, fired up by the patriotic words. A warm glow spread through her. This was where she belonged. She would fight the vile Fascists until the wind of freedom blew through her country.

The sudden rumble of a plane engine vibrated in the air.

'*Lancio*, air drop,' came a cry from the far end of the field.

'Clear the area!' Falcon shouted. 'Light the flares!'

Parachutes were falling from the sky. Parachutes with what looked like wooden boxes attached to their cords.

'Weapons and ammunition!' Antonio yelled, running towards a crate that had just landed.

Falcon came up with a crowbar and cranked the box open.

Cans of food and sundry items of clothing spilled onto the grass.

'*Merda,*' Falcon swore. 'Shit.'

And Lidia's heart sank.

Chapter 13

Charlotte, 2010

We left the hotel straight after breakfast in Alex's Alfa SUV, three bikes mounted on a carrier attached to the boot. Gabriel was chatting non-stop with excitement. I wished I understood what he was saying, and Alex tried to get him to speak a little English—just the few phrases he'd learnt thus far at primary school—but Gabriel was shy.

Alex's fingers on the steering wheel drew my gaze. His nails were short and well-manicured. He took one hand from the wheel to change gear, and heat flushed through me—I was intensely aware of him, his long, lean thighs encased in tight jeans and his broad shoulders hugged by a black t-shirt. I tore my eyes away and gazed out of the window. *Get a grip, girl. You are NOT attracted to Alex.* In any case, he'd shown no sign of being attracted to me. He was just being friendly.

Hair-pin bend followed hair-pin bend as we climbed the steep side of the mountain. The terrain was rugged and fir trees clung to the slopes.

I gasped as a paraglider floated down in the periphery of my vision. 'Oh my God. That looks dangerous.'

'It's a popular sport around here,' Alex said.

'Rather them than me.' I shuddered. 'I'm not scared of heights, but I like the feel of solid ground beneath my feet.'

'Me too,' he grinned.

'My ex was into parachuting.' The words were out of my mouth before I could stop them.

'Your ex?'

'Yeah. We split up last February.'

'Ah, I was wondering if you were with someone…'

'*Babbo, babbo. Guarda!*' Gabriel's high-pitched voice came from the back seat.

'He's telling me to look.'

Alex slowed the Alfa.

A magnificent stag had emerged from the trees.

I took my phone from my pocket and snapped a picture. 'He's beautiful,' I said.

The deer bounded off and we carried on until the road levelled out and a meadow opened before us, dotted with cows. 'It's stunning,' I said. 'Almost like another country.'

'It is,' Alex agreed. 'The top of the Grappa is a self-contained world. A plateau with its own plains, woods, slopes and hills.'

'How high are we?'

'The summit is about 1800 metres.'

I did a rough calculation in my head. 'That's nearly six thousand feet. No wonder my ears are popping.'

'Popping. *Cosa significa* "popping"?' came the little voice from behind.

'Gabriel wants to know the meaning of "popping",' Alex chuckled.

I turned in my seat and pointed to my ears. Then made a "pop" sound by curling my index finger in my mouth and popping it.

Gabriel exploded into a peal of laughter. 'Pop, pop, pop,' he giggled, and I giggled with him.

Alex rolled down the windows and we breathed in the fresh mountain air. 'Nice and cool up here after the storm last night,' he said.

I'd been woken in the early hours by crashes of thunder. 'It was really noisy.'

'Blame the mountains for that.'

'I vaguely remember learning about convection in geography lessons.'

Alex went on to ask me where I'd gone to school and I told him. He mentioned that he'd attended a Catholic institution near Sant'Illaria before studying at the University of Trento.

'Is that where you learnt to speak such good English?' I asked.

'I was lucky enough to get an Erasmus grant and spent a year at Kings College London Business School.'

'That's amazing. I wish I'd studied Italian,' I said wistfully. 'But it was a no-no given Gran's attitude towards Italy.'

Alex was slowing the Alfa now and parking it by the side of the road. 'We've arrived at the partisan memorial.'

We got out of the car. A feeling of unease came over

me. Rosina had written to Grandad about this monument. Therefore, there must be some link to Gran. Was she in any way connected with the partisans?

Gabriel had bounded ahead down a stony path. Alex held out his hand. Just a friendly gesture, I told myself. His warm fingers enclosed mine, dispelling the disquiet within me.

We stopped at a panoramic terrace—a semi-circular platform enclosed by a low wall, which Alex called a *belvedere*. The meaning of the word, beautiful view, wasn't lost on me; the panorama was truly breath-taking. The Venetian plain spread out below us, the towns and villages on a carpet of green. 'It's like we're up in a plane looking down,' I said.

Gabriel was trying to climb the parapet, and Alex dropped my hand and held him back while pointing out the landmarks. 'On the left-hand horizon, you can see Porto Marghera. Venice is directly behind it,' he said. 'Over there, right of the centre, are the Euganean Hills next to Padua. And to the far right the Berici Hills near Vicenza. Those distant hills on the horizon between them, aren't hills at all but the high mountains beyond Bologna. They're the start of the Apennines, which run down the entire length of the Italian peninsula.'

'Wow,' I exclaimed. 'Amazing.'

'I'll take you to the statue now,' Alex smiled.

A mound occupied the area to the right of the terrace, and he led me down a narrow passage lined with cement, which had been cut into the hillock and sliced it in two. We eased ourselves through and stepped onto a stone-paved surface.

At the centre of a concentric pitch stood a statue. Cast in bronze. Abstract, but incredibly powerful. A giant figure, feet planted wide. Stretching his hands upwards. Hands that appeared to have been freed of the bonds that had tied them.

Alex indicated the concrete plaques at the foot of the statue. 'Those are the names of the four partisan brigades which operated up here.'

I read out loud, '*Brigata Italia Libera Archeson. Brigata Matteotti. Brigata Gramsci. Brigata Italia Libera Campo Croce.* I hadn't realised there were so many...'

To the left of the passage we'd come through was a small cave partially blocked by barbed wire, about five foot high and not much wider. 'What's that?' I pointed.

Alex took a couple of steps forward and read the inscription at the entrance. 'It's where seven partisans were burnt alive by flamethrowers during a round-up carried out by the Nazi-fascists on 22 September 1944.' He glanced at me. ''I'm sorry. I should have warned you this was here.'

'It's horrible.' I shivered.

Alex put his arm around my shoulder and I leant into him.

Then, suddenly, with a shout, he dropped his hand.

I gave a gasp. Gabriel had started to squirm his way into the cave past the barbed wire.

Alex leapt forward and grabbed his son by the arm. '*Basta!* Enough!'

Gabriel wriggled from his hold and gave him a cheeky smile. '*Ho fame.*'

'My boy is hungry,' Alex chuckled. 'As if that were an excuse. Let's have lunch then take those bikes off the car and ride them.'

'Sounds like a plan.'

Surrounded by families enjoying a day out, we ate our ham panini, cherry tomatoes and crisps while sitting at one of several wooden tables placed in the grounds of a hotel near the Word War I shrine at the summit of the Grappa. The *sacrario* was composed of five enormous concentric concrete circles laid on top of each other to form a pyramid. Each circle held niches, Alex explained, containing the ossified remains of over twenty-two thousand Italian and Austro-Hungarian soldiers who had been killed up here in 1918. He asked if I wanted to visit the shrine, but I declined, still deeply affected by what I'd seen at the partisans' monument.

I was glad Gabriel was with us. He'd come out of his shell and was curious to know the names of things in English. Interacting with him stopped me from dwelling on that horrific cave and what had occurred there.

We finished our panini, then had a coffee while Gabriel made short work of a chocolate gelato. After using the facilities in the hotel, we returned to the car for a brief drive to the centre of the mountain top, where we unloaded our bikes.

I adjusted the seat of mine to my height, swung my leg over and squeezed the handles in my palms. My bike belonged to the collection Hotel Villa Corradini kept for lending to guests, and it was perfect.

'What about helmets?'

'Got them here,' Alex said, reaching into the boot.

'We'll cycle at Gabriel's pace. He can go in front and we'll bring up the rear.'

The last time I cycled was at boarding school, but the adage about it being a skill you never forget was certainly true. Alex gave me some tips for mountain biking; I should keep my body loose, so the bike could move beneath me, and go easy on the brakes to avoid sliding—which would have catapulted me over the bars. 'Keep your eyes fixed on the path ahead,' he said.

I did as he'd suggested, and exhilaration sparkled through me. The trail alternated between steep and flat ground, and soon I'd worked up a sweat. Gabriel's pace was fast, though, and I was just about managing to keep up.

At the top of the final hill, Gabriel pulled up and jumped off his bike. Both Alex and I did the same. Then Alex handed around his water bottle and we slaked our thirst. The air was filled with the sound of cow bells. Everywhere I looked, cattle dotted the landscape along with numerous farms.

'It's so unique,' I said.

'The Grappa massif is like an enormous island,' Alex explained. 'Surrounded by the Venetian plain in front. The Brenta and Piave river valleys to the sides. And the Feltre valley with Lake Corlo behind.'

A falcon coasting on the thermals above had caught my attention and I shaded my eyes to gaze at it. Without warning, I lost my balance, and I reached for Alex to steady myself. 'Sorry,' I said, feeling the heat of a blush.

'Not a problem.' He glanced at his watch. 'We should head back now or we'll be late for our visit to Rosina.'

We returned to Sant'Illaria and dropped Gabriel off at the Corradini, where Francesca had offered to keep an eye on him until his mother picked him up. I rubbed my nervous palms down the legs of my jeans. Would Rosina remember my gran? And, if so, would she tell me the reason why Gran had been so reticent about Italy?

Rosina's daughter, Michela, was waiting for us outside the Municipio, as arranged. She'd told Francesca she would have a small fox-like dog, a *Volpino*, with her. We recognised her instantly. Alex parked the Alfa and we both got out.

'*Piacere.*' Michela shook my hand after Alex had introduced us. Her greying red hair had been cut in a short, masculine style, and she appeared to be about Mum's age —in her late fifties. She carried on talking while Alex translated. 'My house isn't far. Mamma lives with me as we are both widows.'

'Thank you for taking me to see her,' I said, bending and patting the dog. 'I have a lot of questions, which I hope she will be able to answer.'

Michela shook her head. 'Mamma is ninety years old. Although she is fit and healthy, she tires easily. Her memory sometimes fails her, and she has moments when she goes back in her mind to relive the past. But she has spoken about Elena with great affection from time to time over the years, which is why I agreed for you to see her.' Michela gave me a look. 'My grandparents took Elena in when the Germans had started to deport Venetian Jews to their vile concentration camps.'

I took a sharp intake of breath. 'That was so kind of your family.'

'It wasn't unusual. Many Italians were horrified by what was happening and they did what they could.'

We set off at a brisk walk, and soon we'd arrived at a bungalow at the edge of the village.

After closing the garden gate, Michela let the dog off his lead. It trotted behind her as she opened the front door and we stepped inside.

We entered an open-plan living area, and my eyes were immediately drawn to the old woman who was sitting in an armchair watching a quiz show on TV. Michela went up to her and Rosina turned away from the set to look at us.

'*O Dio,*' she gasped. 'Elena *e il conte.*'

'No, Mamma,' Michela reassured her. 'Remember I told you? Elena's granddaughter, Charlotte, has come all the way from London to see you. And this is not Conte Corradini, but his grandson Alessandro.'

'Ah,' the old lady said with a smile.

Michela offered us a coffee, which we gratefully accepted. She lowered the sound on the television and said to take a seat and make ourselves comfortable. We perched on the sofa, and I suddenly felt awkward. Alex nudged me. 'Show her the letters…'

'Good idea.' I retrieved the envelopes from my handbag and showed them to Rosina.

'I was so sad over the years not to hear from *Leonessa,*' she said, her voice trembling.

Alex translated and I asked, '*Leonessa?* Who was *Leonessa?*'

My heart leapt. Finally, the mystery was about to be solved.

'It was Elena's battle name.' Rosina gave me a poignant smile, while Alex told me the meaning of her words. 'All the freedom fighters took battle names to hide their identities if they were caught,' she said.

'But…why would my gran have a battle name?' I asked, confused.

Alex translated and went on to act as interpreter for the rest of our conversation.

'Your grandmother was a partisan up on the Grappa, didn't you know?'

'No.' My mouth fell open.

'How could you not have known?' Rosina narrowed her eyes.

'Gran didn't want to talk about Italy. Ever.'

'So you don't know what happened?'

'That's why I'm here. I really want to find out…'

'Before I tell you anything more. Please, put my mind at ease. Did Elena live a happy life in England?'

'Oh, yes. She had a daughter, Sara, my mother. Your letters were redirected from my grandad's family home in Herefordshire to London. Gran worked with deprived children in the East End. She was the best.'

'Did she ever go back to Venice? She was a Venetian through and through.'

'As I said, she cut everything to do with Italy from her life. As far as I know she never returned.'

Michela approached with our coffees. Small cups of espresso. We added sugar and drank them down.

Rosina had fallen silent, and her expression had turned vacant.

'I'm so sorry. I didn't expect this to happen so quickly, but Mamma has gone back into the past,'

Michela said, 'I'm afraid you won't get anything more out of her today.'

'It's fine. Your mother has been a great help.' I paused, chewed my lip. 'Would it be okay if I came back tomorrow? I would so love to know more about my grandmother's life in Sant'Illaria.'

'I will ask my mother. Later,' Michela said.

I got to my feet. 'I don't want to be a pest…'

'Not at all. I'll phone the hotel and leave a message.'

Alex and I thanked Michela, and she showed us out. We stood on the front step after she'd shut the door.

'Oh, God, Gran was with the partisans.' My voice shook. 'I hope she wasn't up on the Grappa when the Nazi-fascists were using those flamethrowers.'

'Do you want to give up your quest?' Alex touched my hand.

I shook my head. 'I owe it to Gran's memory to find out. But I think something terrible must have happened. I mean, why else would she have blocked all mention of Italy?'

His gaze locked with mine. 'You're so brave, Lottie. She would have been proud of you.'

He opened his arms, and I went into them. Without thinking, I lifted my head to receive his kiss. I threaded my fingers into his hair—I couldn't help myself—and he deepened the kiss.

We came up for air and stared at each other. Then he moved in for another kiss, hungrier and more possessive. 'You're so beautiful,' he murmured.

His words were like a bucket of cold water thrown over me. Gary had always said those same words as a prelude to sex.

I squirmed out of Alex's hold. 'I'm sorry…'

'Too soon?' he lifted a brow.

I nodded, not trusting myself to speak.

'It's alright,' he said. 'I understand. I'll take you back to the hotel.'

Chapter 14

Lidia, 1944

Lidia and Antonio were helping Fausto prepare the evening meal. Lidia worried as she rolled the dough to make pasta; there were so many more mouths to feed than when she'd first arrived on the Grappa six weeks ago. As the days had passed, increasing numbers of young men had turned up, swelling the ranks of the four partisan brigades to around 1500 in total. Often, they would all go hungry, as the supplies sent up by the National Liberation Committee were barely adequate and ran out before the next delivery was due.

The recent arrivals needed military training; they were so young they lacked experience. And, although there had finally been a few air drops of weapons and ammunition, the British Sten guns they'd received weren't nearly enough to arm everyone. The newcomers hung about the camp during the day and, at night, because there weren't enough tents, Falcon sent them off to hunker down with nearby dairy farmers who let them sleep in their barns. A couple of them had even been allocated sleeping quarters in the same hayloft as her. Falcon had taken their documents for safe-keeping and they'd all chosen a battle name, just as Lidia had opted to be known as *Leonessa*, in honour of the winged lion of Saint Mark.

She wiped a hand across her sweaty brow, fervently hoping she wouldn't be here for much longer. High summer had brought with it a jubilant optimism that the conflict in Italy would be over by the autumn. The Allies had recently taken Florence, helped by the Tuscan partisans, and now everyone believed that, before too long, the British and Americans would advance on Bologna and disembark in Venice.

At night, around the campfire, the men at Campo Croce sang a new song:

> *Years have passed,*
> *Months have passed,*
> *But in a matter of days*
> *There'll be the English, at last.*

Lidia rejoiced with them; the strength of their trust in the Allies was infectious, just like their faith in the war ending soon.

She couldn't wait to go home; she missed the blue colours of the sea. Before her exile, she'd never imagined there could be as many shades of green as she saw every day on the Grappa. She missed Marta and her friends too, but, most of all—it went without saying—she missed Papa. When would she have news of him? She released a mournful sigh.

'What's wrong?' Antonio asked, looking up from chopping carrots.

'Nothing.' She gave him a playful nudge on the arm.

Warmth swelled within her; she'd grown fond of Antonio. He was like a brother to her and came first in the affection she felt for the rest of the young men at Campo Croce. She thought of them as her *lupetti*, wolf cubs; she worried whenever the more experienced of them went on weapons raids and sabotage missions. On returning, they would fire three shots in the air to signal who they were. But the wolf cubs had become complacent, in her opinion; anyone could copy that sloppy warning sign. When she'd mentioned her concerns to Falcon, however, he'd scoffed. The 450 square kilometres of the Grappa were safe from attack, he'd maintained; the Germans down on the plain didn't have the manpower to mount an assault, and the Black Brigades were lily-livered fools who didn't have the guts.

With a shudder, Lidia thought about the vile s*quadrista* who'd tried to violate her at the Zalunardis. He'd returned a week later, Rosina had said, and her parents had informed him Elena Moretti had gone back to Porto Marghera. Lidia prayed she would never set eyes on that hateful man again.

Despite her homesickness for Venice, life in the mountain wasn't so bad. She spent her time liaising with the South Africans, helping print propaganda leaflets, or attending to the scratches, bruises and stomach upsets suffered by the men. If there was anything more serious, like a deep bullet wound, she would help the doctor who'd be sent for from Sant'Illaria. Assisting him reminded her of when she used to help Papa, though, and made her miss him even more.

Among the medical emergencies, she would never forget the occasion when Antonio—battle name, appropriately *Lupo*, wolf—had gorged himself on an entire packet of dried egg from one of the Allies' food parcels. No one else would touch the stuff, but he'd been hungry and said the powder filled him up. A short time later, he'd rolled around in agony, clutching at his belly. Lidia checked the box and read that it had contained the equivalent of forty eggs. *Forty eggs!* She'd decided not to send for the doctor and had made him drink copious amounts of water to wash them through his system. He clearly had the constitution of an ox; he was back to normal the next day, devouring the salami that ginger-haired Fox's mamma had brought up to the Grappa.

Lidia was concerned that, lately, some female members of the families of the men had started to visit. There was always someone's mamma, sister, or sweetheart about the place. They helped in the kitchen and arrived with home cooked food—which the men relished. But what would stop them from talking once they went back down again? Careless talk cost lives, Lidia remembered Marta saying, referring to a British propaganda campaign she'd heard about. If people talked, the Nazis and the Black Brigades would then know the exact locations of the partisans on the Grappa. Lidia sighed. Who was she to question the decisions made by those in charge? Falcon had agreed to the visits, as had the other brigade leaders. She should trust their judgement.

She looked up from the work surface and dusted flour off her hands. Two familiar voices heralded the arrival of Rosina and Signora Zalunardi. Signora Zalunardi approached and enfolded Antonio in a warm embrace, then clutched Lidia to her ample bosom and kissed her noisily on both cheeks. She said she was happy to see them again and produced an almond cake from her wicker basket.

While her mother went to help Fausto with making a pasta sauce, contributing the fresh tomatoes she'd brought with her, Rosina took Lidia to one side. 'An Englishman has parachuted onto the plateau above Asiago,' she said. 'It's the promised adviser sent to coordinate air-drops, apparently. A *stafetta* will bring him up the Grappa tomorrow.' She paused. 'Conte Corradini isn't sure if the Englishman speaks any Italian. So the Count wants you to be there when he meets the commanders of the brigades and act as an interpreter.'

Lidia nodded. Her English had grown even more fluent from speaking with Captain Smith and the other South Africans. 'Of course,' she said. 'Anything to help.'

She would forever be in the Count's debt for billeting her with the Zalunardis and for his understanding attitude when she'd come into the mountain without his permission after the Black Brigades had raided the farm. Rosina said he knew the stocky *fascista* who'd behaved inappropriately towards Lidia; the Count said Rosina had done the right thing to hustle her away that night.

Rosina and her mamma left in the morning. Signora Zalunardi said she'd enjoyed the songs Antonio and the rest of the men had sung but she hadn't enjoyed sleeping in a hayloft. In fact, she'd spent most of the night with her rosary in her hand, praying for the safety of her son and his fellow *partigiani.*

After Lidia had waved Rosina and her mamma *arrivederci*, she went to find Falcon. She came across him sitting cross-legged outside his tent, cleaning a Sten gun. 'Has the *inglese* arrived yet?' she asked.

'He's been taken to the hotel below the *sacrario.* Commander Rocco wants you to question him and make certain he isn't a German spy.'

Falcon was one of those people who spoke slowly, appearing to take all things calmly and never to be in a hurry. But he inspired confidence and, as he spoke, he gave a quiet smile, as if he were someone who'd seen a great deal in life, which Lidia was sure he had done. During the weeks since she'd arrived at Campo Croce, she'd learnt that he'd fought in the African campaign before the Italians were defeated.

Falcon glanced down at the gun in his hands. 'Do you know how to use one of these?'

She shook her head. 'I've only fired a rifle.'

'The main difference between a rifle and a submachine gun like a Sten is, with the latter, if you pull the trigger and hold it down, the business end goes *bang-bang-bang.*' He grinned. 'But this kind of weapon uses handgun ammunition and is basically a dressed-up pistol.'

'Ah,' she said. Her heart hammered. Was he intending the gun to be hers?

Falcon showed her the movements, then added, 'It's best not to drop it when the safety catch is off.'

O Dio, she was about to be given a gun. *Her own gun!*

'If I did drop it with the catch off,' she said, attempting to show herself knowledgeable, 'it might shoot me up the backside.'

'Oh, no,' Falcon said, 'not *might*. It *will* do that.'

'Surely that would depend on how it fell?'

'Not at all.' He went on to explain that if she were to drop the Sten on its butt, it would fire a shot the moment it hit the ground. Then it would leap into the air and during the leap the weight of the breechblock would press on the mainspring causing the gun to reload itself. As it fell again it would fire once more, and so on. Problem was, the Sten was weighted in such a way as to nearly always fall on its butt. It wouldn't shoot straight into the air, either, but rotate, scattering bullets like a fan, or a spiral, gradually lowering the angle of fire until the magazine was finished. 'So, Leonessa, the chances of being shot up the backside are practically certain.'

'I will be careful,' she promised.

'Good.' He got to his feet and handed her the Sten.

She placed the lanyard around her neck. 'I feel like a partisan now.'

'Remember, when you shoot, you must shoot to kill. Otherwise *you* will be killed by the person you've shot at.'

She gulped. 'Of course.'

Could she take a life? All her medical training had been geared towards saving lives. She thought about Papa and set her jaw; she would do whatever it took to defeat the enemy and regain his freedom.

Chapter 15

Lidia, 1944

The two-hour walk started off easy, as Lidia strode with Falcon along the path that overlooked the undulating grassy Grappa plateau. But the hike turned difficult once they began climbing the highest part of the broad mountain. Sweat beaded Lidia's brow, and her breathing became laboured. She focused on the stony track in front, taking one step at a time and telling herself they would get there soon.

Finally, up ahead, rose the five concentric grey circles of the enormous pyramid-shaped *sacrario*. Lidia hadn't been here before. 'It's impressive,' she said.

After showing her the niches in the concrete where the bones of the fallen soldiers had been entombed, Falcon led her to the small chapel perched at the top of the monument. He knelt to pray to the Madonnina del Grappa, his lips moving but no sound coming out. Lidia lowered herself to her knees on the tiled floor. No one knew she was Jewish; she kept Mamma's *Siddur* safely hidden at the bottom of her rucksack in the hayloft, and only took it out when she was alone. She covered her eyes with her right hand and said the words of the *Shema* in her head:

Hear, O Israel, the Lord is our God, the Lord is One.
Blessed be the name of the glory of His kingdom forever
and ever.

She knew all the prayers by heart, having read them over and over when no one was around. They were more an aspect of her culture than a religious conviction; but she found their link to Mamma and Papa a continuous source of comfort.

Falcon crossed himself, and Lidia did the same. It would have looked odd if she hadn't and she had no intention of revealing her Hebrew roots.

With a grunt, Falcon pushed himself to his feet. 'Better get on with it,' he said. 'I expect they'll be waiting for us.'

Clearly expecting no reply from her, he headed down the steep path to the Rifugio Alpino, the inn where the Englishman had been taken. It was a simple structure compared with the hotels Lidia remembered in Venice. Three buildings joined together. On the left towered a gabled roof with a large, shuttered window in the centre, its stucco façade appearing slightly newer than the red bricks of the middle and right-hand edifices.

Lidia followed Falcon through the central door, stepping into a well-lit stone-floored hallway where a bearded man was sitting in a high-backed wooden chair, smoking. 'You took your time,' he muttered as he stood. Then, with a growl of affection, he pulled Falcon into a bear hug and clapped him on the back.

Falcon introduced Lidia to the man. 'Commander Rocco of the Matteotti Brigade.'

'We need you to talk to the *inglese,* Leonessa.' Rocco's voice was gruff. 'Find out if he is who he says he is.' Rocco headed towards a glass door at the side of the hall. 'Ask him why he's the only one in the mission. We were expecting at least two of them.'

'*Va bene,*' she said, her heart swelling with pride at the task she'd been assigned.

They entered a spacious dining room. Sepia photographs of World War I soldiers decorated the whitewashed walls, and the delicious aroma of meat stewing infused the air.

She ignored the sudden rumble of hunger in her stomach—she hadn't eaten her fill in weeks. A fair-haired man was sitting at the rectangular oak table. His khaki-coloured battledress looked smart, and his handsomely chiselled face was clean-shaven. He pushed back his chair and stood to attention. 'Captain Roden at your service,' he saluted.

After introductions, Lidia and Falcon left their weapons by the door, and chairs were found for them.

'I'll leave you to it,' Commander Rocco said. 'Report what you find out to me before we have lunch.'

Lidia sat next to Captain Roden. 'First, we need to establish you are who you say you are,' she said.

The Englishman reached under his shirt and pulled out the metal chain that hung around his neck. He showed her a circular disc inscribed with his name, date of birth, blood group, religion, rank and service number. 'Is that good enough?' he winked.

Lidia prickled at the wink. She wanted to be taken seriously, as a freedom fighter and not as some silly girl to be winked at.

She shot a frosty look into his twinkling blue eyes. 'Good enough? Hmmm. Tell us how you came to be here on your own.'

'My second-in-command landed badly when we parachuted from our Dakota above Asiago the other night. He broke his hip and had to be carried off to a nearby sanatorium.'

'That's unfortunate,' Lidia said before translating.

'Ask him which airport his plane took off from,' barked Falcon.

'Bari,' the captain responded.

'Find out about his war record, Leonessa,' Falcon reminded her.

She questioned the captain, then relayed to Falcon that Roden had served as a gunner in a heavy anti-aircraft regiment before they'd transferred him as a staff officer to GHQ Cairo, where he'd got himself recruited into SOE, the acronym for Special Operations Executive, also known as Special Force One.

'What was his preparation for this mission?'

Lidia translated and the captain explained he underwent basic parachute instruction near Brindisi before being sent to Monopoli—where he trained with his second-in-command by carrying heavy weights on their backs over rough country and engaging in unarmed combat.

'I've brought my radio transmitter-receiver,' Captain Roden indicated the small suitcase by his feet. 'I'll be able to coordinate drops of weapons and ammunition.'

'Good,' Falcon rubbed his hands together. 'We have no radio for communications ourselves.'

The conversation moved on to a discussion of the partisan groups on the Grappa. Captain Roden revealed that his briefing had been minimal. The staff at H.Q knew virtually nothing about the area he'd been sent to work in, had little information about what the partisans were actually doing here, and only had a patchy knowledge of the geography of the mountain. Upon being told there were four brigades, Roden advised they should set up a central command unit. 'We expect our forces to break through the German Gothic Line any day now,' the captain said. 'We'd like you to harass the Germans as they retreat. Also destroy their supply lines by sabotaging the Trento to Bassano railway track.'

'That's exactly what we've been attempting to do,' Falcon huffed. 'Your briefing has certainly been abysmal.'

Roden apologised, and Lidia almost felt sorry for him. But she didn't like the way he was shooting covert looks at her while she translated, as if she were a creature from another planet, so she reined in any sympathy she'd started to feel for him.

'We need more weapons if we are to be effective,' Falcon added. 'We have enough men to make a real impact. Get on that radio of yours and tell the Allies to stop pissing about and step up the air drops.'

'Will do.' The captain blew out a breath.

'What's your battle name?' Falcon cocked his head. 'We all have one up here.'

'Do I need one? I mean, if I'm caught, I'll be held under the Geneva convention.'

Falcon laughed at his response.

'We're in the middle of a civil war in Italy, don't you know? I doubt any of us are covered by the Geneva convention,' Falcon smirked.

'Ah, of course.' Roden appeared pensive. 'How about you all call me "David"?'

'*Va bene.*' Falcon got to his feet. 'I'll go and find Rocco, tell him what you've told me and then we'll have some lunch.'

'So,' the captain smiled at Lidia. A nice smile that lit up his eyes. 'Have you been a partisan for long?'

'Only a few months,' she said, fighting a burgeoning warmth towards him, 'but I'm not supposed to talk about myself…'

He placed a finger to his lips. 'Mum's the word.'

'I've not heard the expression before.'

'It means "say nothing" or "don't reveal a secret".'

'But I haven't told you anything,' she grinned.

He laughed and she laughed with him, warming to him despite herself.

Falcon returned with Rocco and their food arrived, plates of polenta and venison stew. The cook at the hotel had done them proud. The four of them tucked in. Rocco and Falcon talked to each other, and Lidia told David about the South African Captain Smith and his twenty-three fellow countrymen back at Campo Croce.

'I'd like to meet them,' he said. 'Don't fancy staying in this place on my own. It's closed to the general public and

I'd rattle around. Would you mind asking Falcon if I could tag along with you? There's safety in numbers…'

'I doubt he'll agree. We lack accommodation and food.'

'Tell him his brigade will get first dibs when the guns are dropped.' David scrubbed a hand through his light brown hair. 'I'm used to short rations and can sleep anywhere.'

She bent and whispered the Englishman's request into Falcon's ear, adding his promise about weapons.

Falcon nodded. He chewed for a few moments, apparently considering the proposal. '*Va bene*,' he said, eventually. 'If the South Africans can squeeze him into one of their tents and share their food allocation with him, it would be good if he could direct the air-drops to Campo Croce. We can distribute them to the others from there.'

Later, in the still darkness of the chilly September night Lidia and the rest of the fifty or so Italians, plus the twenty odd *sudafricani*, were grouped around the enormous campfire in the middle of the football-pitch sized sloping field. She was perched on a mossy log next to David and the South African captain. Giant flames sent red sparks dancing from the fire; she leant towards the radiating heat and toasted herself warm.

They were waiting in hope for an air drop. The partisans were singing, their songs becoming increasingly sombre as the night wore on and the parachutes bearing weapons seemed ever more unlikely to arrive; the weather conditions simply weren't good enough. Falcon came over and sat on the edge of the log, a bottle of grappa in his hands. He handed it to the burly, sandy-haired South African captain, battle name Douglas, who took a swig and passed it to David. The Englishman tipped his head back and swallowed a mouthful. His eyes bulged. 'What's this made of? Tastes like firewater.'

'Distilled skins, pulp, seeds, and stems left over from winemaking after pressing the grapes,' Douglas chuckled. 'You'll grow to like it. I have. Warms the cockles...'

'Is this mountain named after the drink?' David asked.

'I'm not sure. I'll ask Falcon.' Lidia translated the question.

Falcon shook his head and explained the Grappa's name derived from an ancient word for "crag", whereas the liqueur's name came from "*grappolo*" as in "*grappolo d'uva*", meaning "bunch of grapes".

'Glad I got that cleared up.' David took another swig, made a face, then gave the bottle to Douglas.

Falcon pushed himself to his feet. 'I'll leave the grappa with you. Doubt there'll be an air-drop tonight.' He glanced upwards. 'Can't see any stars. But go easy on the drink. It has a kick like a mule.'

'Don't I know it,' Douglas gave a rueful laugh.

'What are they singing about, Leonessa?' David passed her the bottle.

She took a small sip and the fiery liquid slipped down her throat, setting her insides alight. 'The song is about them not being afraid to forfeit their lives for freedom.' With a shiver, she passed the grappa back to David and hugged her coat to her body. 'I hope it won't come to that.'

'Me too.' He knocked back another swig, then handed the grappa to Douglas. 'How about we give them a rendition of "We'll meet again"'?' he suggested. 'It's more cheerful than singing about dying.'

'I'm game if you are,' Douglas said. 'That's if I can remember all the words…'

'How about you, Leonessa?'

'Sorry. I don't know that song. But I'd love to listen.'

David looked as if he was about to reply, but his eyes lifted to the night sky as a heavy noise droned from above.

'*Lancio, lancio*,' Falcon shouted from across the clearing. 'Light the flares, it's Pippo. He might just see us through the clouds.'

'Pippo is the name we've given to the plane that makes the drops,' Lidia explained to David.

She creased her brow. The droning sound appeared to be fading.

David gave a groan. 'No go,' he said.

Falcon came over. 'As long as they come back tomorrow night it shouldn't make much difference in the grand scheme of things,' he shrugged.

Lidia glanced at David. He must be crestfallen the promised drop hadn't happened. It would have been like the first day in a new job and failing to impress. She touched his arm. 'It's only a small setback,' she said. 'Go and get some rest. I'll see you in the morning.'

Chapter 16

Lidia, 1944

Lidia was in the kitchen, grinding chestnuts to make flour for polenta. Her heart felt heavy; it had been nearly three weeks since David had arrived on the Grappa. Three weeks of almost constant cloud cover which had prevented Pippo from dropping the promised weapons. Falcon had resorted to sending out sorties to steal guns and ammunition from the Black Brigades posted in the villages below. She worried every time the men left and breathed a sigh of relief when they returned. To make matters worse, the expected Allied breakthrough on the Gothic Line still hadn't happened. Radio Londra reported that fierce fighting was taking place near Rimini.

'Falcon wants you to go with us to Central Command, Leonessa.' The voice came from behind. She knew that voice; it was David's. *A joke of a battle name.* She'd seen the name on his dog tag. It was his real name, and she'd pulled his leg about it afterwards. 'Well, Douglas used his first name,' David had chuckled. 'I suppose we aren't accustomed to battle names in the British army.'

'Does Falcon want us to go right now?'

''Fraid so.'

She put down the pestle and covered the mortar with a plate, huffing at the thought of the hike that lay ahead. Then her brow furrowed. 'I hope there isn't a problem?'

'Not sure, to be honest.' He grinned sheepishly.

She poured a glass of water for herself and one for David. 'To set us up for the long walk,' she said by way of explanation.

Her jaw set, she picked up her Sten and slung it over her shoulder—she always kept it with her as Falcon had insisted all armed members of the brigade be battle ready —and followed David out of the kitchen.

Falcon was waiting outside, his face as dark as thunder. 'Let's get going,' he said, turning on his heel and setting off across the field towards the treeline.

Nerves prickled Lidia's skin. Something wasn't right. She couldn't put her finger on it, but there was an ominous feel to the humid early autumn air. Had something happened to one of the other brigades? Perhaps a group of partisans had been ambushed down in the valley? It was a fear that ate away at her constantly, and she lived in dread of it becoming reality.

Lidia caught up with Falcon and asked him what was going on.

'All will be explained when we arrive at Central Command,' he muttered.

A chill crept over her skin.

The hike up to the summit of the Grappa proved just as taxing as the last time Lidia had made the climb. But today she barely noticed she was so worried. She focused on Falcon's feet striding in front of her and listened to David's footfalls behind.

Finally they crested the last grassy rock-strewn knoll and made their way towards the Rifugio Alpino.

Rocco was waiting for them outside. Without saying a word, he led them through to the dining room, where two men were sitting at the rectangular oak table. They glanced up as Lidia, Falcon and David approached.

Rocco introduced Baldo—the swarthy Communist leader of the Garibaldi division of the Brigata Gramsci—and Silvio, the commander of the Italia Libera Archeson Brigade.

Lidia's heart sank.

All three commanders had broken eye contact with her.

With shaky hands, she drew up a chair.

'A *stafetta* arrived this morning with news that the Germans have been massing formidable numbers of troops, heavy artillery and ammunition in Bassano,' Rocco said without preamble. 'Apparently they've been preparing for a good while in secret.'

'A *rastrellamento* from the Wehrmacht is imminent,' Baldo added. 'We've heard they've rounded up the partisans above Asiago.'

Lidia covered her mouth with her hand, stifling a gasp. Falcon had always maintained the Grappa would never be attacked. She translated the information for the Englishman.

David, with the proverbial phlegmatism of the British,

offered a Players to everyone. 'What's the plan?' he asked, striking a match and lighting Lidia's cigarette.

'I think we should bring all the divisions up here to the summit. Establish a fortress-like defence of the position. Turn the stronghold into a type of Verdun, like it was during the First World War,' Rocco suggested, his expression stern.

David exhaled smoke. 'Do you have any heavy weapons?'

Lidia's voice shook as she translated Falcon's grumbled response. 'No machine guns, mortars, flamethrowers, or anything like that.'

David tapped the ash from his cigarette. 'What's your firepower?'

'Maximum eight hours. Would be longer if we had more guns,' Baldo complained.

Lidia expected David to retort that the weather conditions hadn't been his fault, but he calmly said, 'That would be insufficient for any prolonged action. I suggest you focus on guerrilla tactics. The Grappa is so spread out. Vast numbers of ridges and routes crisscrossing it. Makes it ideal for partisan warfare. Especially as your chaps should be more familiar with the terrain than Jerry.'

'I think we should defend the summit to the last man, show the Germans that Italians know how to die,' Rocco insisted.

But Silvio, who'd been quiet up to that point, shook his head. 'Wouldn't it be better we show them we know how to live?'

'I agree.' Falcon banged his fist on the table. 'We should split our brigades into divisions. Assign each to one of the ten approach roads. As my lot are based at Campo Croce, we'll take the southern flank.'

'We'll take the western flank,' Rocco said resignedly.

Silvio nodded. 'The east is our territory. If any *tedeschi* come up from the Piave valley, they'll have us to contend with.'

'We'll take the roads leading up from the Feltre valley.' Baldo played with the knot in his red neckerchief—all the Communists on the Grappa wore one. 'Just let those sons of bitches try anything and we Garibaldini will send them running with their tails between their legs.'

'What's the intel on how long we've got?' Silvio asked.

'We should be ready for action in the morning,' Rocco sighed.

'Viva Italia!' Falcon rose to his feet.

Everyone followed his example, standing and roaring, 'Viva Italia!'

'Viva Italia,' David joined in.

Lidia lowered her voice. 'What do the British say before a battle?'

'For King and Country.' He smiled at her. 'Are you alright?'

'What do you mean?'

'This must have come as a shock.'

'It's a shock for everyone, not just me.' She released a heavy sigh. 'I worry for the new recruits without weapons…'

'Maybe they should go back to their villages?'

'It's a case of damned if they do and damned if they don't.' She gave him a sad smile and slung her Sten over her shoulder.

He gave her a glance. 'You're the first woman I've come across who is armed in this war.'

'Is that why you were giving me those strange looks when we first met?'

'I'm sorry. I apologise for staring. None of our lasses carry weapons.'

'Not even those in Special Ops?'

'Ah. You've got me there. Probably. Just haven't seen any.'

She glanced away from him. Falcon was already heading for the door. 'We'd better get a move on. Thank God, the way back to Campo Croce is mostly downhill.'

On their return to the camp, Falcon gave orders for the next day. He told those without weapons that they should hide in the caves he pointed out on his map. They must stay there until the coast is clear. 'We'll send the *tedeschi packing*. Don't worry.'

After a supper of polenta and wild mushrooms, which the new recruits had picked in the woods that morning, the entire battalion hid their valuables in a cave, then sat around the campfire, singing. But, tonight, their voices rang out with more fervour than usual as they sang a satirical song about Badoglio, the devious Marshal who'd announced the armistice.

Oh Badoglio, Pietro Badoglio
You grew fat on your Fascist bluff,
With your buddy King Vittorio

You've busted our balls enough.

Lidia translated the meaning of the chorus to David, stumbling over the vulgar language, and he laughed.

'Wouldn't it be wonderful if Pippo flew over and dropped a load of guns,' she said wistfully.

He looked up at the sky. Not a star could be seen there was so much cloud cover. 'I'm sorry,' he whispered.

'It's not your fault,' she reassured him.

'Had to hide my radio in that cave just now,' he groaned. 'Couldn't risk it falling into the wrong hands tomorrow, otherwise I'd have another shot at organising a drop.'

She reached for his hand and gave it a squeeze.

'*A letto*, bedtime,' Falcon suddenly called out from the other side of the clearing. 'Everyone is to sleep fully clothed with their rucksacks and weapons ready. We'll be taking up our positions at dawn.'

Lidia said goodnight to David and Douglas, then went to find Antonio. She wasn't sure she would see him in the morning. She found him with his ginger friend, Fox. 'Take care of yourself.' She kissed him on both cheeks. He would be heading for a location to the west of Campo Croce, whereas she would stay here with David and the South Africans.

'You be careful too, Leonessa. I will see you when we've sent the Germans to Hell.'

Her throat tightened. 'Live to fight another day,' she said. 'Promise?'

'I promise.' He gave her a cheeky smile.

She waved him off and went up to the hayloft, where her "roommates" were fast asleep and snoring. She curled up under her blanket, her rucksack and Sten beside her. Her fingers itched to hold Mamma's prayer book, but she didn't want the boys who were sharing the accommodation with her to wake up and spot what she was doing. She slipped the *Siddur* into her pocket and went back down the ladder.

The embers of the campfire were still glowing, and she lowered herself onto the grass. Sitting cross-legged, she took out the prayer book and held it to her chest, feeling the comfort of its link to her past. *Oh, Papa, where are you? How are you?*

'Couldn't you sleep?' came an English voice.

She almost jumped out of her skin. 'David, you gave me a fright.'

He lowered himself next to her. 'What's that?' He pointed to the prayer book.

Should she conceal it? No. He was her ally. She could trust him. She held out the *Siddur*. 'It was my mother's…'

He took the book and turned it in his hands, staring at the Hebrew writing on the cover in the low firelight.

'You're Jewish?'

She nodded.

'I was wondering why an educated girl like you—I mean, your English is perfect—is fighting with the partisans…'

'I'm from Venice. My father was transported by the SS to a labour camp.' Tears stung her eyes. 'The Resistance arranged for me to stay with a farming family in a village at the foot of the mountain.' She took a breath, determined to keep her fear of the imminent attack from showing. 'I came up here because I thought it would be safer…'

'Safer from what?'

'The Black Brigades. I was worried they'd find out about my background.'

'So you're pretending to be a Catholic?'

'Yes,' she said. 'I'm not a practising Jew.'

He took her hand and she let him. His warm palm enclosed hers, and she relaxed into the feeling of comfort provided. 'What is your real name, Leonessa?'

'Elena.' She hadn't been Lidia for so long, her alias tripped off her tongue before she could even think about it.

'Thank you for telling me,' he said. 'I hate Hitler for his antisemitism. But even in Britain, certain sectors of society have shown hatred for the Jews.' He paused, stared down at the prayer book. 'All four of my grandparents were Jewish, but my father changed our surname from Rodenberg to Roden when he joined the British army in 1914.'

'But I saw on your dog tag that your religion is Church of England,' she gasped.

'I was baptized an Anglican. It was a typical move by many Anglo-Jewish families given the subtle anti-Semitism and more obvious anti-Germanism of the English.'

'Man's inhumanity to man,' she quoted Robert Burns.

'You're so well-read, Elena. I'm ashamed of myself for not having learnt any Italian.'

'I meant to ask about that. Why did SOE send a non-Italian speaker to us?'

'Ah, my second-in-command was supposed to be the interpreter.' He squeezed her fingers. 'Although I'm sorry about his accident, I'm thankful now that he isn't with me, otherwise I might not have met you.'

She didn't know how to respond, so she held her tongue. She simply leant into him as he put his arm around her. A strange feeling, to be warmed by another after so long. But it was a nice feeling, and she savoured it as David held her close.

Chapter 17

Lidia 1944

Lidia couldn't sleep. Normally, she was so exhausted when night fell that she ignored the snores of the young men who shared the hayloft with her, ignored the scratchy prickles of the straw and the smell of cow manure wafting from the barn below. The cattle provided the camp with milk; usually she didn't begrudge them their bodily functions, but tonight the odour was keeping her awake. That and her fear of what tomorrow might bring.

She thought about David, how comforting it had been to lean against him with his arm around her. The feel of him was totally different to how she'd felt when she'd snuggled with Renzo, and she was glad about that, glad the two of them were like night and day. In any case, there was no question of her becoming romantically involved with the Englishman. They were brother and sister in arms. Nothing more, nothing less.

She fell into a restless sleep, dreaming that Papa was calling out for her. She blinked her eyes open at daybreak. The hayloft was empty. She rushed down the ladder, her rucksack bumping on her back and her Sten gun in its lanyard across her chest. The sound of distant explosions ripped the air. *O Dio, it has started already.*

David, Douglas and rest of the South Africans were waiting down below. Light rain splattered her coat, and she shivered.

'Falcon and the others have set off for their positions. As you can hear, Jerry has arrived on the Grappa,' David muttered. 'I was about to come and fetch you…'

The rumble of a motor engine cut off whatever he was about to say next. None of the partisans had vehicles up on the Grappa. It could only mean one thing.

He grabbed her hand. 'We're like sitting ducks here.'

He pulled her with him up the slope towards the woods. The men behind them scattered. Some ran downhill, others uphill, and the rest were rooted to the spot.

Lidia ran, her feet slipping on the squelchy ground until she gained momentum alongside David and Douglas. She looked back and peered through the rain.

Two trucks.

Spewing Wehrmacht soldiers onto the field.

Her heart thudded.

Then the firing started. One of the South Africans fell. A ragged wound bloomed red in the middle of his chest. Another crumpled to the ground. He called out and two others put their arms around him to drag him on. But to no avail. They were mowed down immediately.

Lidia had never seen anyone killed before. She took a deep breath to stop herself from throwing up.

'Keep running, Elena,' David yelled, dropping her hand to reach for his weapon.

She looked back again as she ran; she couldn't help herself. The sound of heavy machine guns echoed and tracer bullets flew towards the barn. Seconds later, flames licked through the hay and set the building alight, cows bursting through the open doors.

'Stop looking,' David grunted. 'It's slowing you down.'

Her breath burned in her lungs.

Bullets whistled past her head, flinging wet earth into the air as they landed.

The shelter of the trees was only twenty metres or so away. Douglas had reached it and was lying down with his gun raised.

Lidia made the treeline, with David just behind her. The Germans had stopped further down and were setting up big gun positions.

David grabbed her hand again and they ran. Oh, how they ran. The crumping noise of mortar rounds landing came from the edge of the trees behind them, growing fainter as they put in more distance.

'What do we do now?' Douglas rasped, his breaths coming in short sharp bursts.

'Let's head for Central Command at the Rifugio,' David suggested.

Lidia cried silent tears as they made their way through the woodland. Those poor men gunned down. *And what's happened to Falcon, Antonio and the rest of my lupetti?* Her blood ran cold.

They reached the escarpment. Acrid smoke stung her eyes. She let out a gasp. The entire plateau appeared to be on fire.

Flaming farmhouses.

Burning cow barns.

Animals wandering about, lost.

The echoes of explosions ricocheted off the surrounding hills, and her heart wept.

But it seemed fate was looking out for her. The drizzly mist that had surrounded Lidia and her companions hitherto turned into a thick fog, protecting them while they hiked up the mountain.

Eventually, after a couple of hours trudging in silence through the foggy fumes, they reached the final crest before the summit.

O, Dio!

Lidia's heart hammered against her ribs.

The Rifugio had been bombed to smithereens and was nothing but a burning shell.

She grasped David's arm. 'Where do we go now?'

He appeared to think for a moment. 'Aren't there tunnels around here from the Great War? Perhaps we can shelter in one of them?'

Except before they could start their search for a bunker, Rocco came down the wide concrete steps from the chapel at the top of the shrine.

'The "*sauve qui peut*" order has been given,' he said. 'Everyone should try and save themselves if they can. The *stafetta*, Rosina, came by earlier with a sealed message from Count Corradini, Leonessa. It said, if I saw you, to tell you to take David to him. He'll arrange for him to get to the British Ops mission near Belluno.'

Lidia's stomach lurched with fear for Rosina. 'Where has the *stafetta* gone?'

'To look for her brother. I tried to stop her, but she wouldn't listen.' Rocco shrugged. 'If anyone can slip by the *tedeschi*, it will be her. She knows the paths up here like the back of her hand.'

'How is it that were we overwhelmed so quickly?' David inquired.

'Outnumbered by at least five to one,' Rocco groaned. 'We never expected the Germans to arrive in such numbers and with such force— cannons, mortar bombs, heavy machine guns and flamethrowers—they threw everything they had at us.'

Douglas stepped forward and held David in his gaze. 'I'm going to go and find any survivors from my division. Can't leave them up here on their own.'

'This fog looks set to last the rest of the day and will provide protection,' Rocco said. 'Where were your men when you last saw them?'

Douglas explained that the surviving South Africans had dispersed when the Wehrmacht had attacked Campo Croce. Given that the surrounding area was heavily wooded, Rocco believed there was a good chance they'd simply gone to cover. He'd send a couple of his men with Douglas, killing two pigeons with one stone. He needed to send a message to Falcon, whom he thought might still be in position on a ridge overlooking the town of Romano d'Ezzelino.

'What's the best route down to Sant'Illaria?' Lidia inquired.

'There's a muleteer's path dating from 1918. All you

need do is follow it down to the valley. I'll show you the way.'

After Lidia and David had left Douglas with Rocco's men, he took them to the start of the track, a road made of gravel about as wide as a small car. 'Are you tired?' David asked Lidia after they'd begun the descent.

'I'm fine.' And she was. Nervous energy was keeping her going, as well as the salami and bread that David had pulled from his rucksack. He told her Fausto had given them all a few rations before she'd come down from the hayloft, then went on to say that Fausto had gone with Falcon. She hoped they, Antonio, and the rest of her wolf cubs were alright.

About an hour later, she and David sat on some flat rocks by a gushing stream and drank the fresh cool water by making cups of their hands. Thick fog still surrounded them, and the sound of mortar bombing reverberated from above. 'Let's go,' Lidia said. 'The sooner we are off the Grappa the better.'

Presently, however, she found herself flagging. The track was steep and she lost her footing a couple of times, having to hold on to David to steady herself. She could weep with tiredness, and, when they came across a stone-built shepherd's hut by the side of the way, she suggested they rest for a while.

'I was going to make the same suggestion,' he said, 'but I didn't want you to think I was being bossy.'

'You? Bossy? Never,' she teased. 'But I'm completely exhausted. I didn't sleep at all well last night.'

'With good reason,' he said, pushing open the door of the hut and glancing around. 'It looks dry in here.' He indicated a wooden bench placed against the rough wall. Why don't you stretch out on that while I keep watch?'

She thanked him and did as he'd suggested. Within seconds, she'd fallen asleep. But, also, within seconds, or so it seemed, David was gently shaking her shoulder. He pressed a finger to his lips.

'There are Germans on the road,' he murmured so softly she barely made out what he was saying. 'I counted five of them. I can understand enough of their language to make out they were discussing taking a break from their climb in this hut.'

Slowly, her heart hammering, she swung her legs from the bench and took the safety catch off her Sten.

This was it.

A kill or be killed situation. She remembered Falcon's warning words.

She swallowed, hard. Her hands were perspiring with fear and the barrel of her gun was wet where she held it.

'Ready?' David whispered.

Lidia wiped her sweaty palm on her coat, gripped the Sten's barrel tight. She nodded.

Silently, David opened the door.

The Germans were just outside, lighting up cigarettes.

David unleashed a hail of bullets.

Lidia tightened her finger on the trigger of her weapon. *Bang-bang-bang*. It was just like Falcon had told her it would be. Her eyes widened as the side of a blond German's head blew off.

Before any of the others could return fire, a tall man's

jaw disappeared. *Just like that!* Blood and sinew flew from his neck and he tumbled backwards.

Lidia and David kept firing until all five Germans lay lifeless. She only stopped when the ammunition in her magazine ran out. But her finger remained on the trigger, every cell in her body focused on squeezing it.

David lowered his Bren and went up to the Germans. He kicked their bodies to make sure they were dead, then collected their sidearms and put them in his rucksack.

She'd remained standing, still as a statue. Every muscle in her body seemed to have frozen. Then, without warning, her stomach heaved, and she threw up its entire contents onto the slimy, blood-soaked ground.

David smoothed the damp hair back from her forehead. 'The first time is always the worst,' he said. He opened his arms and held her close, stroking her shoulders and soothing her. 'We should get going, Elena.'

Lidia squirmed out of his hold and flashed him a look. 'Please, call me Leonessa.'

'Can't I call you Elena when we're alone?'

She took a moment to think, then said, 'Alright. Only when there's no one else about.'

He reached for her hand. 'Let me look after you, Elena, you're safe with me.'

'Alright,' she said again before allowing him to lead her down the mountain.

Chapter 18

Charlotte, 2010

Alex drove me back to the hotel after we'd walked to the car from Rosina's. He brought his SUV to a halt in the gravelled car park and gazed at me, his forest green eyes burning with an intensity I found disconcerting. 'Are you still in love with your ex, Lottie?'

Alex's directness floored me, causing me to think for a moment. 'Gary had a fling with my best friend. His betrayal snuffed out all my feelings for him.' I snapped my fingers together. 'Like that.'

'So I have a chance?'

'A chance for what?' I asked.

'To show you not all men are like Gary.'

'Oh, Alex…' A sigh escaped. 'I like you a lot.'

'But?' he raised a brow.

I stared down at my hands. 'I'm sorry,' I mumbled. 'I know it sounds like a cliché, but I'm just not ready for a new relationship. In any case, I'll be going home to London soon.'

'Will you have dinner with me?' he changed tack. 'It's still my day off. I'd like to take you out to one of my favourite restaurants. They specialise in seafood.'

'You've already been far too kind.' I gave him an apologetic look. 'Thank you. I'd love that,' I added, catching the disappointment in his expression.

'Good. I'll meet you in the lobby at seven thirty. No need to dress up. It's a casual type of place.'

We strolled into the hotel together. Francesca was behind the reception desk and asked how we'd got on with Rosina.

'I found out that my grandmother stayed with her family and then become a partisan up on the Grappa,' I blurted.

Francesca let out a squeal. 'Wow! What else did she tell you?'

'That was pretty much it,' Alex smiled ruefully. 'The old dear grew tired and absent-minded. Her daughter will contact us tomorrow and arrange another time to visit.'

'I could go with you to translate, Lottie,' Francesca offered. 'I'm up to date with the bookkeeping, so can take a little time off.'

'Please don't go to any trouble.'

'It's no trouble at all. Besides, I'm fascinated by your grandmother's story.'

After thanking them both, I went up to my room and took a shower. Alex had said not to dress up, so I put on a clean pair of jeans and a fresh blouse. With time to kill before meeting him, I took out my phone and googled Monte Grappa.

What I discovered sent a chill through me.

The restaurant was a split-level establishment, hugging the edge of a picturesque village overlooking the undulating countryside below the Asolo hills. Alex and I sat on the terrace, sipping from flutes of prosecco, the evening sun tinting the panorama with apricot hues.

'So beautiful,' I said, admiring the view of a chain of knolls, seven of them, rippling like a giant Chinese dragon's back.

'Over there is the Rocca,' Alex pointed out the fortress topping a crest to the right. 'We could go there on my next day off if you like. Asolo is a special place. One of the loveliest small towns in Italy.'

He leaned back in his chair and I secretly admired the tailored white shirt hugging his flat chest. My skin was heating up, and I took a sip of prosecco to cool myself down.

He refilled my glass, reached for the menu and handed it to me.

'What do you recommend?' The words came out raspy and I swallowed another mouthful of the sparkling wine.

'The tagliatelle with salmon is delicious.' He licked his lips.

'Sounds yummy.'

'We could have a plate of mixed grilled fish to follow. And a bottle of Pinot Grigio.'

'Great.'

'So,' he said, after a waiter had taken our order, 'how do you feel knowing your gran was with the partisans?'

'I can't get my head around it, to be honest.' I took another sip of prosecco as I struggled to find the right words. 'I looked up Monte Grappa on Wikipedia and read that those who weren't killed on the mountain were publicly hanged by the Nazis in Bassano.' My voice shook. 'Is that true?'

'Oh, Lottie,' he reached for my hand. 'That's not the full story by any means. The reprisals were brutal. The Nazis instigated them, but the Italian Fascists played their shameful role. Not only in Bassano. In all the towns and villages of this area as well.'

Coldness spread through me. 'How terrible.'

Our first course arrived. I stared at my plate, not hungry anymore.

'It's not all doom and gloom.' Alex poured us a glass of chilled Pinot Grigio. 'Your gran survived, didn't she?'

I took a large sip. 'Maybe she wasn't even on the Grappa when the partisans were rounded up?' My words sounded hollow to my ears.

'Rosina should be able to set your mind at ease…'

I took another swig of wine before twirling a strand of tagliatelle around my fork. I knew I should eat or the Pinot Grigio would go to my head. 'This is good,' I said, although I barely tasted it.

Soon, though, I found myself enjoying the meal and relaxing. How could I not, sitting here with this devastatingly attractive, charming man in such a gorgeous location? We chatted about ourselves. Alex told me more about Simonetta and how they'd grown apart after Gabriel was born. She'd suffered from postpartum depression and hadn't coped well with Gabriel as a baby. He was one of those infants who only slept for an hour at a time, suffering from colic and crying constantly. Alex became a stay-at-home dad so she could go back to work. Not long afterwards, he and Francesca inherited the Corradini and he was able to combine fatherhood with his new career. As for Simonetta, she'd become a different mother to Gabriel now he was older, and Alex was happy with her having joint custody of their son.

In return, I told him a little about my life in London. 'I'm not sure teaching high school history is right for me,' I admitted. 'I might look into retraining as a primary school teacher.'

'Or you could try something different,' he stated enigmatically.

A waiter cleared the dishes and served our main course —grilled Adriatic langoustines, sole and monkfish. Alex filled my glass again but didn't pour any for himself. 'Need to keep my wits about me as I'm driving,' he chuckled.

We lapsed into comfortable silence while we ate the fish. It was delicious, and so was the Pinot Grigio. Alex asked if I wanted some dessert, but I declined the tiramisu as well as a refill of wine. 'Sorry, but if I eat any more, I'll burst. And I'm feeling sightly tipsy. I need to keep my wits about me, too.'

'Oh? Why's that?'

'Remember tomorrow morning I'm moving my things over to the annex? Then, hopefully, Michela will get in touch.'

'Ah…'

He paid the bill and we left the restaurant. My legs

gave a wobble as we headed towards the car. He put his arm around me. 'Lean on me, Lottie. I've got you.'

I did as he'd suggested, forcing myself not to lift my face for a kiss. A kiss that would only have led to me inviting him up to my room when we got back to the hotel. I pressed my cheek to his chest and inhaled the scent of his sandalwood cologne instead.

Up in my room, I took out my phone and gazed at the photo of Gran taken in Venice. Part of me dreaded Michela getting in touch tomorrow. Gran must have gone through hell—it was the only explanation there could be for her severing all ties with Italy. The prayer book was in my suitcase, and I flipped through it before putting it away again. Gran was Jewish, and I knew the tradition was passed through the female line so I was Jewish too. The thought sent a warm feeling through me, a sense of belonging to something far greater than myself.

I slept fitfully, and phoned Mum and Dad before going down for breakfast in the morning. They sounded shocked when I told them about Gran's joining up with the partisans and asked me to call them when I'd spoken with Rosina again.

Alex gave me a cheery wave as I headed towards the buffet. Thank God, I didn't proposition him last night—I'd be bright red with embarrassment right now. I'd been drinking and I'm sure Alex would have been too much of a gentleman to have taken me up on my dubious offer.

Tray in hand, I found a table on the terrace. My mobile pinged with a message. Francesca. Telling me to meet her

in front of the annex at nine. I finished my chocolate croissant, drank down my cappuccino and pushed back my
chair. I'd packed my things as soon as I'd woken up. All I
needed to do was go up to my room and fetch them.

Fifteen minutes later, sweating in the heat of the
August morning, I wheeled my suitcase across the lawn
separating the villa from two mews-type cottages
converted from the building that used to be the stables.

Francesca was standing in front of a barn-type door
between olive-green shuttered windows. '*Buongiorno,*
Lottie.' She turned the key in the lock. 'I've just had a call
from Michela that Rosina is happy for us to drop by. So
I'll show you around and we can go.'

Excitement mixed with trepidation rushed through me.
'That's great.'

Francesca led me into the open-plan kitchen, dining,
sitting-room. 'It's lovely,' I said, lowering my case onto
the terracotta-tiled floor. It was cooler in here; the shutters
had kept out the hot sun. The rough stone walls appeared
original and were in keeping with the rustic décor. A
comfy looking sofa, piled high with white cushions, had
been placed in front of the fireplace at one end, and there
was a cooking area on the other side with a fridge, stove,
washing machine and dishwasher.

'Come upstairs,' Francesca said, heading towards the
spiral staircase.

There were two rooms on the upper floor. A spacious
bedroom boasted a brass framed double bed, oak chest of
drawers and a built-in wardrobe. I peeked into the bathroom, beautifully tiled like the one in my old room at the
villa. 'It's perfect,' I said.

Francesca glanced at her watch. 'We'd better get a

move on. Michela said her mamma is more lucid in the mornings and she seemed to be having a good day.'

I proposed driving Francesca in my rented car. The idea had occurred to me that I should get more use out of it, so I told her I was planning on doing some sightseeing after we'd spoken with Rosina.

It was a five-minute drive to Michela's and she answered the door almost as soon as we'd rung the bell. 'Mamma has remembered the *rastrellamento* and wants to tell you about it,' she explained and Francesca translated.

After Francesca had been introduced to Rosina, and Michela had gone down to the basement to get on with some laundry, we perched on the sofa opposite the old lady, like Alex and I had done yesterday. 'I can't get over how much you resemble your grandmother,' she said. 'Are you like her in personality?'

I shook my head. 'I'm not as brave as she was, I don't think. Was she on the mountain when there were those flamethrowers?'

'Oh, yes. She was there.'

And then, the old lady went on to tell us about how she herself was a courier for the Resistance. Her brother, Antonio, had joined the partisans and when Gran had attracted unwanted attention from one of Mussolini's Black Brigade officers, Rosina took her up to the Grappa where it was thought she'd be safer.

'When I found out from Count Corradini that there was to be a *rastrellamento* and he needed me to take a sealed message to the Command Centre,' Rosina said, a melancholic look in her eyes, 'I cycled up the mountain as fast as I could go under cover of darkness.'

'You knew my grandfather?' Francesca gasped.

'I worked for him as a housemaid when I wasn't carrying messages,' Rosina explained. 'The Count was like a reed blowing in the wind one way or the other...'

I was about to ask what she meant, but she carried on with her story and I didn't have the heart to interrupt.

'I reached the Rifugio Alpino in the morning, but the Nazis had already attacked. No one expected it to happen so quickly. Everyone had been preparing for the assault to start at dawn, and the Garibaldi division defending the approach roads from the Feltre valley were caught completely by surprise. They defended their positions until they'd run out of ammunition, then they had to retreat or they'd have been slaughtered.

'I pedalled like mad through the fog—*grazie alla Madonnina del Grappa*, it protected me, otherwise I'd have been seen by the enemy. Eventually, I arrived at the Forcelletto camp, where Commander Rocco told me I might find my brother. He was there with the others who had retreated. I've never been more relieved in my life than I was when I saw Antonio, I can tell you. I asked him about Leonessa, and he told me she was with the escaped Allied prisoners of war who'd joined the partisans a while back.

'At about three in the afternoon a *stafetta* brought the order that we should set off for the Solaroli ridge. Not long after we'd began our march, a shell landed right in the middle of the site we'd just left. We'd escaped by the skin of our teeth.

'We marched the rest of the day and night, Indian file, still protected by the fog. But we could see through the gloom that everywhere was on fire. My heart broke for all those kind dairy farmers who'd let the partisans camp on their land and sleep in their barns. Afterwards, we discovered that a group of unarmed young men who'd hidden in a cave had been burnt alive by flamethrowers. They'd come up to the Grappa to fight for the freedom of Italy and had died for their country.

'Finally, shortly before dawn, we'd come down to the Feltre valley. We wept when we saw so many villages in flames. Death and destruction everywhere we looked. I found out, later, that five thousand Wehrmacht troops came up to the Grappa. It was easy for them…they had ammunition, weapons of all kinds. All we had were rusty guns. We did our best.

'Exhausted, hungry and thirsty—we drank the liquid we found on leaves—Antonio and I got separated from our party. We made our way to Sant'Illaria, playing a cat and mouse game with the *nazifascisti*. There was a roadblock but we knew how to get round it by going under the bridge.'

Rosina came to a halt in her story. She'd paused several times while Francesca translated, sipping from the glass of water Michela had poured for us all. Rosina seemed to have dried up. She fell silent and a sad smile played across her lips.

But she hadn't told me what had happened to Gran. Without thinking, I leant towards the old lady and asked, 'And my grandmother? Obviously, she survived. Did she stay with the POWs?' I marvelled to myself that there had been Allied forces, albeit escaped ones, on the mountain.

'I didn't see her until Antonio,' Rosina took in a deep breath, and her rheumy old eyes suddenly welled with tears. 'It was only when the *nazifascisti* hanged my brother…' She broke into sobs. Heart wrenching sobs. She rocked her body and covered her face with her hands. 'I'm sorry,' she wailed, 'I can't talk anymore…'

Francesca and I leapt to our feet and put our arms around Rosina, who was sobbing as if her heart would break.

And no wonder. Those bastards hanged her brother.

'I'll go and fetch Michela,' Francesca offered, heading out of the room.

I held Rosina, tried to comfort her. I was sorry for the part I'd played in encouraging her to tell more of her story, and I said so to Michela when she rushed up to her mother, her small dog at her heels.

'I was delayed by a phone call or I'd have stopped her,' Michela explained and Francesca translated. 'Usually Mamma doesn't remember what happened to my uncle…'

'It's because I asked her about my gran,' I confessed.

'Ah, I see,' Michela nodded. 'Did she tell you everything you wanted to know?'

'I still have some questions,' I admitted. 'But I don't want to upset your mother again.'

'Perhaps it's best if you don't return for a few days. I can't promise Mamma will want to talk to you again,' Michela said on a sigh. 'If she does, I'll get in touch.'

I thanked Rosina for talking to me, but she was staring into space. I hoped she wasn't reliving those terrible events of 1944.

Michela saw us to the door. Francesca and I stepped into the hot sunshine, then got into my car.

'Well,' Francesca said. 'That was an eye-opener. Such a coincidence that Rosina once worked for my grandfather.' She buckled up her seat belt. 'So many times, I've walked past those trees in Bassano where they hanged the partisans. It's heart-breaking. On each tree trunk is displayed a memorial with the name and photograph of the young man who was hanged and the date of the hanging. So tragic...'

A knot of sadness formed in my throat. 'It's hard to believe such horror existed in this beautiful part of the world.'

'Bassano is a gorgeous town.'

'I'd like to go there.' I came right out with it.

She shot me a glance. 'What? Now?'

'Yes. I owe it to Gran's memory. And to pay tribute to Rosina's brother.'

'I'll come with you to show you the way,' Francesca said.

I thanked her, and, my heart aching, turned the key in the Fiat's ignition.

Chapter 19

Lidia, 1944

It was getting late, Lidia realised, and she despaired of ever reaching the valley before nightfall. To make matters worse, her legs ached terribly and hunger gnawed at her belly. The muleteers' track they were following either cut through the crags via dark narrow tunnels, or became so steep it was as if she and David were attempting to walk down a long slide in a children's playground. The fog was still dense, and what light there was appeared to be fading.

About an hour after they'd encountered those Wehrmacht troops, the track widened and levelled out. A charred farmhouse loomed into view. Two ghostly figures materialised through the gloom. Cows. Their plaintive lowing made a mournful sound.

'Do you think there's anyone inside?' Lidia whispered. The building was still smouldering. Half the roof had collapsed and the rough stone walls had been blackened by flames.

'We need food and somewhere to shelter,' he muttered. 'It will be too dangerous to climb down the mountain in darkness. I'll go and see what I can find.'

'I'll come with you.'

'No, Elena. Stay here and stand guard.'

She did as he'd asked, her Sten at the ready.

Within minutes, he'd reappeared at the door, indicating she should come inside. She took a step forward and her mouth fell open. The ground floor had been completely gutted.

She followed David up to the first floor, the stone steps hot beneath the soles of her shoes. The small kitchen at the front had remained untouched by the fire. A pot of bean soup sat on the countertop. She gave it a sniff. Freshly made, it seemed. She found a spoon and risked a taste. Not bad, although it had gone cold. She discovered two bowls and a ladle in the sideboard and doled out the soup while David searched in cupboards. 'There might be some bread,' he said.

'I suppose the people who lived here ran off when the Germans arrived.' She shuddered, feeling a little uncomfortable eating someone else's food, 'I hope they haven't been gunned down somewhere on the farm...'

David didn't comment. Instead, with a satisfied smirk, he held up a loaf of bread. 'It might have gone stale, but better than nothing.'

They stood at the counter and devoured the soup and the loaf. 'I've been thinking about where we should spend the night,' David said, cleaning his bowl with a chunk of bread. 'This house is too exposed. Let's head into the woods.'

Lidia agreed. She'd been dreading carrying on with their hike she was so tired. She took their dishes to the washing up bowl, filled two glasses with water from a pitcher, and they drank them down before leaving.

Outside, darkness wrapped around them like a blanket, but at least the mortar shelling had stopped. David took her hand. Thankfully, he seemed to have good night vision and he led her in silence the short distance to the treeline. They fought their way through the thickets, catching their feet on fallen branches, their hands and faces scratched by thorns.

'I think we've gone far enough,' David said eventually. 'We need to sleep and it should be safe here.'

Lidia's eyes had grown accustomed to the dark. They'd come to a small clearing and the ground had flattened. She shrugged off her rucksack and placed her Sten by her feet. The partisans always carried a blanket in their bags for rough sleeping. She took hers out and David did likewise.

'Try to rest, Elena. We're going to need every ounce of our energy tomorrow. Lie down next to me. We'll keep each other warm.'

She lowered herself to the leafy damp ground. He stretched out beside her and gently pulled her against him. She stiffened briefly, then told herself not to be ridiculous. There was nothing untoward in what they were doing. On the contrary, it was perfectly sensible.

David fell asleep almost immediately, his breathing deep and reassuring. She didn't think she would sleep; the events of the day were still too fresh in her mind. Except her exhausted body's needs took over from her thoughts and within minutes she'd given in to the tiredness.

She woke with a jolt, every bone and muscle in her body aching. The day had dawned bright and fog-free, thank God. David was already up, sitting on a boulder and examining his gun. 'I've got half a magazine and one spare,' he said. 'Let me look at your Sten.'

'About fifteen rounds left,' he said after she'd handed over her weapon and he'd checked it. 'Hope we don't bump into any more Germans.'

'I'll second that,' she said, getting to her feet and running her fingers through her tangled hair. It had been months since she'd looked at herself in a mirror and months since she'd had a bath. She must look an absolute mess. You're a freedom fighter, she reminded herself. *Your appearance doesn't matter.* She shouldered her gun and fought her way with David through the dense woodland down to the farmhouse.

The cows were still there, their udders looking uncomfortably swollen. She was tempted to try and milk them, but time was of the essence.

David had set out in the direction of the path.

Suddenly, he halted and raised his Bren.

Her heart pounded.

A lone figure was coming towards them.

She gave a gasp.

Signor Zalunardi. His hunting rifle levelled.

'What…what are you doing here?' she stuttered.

'Looking for you, Rosina and Antonio, of course,' he

retorted as if she'd asked a stupid question. 'Have you seen my son and daughter?'

'No, I'm sorry. The Commander told us Rosina had made it to the summit and had left to find Antonio.'

'I came to warn you all about the roadblocks. The Black Brigades are stopping any partisans coming down from the Grappa. Arresting them and putting them on trial.'

'*O Dio!*' Lidia's heart sank.

She translated the conversation and introduced David to Signor Zalunardi. After she'd told Rosina's father that she was taking the Englishman to the Count, Signor Zalunardi suggested they waited until nightfall before entering Sant'Illaria. 'Stay off the road. Follow the stream that you will come across. After it goes under a bridge at the entrance to the village, a path leads directly to Villa Corradini.' He lifted his eyes to the sky. 'There will be a full moon so take care to remain in the shadows.'

'Grazie. I hope you find Rosina and Antonio.'

'They could have gone down any of the roads from the Grappa, but I thought they might have taken this one as it's quieter.'

Lidia explained about their encounter with the Germans, warning him about the bodies beside the track. Before they parted company, Signor Zalunardi reached into his shoulder bag, took out a thick wedge of cheese wrapped in greaseproof paper, and handed it to her.

When she protested that he should save it for Rosina and Antonio, he replied that he had another chunk in his satchel and she should take it with his blessing.

'*Arrivederci.*' She kissed him on both cheeks. 'Be careful.'

'You, too. I will see you in Sant'Illaria.'

'I hope so,' she said.

At around midday, Lidia and David found an abandoned cowshed near the stream Signor Zalunardi had mentioned, where they rested and nibbled the cheese. It was dry inside and they lay curled up under their blankets on the straw, taking it in turns to sleep and keep watch.

In the late afternoon, a nudge woke Lidia and she blinked her eyes open.

'We should go,' David smiled. 'The stream has cut a deep gorge in the mountain side, and it could be tricky to follow if it gets dark.'

'But, what about the Black Brigades?'

'As soon as we can see the village below us, we'll stop and wait until we can continue by the light of the moon.'

They finished the cheese and set off. David's prediction that the way would be difficult was correct. Often, the narrow pathway by the stream disappeared altogether, and they had to climb over slippery rocks to get back on track.

Finally, in the early evening, the church tower of Sant'Illaria came into view. 'We'll wait here until nightfall. Shouldn't be long now…'

They sat on the pebbly ground under the low branches of a wild fig tree. Lidia shivered and David put his arm around her. 'You've been so brave. I'm incredibly proud of you.'

'As I am of you.' She looked him in the eye. 'Are you looking forward to joining the British mission?'

'Yes and no.'

'Why "no"?'

'Because I'll be apart from you, Elena.'

'Oh.'

The silence between them vibrated with words unsaid. She'd never imagined she would ever want a man to look at her in the same way that Renzo had. But now, it was all she could think about in the quiet, still moments when she wasn't fighting for her life and David's. The irony wasn't lost on her when he'd told her he'd been studying law, the same as Renzo. But Renzo was doing it for the money, whereas David wanted to help people.

She closed her eyes and memorised the manly scent of him. It might be the last chance she got. Once they arrived at the villa, he would leave for Belluno as soon as possible.

'Come on,' he said, pulling her to her feet.

As Signor Zalunardi had predicted, a full moon had risen and lit their way. They reached the bridge spanning the gorge with the roadblock manned by guards. Stealthily, keeping to the shadows, they slipped beneath the arches.

'There's the villa.' Lidia had only been there once before, not long after she'd arrived from Venice, but it was unmistakable for the grandeur of its structure.

They climbed the steep path leading up from the stream.

Without warning, Lidia slipped.

She yelped before she could stop herself.

A search light beamed from the Black Brigades on the bridge.

'Lie down,' David lowered his voice. 'Flatten yourself as much as possible.'

The searchlight missed them by centimetres, and she heaved a sigh of relief.

David grabbed her hand and pulled her with him the rest of the way up the slope.

Soon they'd arrived at the villa's stable block. A horse whinnied and then a dog started barking loud enough to wake the dead.

'Who's there?' A man came out from the side of the building, a growling mastiff pulling at its lead.

Lidia froze, but David manoeuvred her behind him. 'Captain Roden, at your service,' he saluted the man.

'We've been waiting for you to arrive. The Count is expecting you.' The man soothed the snarling mastiff while Lidia translated. 'Come with me.'

Chapter 20

Lidia, 1944

The Count's steward introduced himself as Orazio Fabbris. He returned the guard dog to its kennel, then took Lidia and David to his employer.

Count Corradini was having dinner in the opulent, red-carpeted dining room, a porcelain tureen of minestrone steaming in the centre of the table. 'Glad you made it.' His smile was welcoming. 'Please, leave your weapons by the door and take a seat. You must be hungry.'

The aroma of the vegetable soup made Lidia's mouth water, but she asked, 'Can I go and wash my hands first?'

'Of course.' He picked up a silver bell from the table and rang it.

Within seconds a thin, grey-haired woman appeared. 'My housekeeper, Signora Bernardi,' he said by way of introduction. 'She will take you both to the cloakroom.'

David waited outside while Lidia used the facilities. Her reflection stared back at her in the gilt-framed mirror. She recoiled in horror. Her filthy face was covered in scratches from the thorns last night; her unkempt hair resembled a bird's nest; the English overcoat she'd been given after an air drop was splattered with mud; her trousers and jumper were disgustingly dirty. Up on the Grappa it hadn't mattered; they'd all looked like tramps. Here, in this sumptuous villa, though, she suddenly found herself mortified by her appearance. She turned on the tap and her breath stalled. *Running water!* She lathered her hands with the almond-scented soap, her heart singing at the pure pleasure of it.

It was her turn to wait for David while he was in the cloakroom; she insisted. She didn't want to face the Count on her own. He was only in his early thirties, but his aura of sophistication the first time she'd met him had been intimidating. She told herself not to be silly; she'd faced the enemy with her Sten levelled, hadn't she? She could deal with the Count.

Lidia and David left their muddy shoes and coats by the door and walked across the tiled hallway back to the dining room. Places had been set for them at the table and Signora Bernardi was ladling minestrone into their dishes.

The Count, speaking impeccable English, said he'd received a message from the British mission that they were expecting David forthwith. As soon as a *stafetta* became available, she would take him to them.

David gave the Count a thumbs-up sign. 'Elena and I haven't discussed this, but I was hoping she'd be able to come with me…'

'To do what?' The Count gave Lidia a curious glance.

'I'm a freedom fighter now,' she said, thrilled by David's suggestion. 'I'd like to join up with the partisans in Belluno.'

'I will see what can be done,' the Count said before going on to ask Lidia and David about their experiences during the *rastrellamento*.

They told him everything: how the attack came out of nowhere; how they were greatly outnumbered by the Wehrmacht forces; how the partisans' lack of weapons and ammunition had made resistance futile.

'It's time the *partigiani* altered their tactics.' The Count wiped his Clark Gable moustache with his napkin. 'By isolating themselves up on the Grappa without any means of communication other than girls on bicycles, they inevitably exposed themselves to encirclement by the *nazifascisti.*'

'I found the partisans I met to be extraordinarily brave.' David took a sip of the red wine Count Corradini had poured for him and Lidia. 'They have to suffer greater hardships and run greater risks than regular troops.'

'I agree,' Lidia dared to comment. 'The conditions up there were terrible. I couldn't help admiring their spirit of determination, self-sacrifice, patriotism and passion for the cause of freedom.'

'Most definitely,' the Count nodded. 'The National Liberation Committee has great faith in the partisans and what they will achieve when the Allies reach the Veneto and the Germans start to withdraw.'

'Any news on that score, Count Corradini?' David asked.

'Please, call me Guido. We are equals, are we not?' He shook his head. 'Rimini has turned into a second

Monte Cassino, by all accounts. Now the British Eighth Army has paused action to reorganise.' A smile played across his lips. 'But the Americans are on the outskirts of Bologna.'

'That's wonderful,' Lidia exclaimed. 'It will all be over soon.'

The Count—she would never think of him as Guido—reached across the table and patted her hand. 'We live in hope. That is what sustains us. But, in the meantime, we must fight on.'

'I was devastated by the reprisals,' Lidia sighed. 'All those burning farmhouses…'

'I'm afraid there are more reprisals to come.' The Count took a sip of his wine. 'The Black Brigades have over fifteen thousand men forming a noose around the Grappa. The roadblocks aren't picking up as many of what they call *banditi*, or outlaws, as they'd hoped. But there are informants in the villages who are reporting the presence of partisans in their midst.'

'That's terrible,' Lidia stifled a gasp. 'Why would they do that?'

'Because they are Fascists. They cling to the ideology and it serves their interests to do so.'

The door to the dining room opened, and Signora Bernardi bustled in to clear their dishes and serve them succulent slices of roast chicken. But what the Count had said about the Black Brigades had made Lidia lose her appetite, and she toyed with the food on her plate.

'Are you alright?' David shot her a worried glance.

'Just tired,' she yawned. 'I'd like to go to bed…'

The Count rang his silver bell again and Signora Bernardi reappeared. 'Please take the young lady to her room. Captain Roden and I will have a brandy and a cigar before we retire.'

Lidia followed the Count's housekeeper upstairs to a beautiful bedroom. Exposed ceiling beams, waxed parquet floors, and gorgeous Venetian style handcrafted furniture. Her eyes filled with tears of nostalgia as she remembered the lovely pastel shades of her chest-of-drawers at home, so like the one she was looking at now.

'There are some clothes in there,' Signora Bernardi indicated the wardrobe. 'They belong to Count Corradini's sister. She's a similar size to you. He said she won't mind at all if you wear them.'

'The Count is so kind,' Lidia thanked the housekeeper.

'I'll run a bath for you,' Signora Bernardi offered. 'The bathroom is next door.'

Within minutes, Lidia was luxuriating in warm water scented with dried rose petals. She washed her hair with the shampoo provided and thought about David's suggestion that she go to Belluno with him. Relief spread through her—she would miss him dreadfully if they were separated. He was her brother-in-arms. The notion of being apart from him had been festering in her like an open wound.

She dried herself with a fluffy white towel, wrapped it around her body and returned to the bedroom. A woolly pink nightdress had been left on the bed. She put it on before retrieving Mamma's prayer book from her rucksack and placing it on the nightstand. She would find a hiding place for it tomorrow. Then she climbed under the sheets and eiderdown to surrender herself to sleep.

∽

Lidia rolled over and buried her head in the feather-filled pillow. Where was she? She was used to rough, prickly straw not crisply laundered bedlinen. The soft mattress under her felt strange and the smell of the bedroom was all wrong. What had happened to the odour of cow manure? Why couldn't she hear the rumbling snores of the young men? She blinked her eyes open and her chest hitched. The events of the past couple of days came back to her in a rush—the whistle of the bullets, the thump of the mortar rounds, the acrid smoke of the fires. *The Germans she and David had killed.* A bitter taste filled her mouth.

She swung her shaky legs from the bed and went to open the wardrobe. She flicked through the clothes. Elegant dresses. Stylish skirts. Gorgeous blouses. She found some cotton underwear and a cashmere cardigan in the chest-of-drawers, then returned to the wardrobe to select a tartan A-line woollen skirt and a cream-coloured silk blouse. There was a pair of stacked heel black leather shoes in the bottom of the cupboard and she tried them on. They were a little on the big side, but were certainly better than the worn-out mud-caked Oxfords she'd arrived in.

After washing her face and brushing her teeth in the bathroom, she made her way downstairs. The wall clock in the hall displayed the impossibly late time of midday. She hadn't realised she'd slept so long. Her heels tapped on the tiled floor as she went to look for David. She found him in the living room, sipping coffee with the Count.

'Ah, there you are. Hope you slept well.' David got to his feet. He was dressed in a smart pair of grey slacks and a light blue jumper he must have borrowed from the Count.

Count Corradini rang his ubiquitous silver bell. 'Coffee

for the signorina,' he said, when Signora Bernardi came through the door.

'Guido has been filling me in on what happened to our comrades up on the Grappa.' David's tone was serious and Lidia's heart sank. 'Not good news, I'm afraid. Douglas has been killed along with two of his men.'

'Oh no!' Her hand flew to her mouth. 'That's awful.'

'There was only one Black Brigades battalion involved with the Germans in the *rastrellamento*,' the Count muttered. 'An eye-witness who was hiding under some dead bodies came down from the mountain this morning. He reported to me that the South Africans had surrendered, but the Fascists shot them.'

'The bastards.' David shook his fist. 'That's completely against the Geneva convention.'

Tears trickled from Lidia's eyes. She knuckled them away and took a deep breath. 'Any news of Commander Falcon?'

'As far as I'm aware, he's still alive.'

'Thank God for that,' David said.

With trembling hands Lidia stirred sugar into the coffee Signora Bernardi had just placed in front of her. 'Do you know if Rosina and Antonio have managed to get home?'

'The Fascists' roadblocks have turned out to be ineffective,' the Count said. 'The *partigiani* know how to get round them. I haven't heard from Rosina, but I expect she and her brother are safely back.'

'And their father too, I hope,' Lidia gave a sigh.

Later, after lunch, Lidia and David were in the sitting room, talking about what had happened to Douglas and how much they hoped Falcon, Rosina and Antonio had made it back down the mountain. Count Corradini had explained to them over a meal of pork loin cooked in white wine sauce, that the local *fascisti* thought he was one of them. He maintained the pretence in order to get information that he would relay to the regional H.Q of the National Liberation Committee. He warned David and Lidia that they would need to keep a low profile if ever he had guests.

'What do you think of Guido?' David whispered to Lidia as they sat next to each other on the sofa.

'I'm not sure, to be honest. I mean, it's kind of him to let us stay here. But, if he's pretending to be a friend of the Fascists, I'm wondering how much of that is a pretence? The Italian upper classes have been ardent supporters of Mussolini since the outset...'

'That's what I heard. But then, the disastrous war put paid to their support.'

'Hmmm...' Lidia drew her brows together. 'H.Q trusts the Count so I suppose we should too. I owe him a debt of gratitude for helping me when I had to leave Venice.'

'And I owe him that same debt or I wouldn't be here with you right now.' David's eyes smiled into hers. 'You're looking incredibly beautiful, Elena.'

She felt her cheeks heat up. 'I feel more human after a bath and wearing these clothes. They belong to the Count's sister,' she explained.

She was just about to compliment David on how handsome he was in his borrowed outfit, freshly shaved and with clean hair, when the door to the living room crashed open and the Count burst into the room.

'I've just received a phone call from a contact,' he huffed out a breath. 'The German Command and Black Brigades are using a ruse to catch the partisans who've taken refuge with their families. They've spreading the word that they'll be offered an unconditional pardon if they hand themselves in. They won't be put on trial but given the chance to do military service or work on engineering projects.'

'Surely they realise it's a set-up?' David shook his head.

'They've enlisted the help of village schoolmasters and people like that. They're going around persuading families to encourage their sons to present themselves and receive a pardon.'

Lidia's blood ran cold. 'What's happening to them?'

'Reports are that, after a kangaroo court trial, the bastards are hanging the poor lads in village and town streets and squares as "a warning to the populace".' The Count's voice had risen.

Lidia was out of her seat before she'd even thought about it. 'I've got to warn the Zalunardis.'

She belted out of the villa and down the driveway, running as if the hounds of Hell were at her heels, not even realising David was behind her until she was well on the way to the village.

Fear twisted her stomach into knots.

The gardens of Sant'Illaria, normally filled with people tending to their vegetable plots, were eerily empty. A heavy silence hung in the air, becoming more pronounced the closer they got to the main square. A fierce breeze had sprung up, whipping her hair across her eyes. A rumble of thunder heralded the imminent arrival of a storm.

'Take care, Elena,' David lowered his voice and held her hand.

In the piazza, she froze in disbelief. '*O Dio…*'

Two bodies.

Each hanging from a separate lamppost.

Their hands tied behind their backs.

Their legs swinging in the wind.

She wanted to turn and run. She wanted to get closer to be sure. She wanted to hide. So many emotions rippled through her, but, in the end, she walked towards the macabre sight, as if pulled by an invisible thread.

Antonio and his comrade, ginger-haired Fox.

Heads twisted to an unnatural degree by the ligatures around their necks.

Their eyes stared blankly.

Their tongues protruded.

Lidia's stomach heaved. She took a breath, forced herself not to vomit.

Villagers had gathered, and there were the Zalunardis —Rosina and her parents— clutching each other, their mouths open in shock.

Without warning a squad of Black Brigades marched into the square. At the front strutted the vile man who'd tried to force himself on Lidia. She gave a gasp.

'Come, Elena,' David murmured. 'We've got to get out of here. There's nothing to be done.'

He dragged her away. As soon as they'd reached the safety of the villa's driveway, he opened his arms and she went into them.

She sobbed against his chest. 'How can people be so cruel?'

'It's dreadful, I know.' He lifted her chin and gazed into her eyes. 'But you must be more careful. Not draw attention to yourself.'

'I wasn't thinking. I only hoped I'd be in time to warn the Zalunardis.'

'I'm sorry about Antonio. He was a good lad.'

Tears ran down Lidia's face. David bent and kissed them away. 'Oh, God, Elena. I love you. You are the most incredible, courageous, wonderful girl.'

'I love you too, David.' And she did. He'd become her harbour in the storm. She loved him with every particle of her being.

He kissed her properly, his mouth claiming hers. This was where she should be, she realised, in David's arms. He'd peeled back the defences she'd put up after Renzo had stopped writing to her. Renzo had been a boy, she knew that now, whereas David was a man. She gave herself over to his kiss, threading her fingers into his jumper and clinging to him.

He stroked a finger down her cheek. 'My girl from Venice,' he smiled.

She angled her face towards his palm and kissed it.

Thunder cracked. 'We'd better get inside or we'll be soaked,' David groaned.

'And we need to tell the Count what's happened.'

Chapter 21

Charlotte, 2010

Francesca directed me to a car park opposite the Bassano train station. After I'd found a spot for the Fiat, we set out on foot, making our way into the old town centre down a narrow street lined with stalls.

'Market day is only on Thursdays and Saturdays.' Francesca linked her arm through mine. 'It's a good place to shop for cheap clothes.'

The hot sun beat down on us and I wiped sweat from my brow as we strolled past vendors selling everything from cotton dresses to jeans, socks and t-shirts as well as a variety of vans offering fresh fish, cheese, fruit and vegetables. I expected the stall keepers to be shouting out, touting their wares, but they didn't appear particularly bothered about business and were chatting among themselves, smoking or even reading newspapers.

We'd arrived at a rectangular piazza with a statue of the winged lion of Saint Mark on a pillar in the middle. We bought ourselves bottles of chilled water from a vending machine and drank them down.

Francesca led me up a side street lined with designer boutiques. Bassano was obviously a prosperous town.

'The Viale dei Martiri is this way,' she said, linking my arm once more.

Martyr's avenue. It wasn't difficult to work out the meaning of the words. Despite the heat, I shivered at the thought of what I would find.

The ramparts of a castle rose on my left, sand-coloured against a cerulean blue sky. A line of trees edging the wide road pulled me like a magnet. Twelve holm oaks, their foliage pruned to look like soldiers' helmets. My stomach churned and I unhooked my arm from Francesca's.

I stepped up to the first tree. A tubular metal structure encircled the trunk. A cross, enamelled in black, had been fixed to the centre. The name, *Fiorenzo Puglierin,* on a brass plaque with the date of his death, spanned the middle of the cross, and his ceramic photo in an oval bronze frame had been attached above it. A miniature hangman's noose, cast in steel, hung below the photo down the centre of the structure, under which a vase had been strapped where someone had placed fresh flowers. Sadness bloomed in my chest.

We walked the entire length of the avenue, checking the names of the fallen: Giovanni, Giacomo, Pietro, Girolamo, Cesare, Albino, Francesco, Pietro, and three "unknown".

'Could Antonio be one of the "unknowns"?' I asked.

Francesca shook her head. 'Rosina categorically stated that her brother had been hanged. So his name would be here.'

'Maybe she was confused?'

'I don't think so. Michela also mentioned it.'

'She didn't say he died in Bassano, now I think about it.' I drew my brows together. 'Do you know if they executed partisans anywhere else?'

'There are memorials in many of the towns and villages of the area. I'm sorry, but I've never paid much attention to them.' Her eyes met mine, and they were filled with sorrow. 'It all happened so long ago, and not knowing anyone involved made everything seem remote.'

'That's understandable,' I said. 'I guess it's the same for me when I go past the cenotaph in London.'

We'd come to the end of the line of trees, where we found a metal-framed poster under glass. A description in Italian and English of the events on Monte Grappa in September 1944. I read out loud, '*Most of the partisans came down from the mountain, passing the roadblocks and returning to their families. The German Command spread the word that if they handed themselves in, they would receive an unconditional pardon. The local populace greeted the news with relief. They convinced their young men to come out of hiding. But it was a trick. Hundreds of partisans were shot or hanged.*' My voice shook. '*Hundreds of others were sent to Nazi concentration camps. In Bassano itself, seventeen men were killed by a firing squad in the military barracks and thirty-one were strung up on trees in the city with "Outlaw" written on a placard attached to their chests.*'

'It's tragic.' I blinked the tears from my eyes. 'Those photographs on the trees showed how young they were. I'm shocked this could have happened here…'

Francesca gave my arm a squeeze. 'Italians pitted against Italians. Germany pitted against the Allies. Young people fired up by the spirit of insurrection. It was a terrible time in Italy.'

'And it's happening again today in other parts of the world.'

'Come on,' she said, turning and leading me back up the road. 'Enough with the sadness. Let me show you more of Bassano. Life goes on, as they say…'

We headed down a steep road to where a picturesque wooden bridge, balanced on pontoons, spanned the rushing River Brenta. We strolled from one side to the other, and Francesca told me about the Ponte Vecchio's history—the structure had been designed by Palladio, a famous 16th century architect, apparently. We posed for selfies on a kind of balcony overlooking the fast-flowing water, in front of a magnificent panorama of pastel-coloured buildings and the mountain crags beyond.

Francesca suggested we stop for an aperitivo in the Nardini Grapperia. 'They have a bar like the one in *Cheers*, where everybody knows your name.'

'Great idea,' I agreed, wiping my sweaty hands down my shorts. 'I'm parched.'

The grapperia was crowded with locals, their melodic voices creating a hubbub of sound. 'This place is amazing,' I said, breathing in the heady grappa fumes. 'It has an olde worlde feel to it.'

'Dates from the 18th century and was where grappa was distilled on a commercial basis for the first time.'

'You are a fountain of knowledge,' I chuckled.

'It's information I relay to our guests in the hotel when I give them ideas for day trips,' she winked. 'Just like I tell them that the name of the mountain has nothing to do with the drink.'

I was about to ask her for an explanation when our own drinks arrived, *Mezzo e Mezzos*, which Francesca explained were cocktails of grappa mixed with fruit juices and topped with soda water.

She clinked her glass with mine. '*Salute,* to your health, Lottie.'

'*Salute,*' I responded.

'Alex likes this place.' She gave me an unreadable look. 'He's fallen for you,' she added. 'I know he only met you a few days ago, but I've never seen him so besotted.'

I sipped my drink to cover my surprise at her forthrightness, gathering my thoughts while the bitter sweetness rolled on my tongue. How could I tell her I feared getting hurt again? She would think I was being corny. But I risked it and told her about Gary, then said, 'I'm not saying Alex is like him. Far from it. I'm just not up for a new relationship.'

'Just give him a chance, bella. He's worth it. My brother hasn't had much luck where women are concerned. He married Simonetta when she became pregnant with Gabriel. They were together for a long time beforehand, since university, more from habit than because they were in love.'

'I'm honoured you think I'm worthy of him,' I said. 'But my life is in London. Starting a relationship with Alex would be totally insane.'

'Haven't you heard of "long distance"? Nowadays with

the internet and cheap flights, everything is possible.' She laughed.

'Hmmm.' *Time for a change of subject.* 'How are your wedding plans coming along?'

A smile dimpled her cheeks. 'I need a final fitting for my dress, that's all. Everything else is in hand.' She took a sip of her *Mezzo e Mezzo*. 'Why don't you come for dinner next week and meet Lorenzo? I'd love you to see the farmhouse we've renovated on the hill behind Sant'Illaria.'

'That would be amazing. Thanks. If I'm still here. I hope Rosina will agree to see me again in a day or two.'

'I hope the old dear will remember more about your grandmother.'

'She said Leonessa had come down from the Grappa with the rest of the partisans, I'd really like to know what happened to her next.'

Francesca and I stopped off for a pizza on our way back to the car park. Once she'd started talking about Lorenzo and her upcoming wedding, it was easy for me to distract her from pressing me about Alex. I couldn't believe he was "besotted". More likely up for a fling. *A fling that would be a disaster.*

On our return to the Corradini, I went to my new accommodation, unpacked, then had a short rest. The bed was lovely and comfortable, and the shutters had kept the room cool. After I woke up, I drove the short distance to the supermarket Francesca had shown me on our way back from Bassano where I stocked up on essentials—coffee, milk, tea, fruit, salads, cold meats, cheeses, etcetera. It didn't take long for me to put everything away in the fridge when I got back, but I was feeling hot again and decided to go for a swim.

I changed into my bikini, left the annex, and sauntered across the lawn to the pool. Half a dozen or so hotel guests had stretched out on the sun loungers, but there was only one person in the water.

Alex.

Ploughing up and down, swimming lengths.

He stopped when he saw me and gave me a wave.

I dived in and swam up to him.

He shook the droplets from his hair, and my heartbeat raced. God, he was gorgeous. Francesca said he was besotted with me, but that couldn't be true, could it?

'My sister filled me in on what happened at Rosina's and then your visit to Bassano,' he said.

'So sad.' The words sounded hackneyed to my ears. 'It must have been terrible to live through those times. No wonder my gran decided to forget all about the past...'

'Our grandparents' generation had a common purpose once the war was over. They wanted to put it behind them and move on.'

'I know. I'm a history teacher, remember?'

'Ah, yes. Of course.'

I touched his shoulder. 'Sorry. That came out all wrong. I didn't mean to be curt.'

'No offense taken,' he said with a smile.

'Race you,' I said, covering my discomfort by setting off at a fast crawl.

I left him in my wake.

'Speedy Gonzalez,' he laughed low in his throat when he'd caught up with me at the other end of the pool.

'Where's Gabriel?' I asked, looking around for Alex's mini-me.

'With Simonetta. She fetched him last night before we went to the restaurant.'

'About last night…' I felt the heat in my cheeks. 'I hope I didn't give you the wrong impression.'

'I don't know what you mean, Lottie.' The words came out so serious, but the twinkle in his eye told me he was joking.

'Think I'll head back to the annex,' I said. 'Catch you later…'

I climbed the ladder and fetched my towel, then made my way towards the stable block.

Alex fell into step beside me. I couldn't help glancing at his swimming shorts clinging to his rounded buttocks, the water dripping down his toned chest.

'You don't need to walk me home,' I muttered. 'I know the way.' I didn't know why I was being so prickly.

'Oh, didn't Francesca tell you?' he smiled broadly. 'I live in the maisonette next door to yours.' He stopped and held me in his gaze. 'My sister insisted on giving me the night off. Most of our guests have gone in the hotel's minibus for a night at the opera in Verona, and she says she'll cope fine with those who are left.' He touched my hand. 'So, I'd love to make dinner for us. Nothing fancy. A plate of spaghetti with fresh tomato sauce. Would you like that?'

'Thank you.' What else could I say? He'd taken me completely by surprise. 'That would be lovely.'

He waited at my door while I unlocked it.

I turned to say I'd see him later.

Before I could utter a word, he tilted my chin up, his green eyes questioning.

I nodded and he brought his mouth to mine.

My heart hammered and I arched up on the tips of my toes, kissing him back, looping my arms around his neck as he pulled me against him.

He pulled me closer.

I tugged at the back of his hair. *I want him so badly it hurts.*

He held me even tighter, manoeuvring me backwards, kissing me until my spine pressed against the wall. His lips grew more demanding, and I opened myself up to him, my skin tingling with need.

With a sudden chime, his mobile phone rang.

Gasping, we sprang apart.

'Sorry.' He checked the caller I.D. 'It's Michela.'

He spoke in rapid Italian, then disconnected the call.

'What's wrong?'

'Rosina's in hospital,' he said, his expression grave.

I came down to earth with a thud. 'Oh, no! Is it serious?'

'She had a fall at lunchtime and broke her arm. She's very confused, so they're keeping her in for observation.'

'Will she be okay?'

'Michela thinks so. She just wanted to tell us that it will be a while before her mamma can talk to you.'

'That's absolutely fine,' I said in a false-bright tone. 'An excuse for me to stay here longer. Not that I'd have wished this on poor Rosina...'

'Neither would I. I'm relieved you aren't about to

leave for London. Although I'd have preferred it if you hadn't needed an excuse.'

I looked him in the eye. 'Can we take this slowly, please, Alex? Whatever "this" is?'

He bent and brushed a kiss to my lips. 'As slow as you like, Lottie. You have my word.'

Chapter 22

Lidia, 1944

Lidia woke in the middle of the night, shivering. A draught of cold air was coming through the bedroom window and she went to close it. Still half asleep, she reached for the latch. Something caught her eye—a flicker of shadows across the lawn. Her skin prickled as she saw German soldiers, lighting cigarettes. But when she looked again, the shadows had gone. Her mouth twisted. Of course Zeno, the Count's mastiff, would have been barking his head off if there'd been anyone there. Her imagination had been getting the better of her. Shaking her head, she returned to bed.

She closed her eyes and waited for sleep to take her. But to no avail. She had taken a life. *More* than one life. Men sent to war. Kill or be killed. It was the most terrible thing.

Mamma's prayer book was at the back of the wardrobe, hidden in a pair of boots. Lidia swung her legs from the bed and went to fetch it. She held it to her chest and slipped under the covers again.

A wave of sorrow brought tears to her eyes. Everyone she loved ended up being taken from her. First, Renzo. Then, Papa. And now, David. He was leaving tomorrow. Despite his request, she hadn't been permitted to go with him. It didn't bear thinking about. Yet, think about it she did. And it made her chest ache. She wiped away the tear that had escaped. She would give anything for him to be here with her. In her bed. But she'd been too shy to ask and he was too gentlemanly to propose such an idea. And now it was too late. In a few hours he'd be gone, leaving her bereft of his protection, bereft of his kisses. She might never know what it would be like to be physically loved by him.

She touched a hand to her lips. Her feelings for David were more sensuous than anything she'd ever experienced. She loved being kissed by him; she loved it when his hands slid around her back; she loved the warmth and press of his mouth. Their tongues would play chase in endless rounds of swollen embraces until the pounding of her heart trembled in her mouth and quivered in her belly. She wished she could share her love for him with the world, but he'd said that if she wanted to carry on fighting by his side, their kisses could only be snatched in secret.

A sigh swelled in Lidia's chest. Shortly after they'd arrived at Villa Corradini over a month ago, a message came that the British mission had stood down temporarily after combatting with the Gramsci Brigade in the Dolomites. That campaign had not gone well and David had been told to wait until a different H.Q had been set up. It took weeks. During that time, most of the partisans who'd survived the roundups had gone to ground. There'd been enough killing and burning to lower everyone's morale, and there was widely expressed dissatisfaction directed at the National Liberation Committee because of the obviously faulty tactics they'd insisted be employed.

Finally, however, a new organisation had been established in the Cansiglio Forest above Vittorio Veneto overlooking the river Piave, where the freedom fighters were reconvening and waiting for the Allies to drop weapons and supplies. David's help was now needed. He'd promised Lidia that, as soon as he'd re-joined his comrades, he would persuade his Commander to send for her on the strength of her language skills, her medical knowledge, and last, but not least, her courage.

She'd said her bravery had been insignificant in comparison with the young men up on the Grappa. Her heart broke every time she thought about her wolf cubs and what had occurred in the towns and villages at the foot of the mountain. So many executions and deportations to labour camps. She would never forget the sight of Antonio swinging from that lamppost, Rosina and her parents' faces frozen in horror.

Lidia deeply sympathised with her friend. Rosina had come back to her housemaid job at the villa, but she no longer carried messages as a *stafetta*. It was her parents who'd persuaded Antonio to hand himself in. They, like many of the families in the area, couldn't forgive themselves for what they'd done, despite having been duped into doing it by the *nazifascisti*. Signora Zalunardi hardly moved from her chair by the fireplace these days, and it was up to Rosina to look after the farmyard and animals.

Lidia and David had been confined to quarters. He didn't seem to mind as he got on with the Count "like a house on fire" (his words not hers) and enjoyed their chats over brandy and cigars in the evenings while Lidia would go up for an early night. Thank God, there was a library full of books, and David to talk to when she wasn't reading. She smiled to herself; they'd shared everything about their lives with each other. She'd told him about Renzo, and David had confessed that he'd once been engaged to a girl in the WAAF. To Lidia's relief, the girl had broken off their engagement. In a spirit of optimism, both said they wanted to go back to university after the war—David to complete his law degree in Cambridge and Lidia to finish her medical studies. The fact that they would be living in different countries hadn't been lost on her, but she'd put it to the back of her mind. The future would take care of itself, she has hoped.

She tossed and turned under the eiderdown, sleep still eluding her. She needed to go to the bathroom, so she turned on her bedside light and got out of bed. After using the facilities, she returned to the corridor. She almost jumped out of her skin. David was standing in her open bedroom doorway. 'Is anything wrong?' she asked.

'Yes,' he said morosely, 'I woke up as I thought I'd heard a noise. Now I can't sleep for thinking about tomorrow and how much I'm going to miss you.'

She took a step to close the distance between them and curled her fingers into his silk pyjama top. 'I will miss you too, *amore mio*.' Her heart raced. 'Promise me you'll be careful. I couldn't bear it if anything happened to you.'

'You be careful too, my girl from Venice.'

'You didn't promise me,' she said.

'I promise I'll be careful.' He bent and whispered. 'Good night, my love. If I don't go now, I might do something I'll regret.'

'Go where?'

'I was heading down to the kitchen to heat up some milk.'

'Don't go.' She pressed her hand to his chest, feeling the beat of his heart. She decided to be direct, to give voice to the thought that had been uppermost in her mind. 'I want you to stay with me the rest of the night. All the promises we make don't count for anything in this terrible war. None of us knows what will happen. I want a memory I can hold onto in the dark times ahead.'

Then his lips were on hers, his hands cupping her face.

She drew herself up onto the balls of her feet to align her body to his.

Their mouths clashed and slid. Their tongues teased hidden corners before their frenzy gave way to a quiet fervour.

He nuzzled the base of her throat and pressed kisses along the neckline of her nightgown, making her gasp. Kissing his way downwards, he dropped to his knees and knelt with his face close to her most intimate part. He pressed kisses there, ran his tongue over her nightdress, creating a hot wetness that sent tingles to her core.

'Oh, David,' she whimpered.

He rose to his feet and lifted her in his arms, closing the bedroom door behind them with his shoulder before carrying her to the bed.

'Is this what you want, Elena? Tell me to stop now, and I will.'

'Don't stop.'

He removed her nightgown and gazed at her in the soft light. 'You are so beautiful, my darling girl. I love you so much.'

She basked in his gaze. 'I love you too, David. *Ti amo.*'

He undressed quickly and took her in his arms, skin against skin, kissing her passionately once more as they fell to the bed, her thighs falling open for him. 'I don't want to hurt you, my love.'

'I'm not afraid of pain.' And she wasn't. She wanted this more than she'd ever imagined possible.

He covered her with his firm body.

She threaded her fingers through the silky strands of his hair.

He kissed her, his tongue caressing hers with such love she wanted to weep.

And then he was rocking into her so gently she scarcely felt the twinge. He moved like waves licking at the shore, creating a tide of sensation that took her breath. A hot liquid feeling lapped and retreated, building in intensity. He kissed her without stopping, running his hands over her breasts, down her sides to the curve of her hips.

She felt everything tighten inside her, coiled like a ball of string. Then the tightness unravelled in ripples and it was so beautiful it made her cry.

David stroked her hair and his body stilled. Looking deep into her eyes, he told her how much he loved her. 'I hope I didn't hurt you,' he added, brushing the tears from her eyes.

'You could never hurt me, *amore*.' As she said the words, she knew how true they were. This man. This wonderful man. How fortunate she was to have met him. 'My tears were tears of love.'

Lidia rolled over and opened her eyes. Dawn light came through a gap in the curtains. Her heart sank. David was leaving today, she remembered. Leaving without her. She'd grown so used to him she didn't know how she would manage on her own.

He was already awake. His gaze was gentle, his mouth gentler, his touch to her back the gentlest of all. 'Good morning, my love.' He kissed her forehead.

Her throat was so swollen with sadness she could barely speak. '*Buongiorno.* I am wishing you a good day, but for me it will not be a good day. In fact, it will be an awfully bad day…'

'As for me, Elena.'

She felt a tremor run through him. He pressed his lips to hers and his sigh vibrated against her tongue. He murmured into her mouth, kissing her even as he spoke, 'Marry me, Elena. As soon as the war is over—and it will be over soon, mark my words.'

Her breath hitched. Of all the things she thought he'd say, asking her to marry him wasn't one of them. She searched his eyes, saw the earnestness and honesty. He was waiting for her answer, but she didn't know what to say. Could she leave Italy and live in England? His life was there and hers was here.

He must have caught the doubt in her expression, for

he said, 'I'll learn Italian. Move to Venice. Study Italian law instead of English.'

'Oh, David. You would do that for me?' the words trembled on her lips.

'Elena.' He cradled her face in his hands. 'I love you. So very much. I want us to spend the rest of our lives together. Tell me you want that too.'

'I do,' she nodded.

'So you'll marry me?'

'Yes,' she smiled. Then laughed at the pure joy of it. 'I will marry you, David Roden. I can't wait for you to see our apartment in Venice. But, most of all, I long for you to meet my papa. He will love you as much as I do.'

David rolled her over and smothered her in kisses. 'I'd better go back to my room before it gets any later. I will see you at breakfast, my love.'

He dressed and she watched him leave, unable to hold back her tears. She reached for the prayer book on her nightstand, holding it to her chest and praying to the God of her ancestors to keep David safe.

Chapter 23

Lidia, 1944

It was two days before Christmas, two months after David had left for the Cansiglio. Lidia woke early, a bubble of excitement in her chest. A *stafetta* had arrived last night with a letter for the Count and one for her. Finally, the British Mission Commander had agreed to David's request. Lidia had packed her rucksack straight away; she couldn't wait to go. She'd missed David so much and life closeted in the villa without him had been monotonous in the extreme. Although she'd told herself again and again that she'd been lucky to have escaped the *nazifascisti* reprisals, she'd chafed at her enforced idleness. She must have read every Agatha Christie and the entire collection of Jane Austen and the Bronte sisters' work in the Count's library.

Against all her expectations, the highlight of her days

had been when she would have dinner with Guido, as she'd eventually become relaxed enough in his company to call him. He was an interesting man, and his insight into the war had been informative. According to him, the Allies' strategic aim was to force the Germans to deploy so much strength in Italy that it took away from their defence of occupied France. Otherwise, the balance would have been tipped against the British and Americans in their cross-Channel campaign. It was Guido's belief that the partisans' harassing of Jerry had been vital and would continue to be so.

Lidia smiled wryly to herself, remembering the evening in mid-November when she'd listened open-mouthed to a broadcast, a transmission from the Allied radio station *Italia Combatte.* A proclamation on behalf of General Harold Alexander, Supreme Commander of the Allied Forces in Italy, came over the airwaves, requiring a coordinated response from the partisans. Because the rain and mud couldn't but slow down the British and American advance, the partisans must cease their prior activities in order to combat a new enemy: winter. The nights during which the Allied planes would fly might be few and far between, necessarily limiting airdrops, although they would do what they could. Guido had commented dryly that war against the Nazis was not a "summer sport". Lidia had agreed with him, frustrated that the expected end to hostilities still seemed a long way off, given that the British and Americans had yet to take Bologna.

Sometimes, when Guido was entertaining Germans and their Fascist toadies, Lidia would eat in the kitchen with Signora Bernardi. Guido explained that it was all an act on his part—otherwise he would have fallen under suspicion. Other times, one of his lady friends would visit, and, again, Lidia kept out of the way. Although she'd grown to like the Count well enough, she couldn't make him out. Perhaps it was his background? She'd never met anyone like him before.

Dawn light was filtering through the gap in her bedroom curtains now. She was too excited to sleep. She got out of bed and dressed in the plainest clothes she could find, ready for her journey. A simple grey woollen skirt, a cotton blouse and a thick navy jumper. David's letter was on her nightstand, calling to her. She switched on her bedside light and reread it for the umpteenth time.

Dearest Elena

I hope this letter finds you safe and well. I miss you so much, and the past two months have been hell without you. Oh, how I've wanted to hold you in my arms. There hasn't been a minute of every day when I haven't thought about you, my darling.

But, before you decide if you want to join me, I must warn you about conditions here. Our barracks consist of two log cabins about 100 yards apart. The larger cabin has two tiers of bunks to take about twenty, the other forms the kitchen and mess room. Water comes from a pond 300 yards away. This is now snow-covered, for we're over 4,000 feet up and Cansiglio Forest is a notoriously cold place. We're kept busy with patrols, ciphering, chopping wood, fetching water and hay for Henry, our mule, and visiting the nearby partisan battalions. Your language skills are sorely needed, my love. The dropping ground for parachute drops is close, but our bad luck on that score continues. A couple of weeks ago, two planes dropped their loads, including our wireless stores and three months' mail, to a Fascist garrison ten miles away by mistake. The partisans were disgusted by this tragedy, especially when visitors from the plain below regaled them with details of how the fascisti are smoking English cigarettes and eating English chocolates, while they busy themselves stripping and reassembling handsome new Bren guns and Stens for use against us. I'm glad to say, though, that despite this deplorable record of failure, we remain good friends with the partisans—although they clearly find it difficult to believe that the R.A.F., in whom they had such confidence, could be so bloody incompetent.

Christmas will be here in a couple of days and preparations are in full swing. I long for you to be with me again, my darling girl, but if you should decide against the hardship and danger, I will fully understand. No need for explanations, and I will come to the villa to find you as soon as the war is over.

Please destroy this letter once you have read it, my love. For obvious reasons.

Your loving David.

The time had come for her to follow David's instructions. With enormous regret, she tore the letter into tiny pieces. Cupping them in her hand, she went to the bathroom and flushed them down the toilet. Of course, she would leave with the *stafetta*. She didn't care if she had to sleep in a bunk bed surrounded by snoring men who stank of sweat. She didn't care if it was freezing. She didn't care if there wasn't enough food or clothing. All she cared about was being with David.

Back in her room she went to pick up her rucksack and go down for breakfast. Loud banging at the front door stopped her in her tracks. She rushed to the window and peered through the gap in the curtains.

O, Dio!

Two men on the doorstep. Dressed in the National Republican Guard uniforms—the Fascist police force established by Mussolini to take over from the Carabinieri.

Lidia's heart hammered. Had they come for her? Her blood turned to ice.

She contemplated hiding in the wardrobe, but that would be the first place they would look. Quick as lightning, she rummaged in her rucksack and found Mamma's prayer book. Her only option was to return it to its hiding place, which she did quickly, stuffing it in the boot. She returned to the window and opened it, checking to see if she could climb out. But her room faced the front garden and it was a sheer drop to the ground.

Shouts reverberated from the lower floor. Doors banged. The heavy thud of feet echoed from the tiled hallway.

Oh, good God. Lidia's eyes almost popped out of her head. The policemen had handcuffed Guido and they were marching him down the driveway.

She raced downstairs to find Rosina. 'Come,' Rosina grabbed her hand at the foot of the stairs. 'The Count told me that if this were ever to happen, I was to destroy all the incriminating documents I could find in his study.'

'I'm surprised the guards haven't made a thorough search.'

'They are too lazy. All they were interested in was arresting the Count so they could return to the police station and put their feet up.'

Rosina went to the Count's desk. She opened all the drawers and took out every document. 'I don't know if these are incriminating or not. So I'll burn them all.' In the top drawer she found a wad of Lira notes. She handed them to Lidia. 'Here, take these. You will have to go to Venice to the Count's sister. She knows influential people who might be able to help the Count.'

'But…but I'm supposed to be leaving for the Cansiglio. The British Mission is expecting me.' Lidia's voice trembled.

Rosina tapped her foot on the parquet floor. 'The *inglesi* will have to wait. You can go to them when you get back from Venice. I will ask the *stafetta* to relay a message to them.'

Lidia couldn't refuse. It would be ungrateful. Guido had helped her; she must help him in return. Rosina couldn't go; she had to take care of her parents and look after the farm animals.

'I'll do it,' Lidia sighed. 'I'll leave straight away.'

Unlike her journey to Sant'Illaria nearly a year ago, when she'd travelled via Treviso, Lidia cycled to Castelfranco this time. The town was closer and there would be fewer Germans about. At the station ticket office, she showed her new fake I.D—which the Count had organised for her planned transfer to the Cansiglio—and then, her heart heavy with disappointment and not a little trepidation, she boarded the train.

The locomotive's whistle blew and, with a lurch, they set off. The train stopped repeatedly, taking on passengers until they filled every seat. Nausea swelled in Lidia's stomach at the stench of unwashed bodies and clothes. Soap was expensive because of the war, she reminded herself. There was a long stop at Mestre. Almost everyone got off and Lidia felt conspicuous sitting staring out of the window with no one next to her. But soon the train left the station and they were crossing the causeway to Venice.

At Santa Lucia station, she presented her I.D at the barrier without a blink. A year ago she would have kept her eyes down, every nerve in her body on edge. But that had been the old Lidia. Now she'd become a different person. All she needed to do was think about David and courage stiffened her spine. She took the vaporetto that entered the Guidecca canal via Santa Croce, then alighted at Redentore and walked the rest of the way to the Pivettas' house.

Marta answered the door with a gasp. '*Dio buono*. Is it really you?' She grasped Lidia's arm and pulled her indoors.

Lidia hugged her dearest friend, tears of emotion in her eyes. 'I need your help,' she said, after Marta had taken her into the kitchen to greet her mother.

Lidia then told Marta the whole sorry story about Count Corradini's arrest, pausing only to sip from the glass of water Marta's mamma had fetched for her. Lidia remembered to ask Marta about Giorgio. 'Do you have news of him?'

'No. Nothing.' Marta's voice was filled with regret.

Lidia reached across the table and squeezed her hand. 'He will return to you, I'm sure.'

'I hope you are right.'

Lidia debated whether to tell her about David, but now was not the time. Instead, she asked, 'Will you be able to help me get to Beatrice Corradini?'

'Of course,' Marta smiled. 'And you must stay here tonight. It will be too late for you to catch a train this evening and cycle back to Sant'Illaria in the dark. We'll take Babbo's boat. It will be safer.'

Lidia thanked her, declining Marta's offer of some food; she couldn't stomach it. They left the house almost as soon as she'd retrieved Guido's sister's address from the heel of her shoe—where she'd hidden the piece of paper on which Rosina had written it.

Signor Pivetta's small boat bumped over the frothy white horses topping the emerald-green waves. A blustery wind whipped Lidia's hair back from her face and she tasted the salt of the sea on her lips. She'd missed this so much, except it counted for nothing in comparison with her missing David.

They took a short cut across Dorsoduro to the Grand Canal, where Marta tied her babbo's boat to a wooden pole by the Accademia Bridge jetty. Lidia followed her up the steps to the pontoon. 'I hope the Count's sister is home,' she said.

'It's still afternoon rest time, bella. I expect we'll find her with her feet up. Ladies like her take their leisure seriously.'

Lidia nudged Marta's shoulder. 'Do I detect a hint of sarcasm?' she gave a wry chuckle.

'Me? Sarcastic?' Marta chuckled with her.

They pushed open the heavy wooden door at the foot of an imposing palazzo overlooking the waterway and traipsed up the marble stairs. A maid answered the bell and told them to wait on the landing while she went to check with her mistress.

Within minutes, a slender woman appeared, her dark hair elegantly styled in a fashionable bob and a string of pearls around her neck. Lidia took her coat off and showed the Count's sister what she was wearing. 'I hope you don't mind, but I had to borrow some of your clothes.'

Beatrice Corradini raised a brow. 'Come in, my dears, and tell me the purpose of your visit.'

She ushered Lidia and Marta into a sumptuous living room with Murano glass chandeliers. The Palladian windows with an arch in the centre and columns at the sides reminded Lidia of the window overlooking the lagoon in Papa's and her apartment. She breathed out a sigh; she only hoped Signor and Signora Rossi were taking good care of the place.

After she'd taken the seat the Count's sister had offered her, Lidia launched into the reason for her visit. When she'd finished explaining, Beatrice Corradini stared at her, wide eyed. 'I always knew my brother would get into trouble, one day.' She shook her head. 'Whatever was he thinking, dragging our family name into disrepute?'

'He's a patriot,' Lidia said firmly.

'Depends on what you mean by the word,' Beatrice Corradini huffed. She picked up a cigarette case from the coffee table, offered one to Marta and Lidia then took one herself.

Lidia inhaled one puff of her *sigaretta*. It made her feel sick, so she put it out. 'I hope you will be able to help your brother,' she said, sending Beatrice Corradini a pleading look.

'My husband is away until the day after tomorrow. He knows the Commander of the *Decima MAS*, Don Junio Borghese. I'm sure he'll agree to have a word. Junio is an old friend of his and almost certainly owes him a favour or two…'

'*Grazie*,' Lidia thanked her. She needed to get Marta out of here. Her friend's face had turned as black as thunder. What had put her in such a foul mood?

All was made clear as soon as they'd left the apartment. 'The *Decima MAS* was Giorgio's old unit, the Assault Vehicle Flotilla,' Marta muttered. 'Borghese is a *maledetto* die-hard Fascist.'

'If he's that powerful, surely he'll have the clout to get Count Corradini released?'

'That's if he agrees. The *Decima MAS* are collaborating openly with the Nazis and fighting the partisans…'

'*O, Dio,*' Lidia's heart sank.

They returned to the Pivettas' house where they spent the rest of the afternoon in Marta's bedroom, filling each other in on their lives. After telling her best friend all about her experiences on the Grappa, Lidia confessed to Marta about David. Marta enveloped her in a warm embrace. 'I wish you every happiness with your *moroso inglese,*' she smiled. 'But I hope you won't go to live in England.'

Lidia explained about her and David's plans and Marta told her about the Venetian Resistance, how they were getting stronger. 'We will be ready to take the city back when the time comes,' she said. 'I'm working for the Municipality now,' she added. 'I get to read all kinds of important documents and anything of interest I report back to H.Q. You are lucky today is Saturday and I am home.'

'Take care, bella,' Lidia warned. 'What you are doing is dangerous.'

'You be careful too when you go up to the mountain. I wish you would stay here, though. We have a network of safe houses where you could live.'

Lidia shook her head. 'I'm sorry…'

'Yes. Yes. You must follow your heart.'

'Dinner is ready,' came Signora Pivetta's voice from downstairs.

The aroma of seafood risotto wafted from the tureen at the centre of the dining table as Lidia followed Marta into the room. It was one of her favourite dishes and she tucked in gratefully. But, after a few mouthfuls, her stomach turned and her skin became clammy. 'I'm not feeling well,' she said, pushing her chair back and running to the bathroom. After she'd vomited, she returned to the dining room and apologised to Marta's family. 'I must have caught a chill out on the water,' she said. 'If you don't mind, I think I'll go to bed.'

'I'll be up presently,' Marta said. 'Lie down and get some rest, bella. I'll join you as soon as I've helped with the washing up.'

Lidia stretched out on the bed and closed her eyes. It must have been stress and worry that had make her ill. Or could it have been the chicken casserole Signora Bernardi had prepared for dinner last night? Perhaps the meat had gone off?

Lidia's brows furrowed and she made a list in her head of all the medical reasons for nausea. With a gasp, she clutched her arms to her stomach. Her sickness couldn't mean she was pregnant, could it?

She tried to remember when she'd had her last period. It was an inconvenience when she'd been living rough with the partisans, and she'd been glad when her bleeding had become an irregular event. No, she couldn't be pregnant. It was impossible. She hadn't bled for ages so probably hadn't been ovulating; she must have simply caught a chill.

In the heat of the moment, though, when David had made love to her before leaving for the Cansiglio, he'd spilled his seed inside her. She shouldn't have invited him into her bed so rashly. Could she be having a baby? She wanted to laugh with joy and cry with despair at the same time.

Chapter 24

Lidia, 1944

Lidia's legs ached as she cycled into Sant'Illaria early the following afternoon. After a sleepless night worrying that she might be pregnant, she'd woken up feeling so much better. She'd tucked into a breakfast of freshly baked bread rolls and grain coffee with Marta, who then took her to the train station in her babbo's boat. 'Be careful, bella,' Marta had said, kissing her on the cheeks as they'd bid each other farewell. 'When spring comes, we will be together again in the new, free Italy,' she'd smiled widely. 'And both of us will be with our *moroso*.'

'I hope so,' Lidia had responded. 'And my papa will have come home too.'

Perspiration beading her brow, she hopped off her bike at the gates to the front of the villa before wheeling it up the drive. The door to the house was wide open. *How odd.*

She rolled her bicycle to the stable block and looked around for Orazio, but he was nowhere to be seen. Neither was Zeno the dog.

She went around to the back entrance, hoping to see Rosina. The kitchen was empty. No sign of Signora Bernardi. With a shrug, Lidia picked up a glass and filled it with tap water to slake her thirst. She'd eaten the panini Marta had made for her to take on the train, so she wasn't hungry. But she was tired. *So very tired.* She decided to head for her room and have a rest.

She stepped into the hallway, expecting to find Signora Bernardi and Rosina doing their chores. She called out for them, then gave a gasp.

O, Dio!

Two Republican Guards had come out of Guido's study, their guns raised.

Lidia felt the blood drain from her face.

'Elena Moretti?' the taller man inquired. His black uniform and the jagged shape of his silver collar insignia sent a chill down Lidia's spine.

'Yes.' Her mouth had gone completely dry.

'We are taking you in for questioning. Hold out your hands.'

She contemplated making a run for it, but she knew that wasn't an option—the policemen had guns and the Count had locked up her Sten with his hunting rifles. She held out her hands, shrinking as the cold steel of the hand-cuffs met her skin.

The guards led her through the front door, and it was only then that she saw the splintered frame. The bastards had forced their way in. Thank God Rosina, Signora

Bernardi, Orazio and the dog had obviously managed to escape.

She kept her head high, meeting the stares of curious villagers, but every cell in her body was quaking with fear while the guards marched her to the Fascist military barracks behind the Municipio.

Her pulse thudded. The stout Black Brigade squad leader who'd come up to the Zalunardi farm and whom she'd seen in the square at Antonio's hanging was there, in front of her, sneering. 'Ah, Signorina Moretti. We meet again.' He paused. 'Let me introduce myself. I am Commander Quinto.'

She shot him a defiant look. It was all she could do; she had her pride and she would cling to it.

The officer and guards took her upstairs to a room overlooking the rear of the building. 'Take off your clothes so we can search you,' Quinto barked.

'I can't. You've handcuffed me,' she retorted.

He clamped his hand down on her arm. 'Do not answer back.' He indicated to the shorter guard. 'Free her.'

The guard did as he'd asked, and Lidia managed to pull off her jumper.

'More,' the Commander growled. 'Take everything off.'

With trembling fingers, Lidia undid her blouse and unbuttoned her skirt. The clothes fell to the parquet floor and she stepped out of them. She pulled down her woollen socks and removed her shoes. She was only wearing her bra and knickers now. She shivered and wrapped her arms around herself.

'I said take everything off,' Quinto yelled in her ear, spit flying from his mouth.

She flinched but complied with his order, her hands shaking but looking him boldly in the eye.

Naked and embarrassed, she covered her breasts with one arm and her privates with the other.

Quinto came to stand by her side. 'Bend over,' he said, 'I need to check for hidden weapons.'

Lidia didn't move. All she could do was tremble.

'Bend over!' he bellowed in her ear, pushing a hand into her back.

Lidia did as she was bid, the guards laughing as Quinto's searching fingers assaulted her.

'Stand up straight,' he eventually said, positioning himself in front of her. He swatted her hands from her breasts and raked his eyes over her.

'Get dressed,' he said. 'It's Christmas Eve and I'm due some time off. I will question you after the holidays.'

She put her clothes back on and the guards handcuffed her again. Their gazes were fierce, but she gritted her teeth. They led her down to the basement, to an empty cell. Light from a bare electric bulb showed a chamber pot in the corner, a cot with a rough looking blanket against one wall and a table with a wooden chair opposite.

'Don't move,' the tall guard said. 'I will take off your cuffs.'

She did as he'd ordered and rubbed her wrists when the handcuffs had been removed.

The other guard had planted his feet wide and was giving her looks that made her flesh crawl.

With a clang, the two men closed the cell door, locked it and left her on her own.

O, Dio, why have I been arrested? What do they know about me? And, more to the point, who has betrayed me?

The questions went round and round in her head in an endless cycle. She paced the concrete floor, chewing her thumbnail and trying to be brave. She knew what happened to partisans who were caught, though. Her pulse pounded. She would be tortured and then executed.

Perhaps it was all a mistake? A misunderstanding. She'd kept a low profile since coming down from the Grappa. The Fascists might not know she'd been up there. But, why would they have locked her up in a cell if that were the case? She slumped down on the cot and curled herself into a ball, a cold feeling of dread spreading through her.

After an hour or so, her jailors returned with a jug of water and a tray of food: bean soup, cheese and black bread. A sour taste filled Lidia's mouth; if she ate anything, she'd be sick.

She woke after a restless night spent worrying. She would be tortured, she was sure of it, but she would rather die than betray anyone.

The tall guard brought her bread, jam and grain coffee for breakfast. He wished her *Buon Natale*. She went to spit in in his face but stopped herself in time. She tried to sip the coffee and nibble the bread, but her stomach heaved and she hurried to the chamber pot to throw up. She spent the morning curled up under the blanket, willing herself to stay calm.

At lunch, the shorter guard arrived with a meal of rabbit stew and there was even cake with marsala wine. She couldn't eat—the food stuck in her throat and she couldn't swallow. It occurred to her that they were probably treating her well so she would talk. She would never talk. Even if they broke every bone in her body, she would stay silent.

In the evening, the tall guard returned with a bowl of soup. 'Because it's Christmas, we won't do anything to you today,' he smirked. 'Tomorrow you will be interrogated, and you must tell the truth, or else...'

She laid on the cot, lonely and afraid. To stop herself from crying, she thought about David. Stay strong, she told herself. She closed her eyes, waiting for sleep to claim her. She needed to rest if she were to resist what was surely to come.

The next morning, the guards took her to a separate room, where they sat her on a chair. They tied her hands behind her back and shackled her feet. She squirmed and the shackles bit into her skin.

The portly Commander arrived. He came and stood in front of her. 'Tell us where the partisans are hiding and we'll let you go.' He fixed her with a steely look.

She held his gaze. 'I don't know.'

The slap came from nowhere, knocking her head sideways, the sting so sharp it brought tears to her eyes. The metallic taste of blood filled her mouth.

'Where is the Englishman who was staying at the villa?'

'I don't know who you are talking about.'

A punch landed on her stomach that took her breath away.

'What is your connection to the Count? We are holding him in a room upstairs, and he's sung like a canary, told us everything about you. That you were up on the Grappa with the Campo Croce brigade. That you fought with the escaped POWs and a British Special Force One officer.'

'No comment,' she said.

Quinto twisted his hand in her hair, yanking her head back. Her scalp burnt like fire and tears of pain gushed from her eyes. He bent and licked his tongue down her neck, the stench of his breath so vile it made her gag.

He stared at her, watched the tears sliding down her cheeks with cold eyes.

'Talk,' he snarled. 'Tell us the real names of the partisans you were with!'

'Never!' she shouted.

'What is your connection to the Zalunardi family?'

'I am their cousin. You know that already.'

'Where has the Englishman gone?'

'I don't know any Englishman.'

Oh, God, Quinto had pulled his gun on her. Bullets flew, whizzing past her head. He was deliberately trying to frighten her by aiming wide.

'Talk!' he bellowed.

More slaps landed on her face and punches to her belly. Quinto repeated the same questions again and again. She screwed her eyes shut to contain the tears.

'Speak or we will hang you by the neck until you die.'

She could only shake her head.

'Untie her. Strip her naked and bend her over the desk,' Quinto ordered his men.

She heard the crack of a whip and her heart almost

gave way. She sensed the Commander moving behind her and she braced herself.

'Who are you, Elena Moretti? Is that your real name?'

'No comment.'

Sharp pain sliced into her as leather hit the flesh of her shoulders. She let out a squeal.

'Talk!'

'Never!'

Rage and hatred boiled inside her. How she wanted to turn on the man, grab his gun and kill him. But she knew he would shoot her dead before she got the chance.

She took a deep breath, blew it out. The next hit came, striking like a hot knife across her back. She cried out and her feet twisted.

'Tell us what we want to know,' Quinto spat out the words.

'No!'

Another crack of the whip. Harder this time. She shrieked at the burn.

'Ready to talk now?'

She remained silent.

The Commander carried on whipping her, harder and harder as he appeared to get into his stride. She whimpered, and her legs felt weak and shaky.

Without warning, he grabbed her, turned her around so she was half lying on the desk with her legs dangling.

'Hold her,' Quinto ordered his men.

They stood, one on each side, and pinned her arms down. She struggled and twisted her head.

Oh, dear God.

Quinto was staring at her, lust in his eyes.

'Don't touch me!' she yelled.

'You aren't in a position to tell me what to do,' he laughed.

He angled himself between her legs and unbuttoned his trousers.

O Dio, no!!!

This couldn't be happening.

She screamed.

He clamped his hand over her mouth.

She sank her teeth into the fat flesh of his palm.

'Bitch!' he roared and slapped her face hard.

He fetched a gag from the drawer and tied it around her mouth. All she could do now was plead with her eyes.

Quinto ignored her. He only had one thing on his mind. He pushed into her and it was agony. She let out a muffled shriek. Tears ran down her face as he pumped like a madman, grunting while the guards whooped and cheered. He juddered and pulled out of her. 'Your turn,' he said to the guard on her left.

She begged him with her eyes. To no avail. The guard unbuckled his belt and thrust into her. Soon he had finished and the other guard took his place.

Lidia detached herself. It was as if she'd left her body and gone somewhere else. All she could think about was David. Except now she knew they could never be together. She felt dirty, spoiled. She no longer cared if the Fascists killed her. After what they'd done to her, she'd rather be dead.

When it was over, Quinto made her get dressed and the tall guard took her back to her cell. She could barely walk from the abuse she'd suffered. Her face felt swollen. Her inner thighs were streaked with blood and semen.

Somehow, she managed to find her strength. She threw

herself at the guard and raked her nails down the side of his face.

'*Stronza!*' He slammed her to the floor and pummelled her with his fists. His foot crashed into her skull. After that, she lost track of where the blows landed. Eventually he stopped. The inside of her mouth tasted tangy, and blood trailed down her chin. One eye felt as if it had been sewn shut.

'You filthy whore.' He pointed to the basin of water and cloth that had been provided for her. 'Clean yourself up.'

The guard spun on his heel and left her prostrate on the floor of her cell. She crawled over to the bowl, picked up the cloth and wiped off the dirt as best she could. The water turned red.

She curled herself into a ball on her cot and closed her eyes.

Against all reason, she must have slept. She blinked her eyes open, her head throbbing and every muscle in her body aching. Totally disorientated, she tried to focus—but she was too dizzy.

Sudden nausea assailed her. She swallowed down the bile that had made its way from her stomach to her throat.

Gradually, her mind cleared, and she remembered what had happened.

The maledetti raped me!!!

She choked on a sob. She'd gone to Venice to help the Count, but he'd betrayed her to the Fascists. How could he?

The pattern was repeated for the next four days. The Fascists questioned her, she refused to answer, then they beat her and raped her. On the fourth day, after abusing her as usual, the guards took her back to the cell. One of them let slip that the Count has been freed. She couldn't bring herself to feel any happiness for him whatsoever.

Five days after the abuse had started, she woke with severe cramps in her belly. She rolled over on the cot. She was lying in a sticky pool of blood. Great red clots had been expelled from her body. And she knew, she knew with absolute certainty, that she'd been pregnant and now she'd lost her baby. She wept, then. Not for herself, but for the unborn child whose life had been sacrificed to the cause.

Chapter 25

Charlotte, 2010

I opened the door to Alex; he looked so handsome in his black jeans and tailored white shirt. I was more relaxed in his company now. He'd been true to his word, taking things slowly this past week. We had got into the habit of spending the late evenings together after he'd handed over his hotel responsibilities to the night manager. When we wished each other, *buonanotte*, his hands would slide around my back while he lowered his mouth to mine. I revelled in the warmth and presses of his kisses, my body quivering with need. But we always drew back.

A warm glow spread through me. The feelings I was developing for him weren't just physical. I loved his sense of humour; I loved the fine balance of persistence and respect he showed towards me; and I loved the ease of his company. Only yesterday, he'd taken me with him to the prosecco vineyards when he'd gone to visit a supplier. We'd had lunch in a rustic restaurant overlooking the UNESCO World Heritage site of the rolling hills where the Glera grapes were grown. On returning to the hotel, we'd cooled off in the pool before he went back to work.

When I wasn't with Alex, I'd spent my time exploring the picturesque towns of this part of the Veneto, taking an online Italian course, and reading e-books. The longer I was here, the more I was falling for this beautiful part of Italy and its inhabitants. Francesca had become a real friend; she'd kept her promise of inviting me over to meet Lorenzo. Alex had been included in the invitation, of course, after the night manager had taken over in the hotel. Lorenzo had grilled ribs and chops on a traditional wood-fired ceramic barbecue, and we'd sat outside under the stars, sipping rich red wine.

'Ready to go?' Alex asked now, his cheeks dimpling with an encouraging smile as he waited in my doorway.

'As ready as I'll ever be…'

Finally, Michela had phoned to say that her mamma was feeling more like her old self and had remembered what had happened to Leonessa after she'd come down from the Grappa. Alex offered to go with me and I'd gratefully accepted; Francesca would cover for him at the hotel. He'd done the same for her yesterday when she'd gone for a wedding dress fitting.

'How are you feeling?' Alex asked as we made our way to his car.

'I'm a little nervous, to be honest. I mean, I might eventually learn why Gran cut herself off from her roots.'

He took my hand, gave it a squeeze. 'Don't forget I'm here for you, Lottie. I'll help you get through it.'

'Thanks. You're so nice.'

'Just nice?' A teasing smile crossed his face.

'Okay,' I smirked. 'You're pretty amazing.'

'That's more like it,' his eyes twinkled.

He drove me the short distance to the village; we'd decided beforehand the weather was too hot for walking.

Michela opened the door before we'd even pressed the buzzer. '*Buongiorno,* come through to the garden. It's lovely and cool out there.'

We followed Michela through the sliding glass doors leading off the living area. Rosina was sitting under a patio umbrella shading her from the sun, her arm in plaster held by a sling around her neck. The little dog gave us a warning woof before going back to sleep by her feet.

With Alex translating, I asked her how she was feeling. 'A lot better,' she said. 'I tripped over a pair of shoes I'd left by my bed and stretched out my arm to break the fall.' She huffed. 'Stupid of me.'

'Not at all,' I told her.

'I had a long sleep this morning,' she added. 'So I feel strong enough to tell you everything.'

Michela offered us a coffee, but we declined. So she sat with us and we waited for Rosina to speak.

Rosina took a deep breath. 'Your grandmother, she was incredibly brave…'

And then, she told us. Told us how Gran was supposed to join the British in a forest on the mountain behind the town of Vittorio Veneto, but the Count was taken in for questioning so she agreed to go to Venice and seek help from his sister instead.

Alex visibly stiffened as he translated Rosina's words. 'Incredible. What did they suspect my grandfather of?'

'After he was freed,' Rosina gave him a sympathetic look, 'thanks to Leonessa, we worked out that it was his steward, Orazio, who must have informed on him. The bastard ran off almost as soon as the Count was arrested and took his dog with him. The *nazifascisti* were paying people for information at the time. Orazio probably told the Black Brigades that Count Corradini had contacts with the partisans and the Allies.'

'That's terrible,' I stumbled over the inadequate words. 'What happened next?'

'Well,' Rosina's eyes met mine, 'shortly before your grandmother returned from Venice, two Republican Guards forced their way into the villa. Signora Bernardi, the housekeeper, and I heard them banging on the front door. We managed to run out the back way, but it was too late to warn Leonessa and she fell right into the trap.'

Shock ricocheted through me. 'W…was she arrested?'

'Yes, my dear.' Rosina paused, clearly mulling over what to say next. 'It was the Count who betrayed her.' Another pause. 'I found out from him afterwards. He'd been certain Elena would have already left to join the Allies as planned. He believed he was giving the Fascists information of no use whatsoever.'

Rosina waited while Alex translated, the words catching in his throat. Then she said to him, 'Your grandfather was devastated when he learnt what had happened to Leonessa and immediately put the wheels in motion to get her released.'

'So no harm done?' I risked asking, although I knew I was clutching at straws. From what I'd learnt about the *nazifascisti*, and given Gran's need to forget the past, I feared that harm had very much been done. My skin tightened with apprehension.

'The Count sent me to bring her back to the villa when those bastards let her go. It was New Year's Eve and he'd thrown a party for about fifty Germans—it was a ruse on his part to convince the Fascists he was on their side.' Rosina waited while Alex translated, an incredulous look on his face.

'There's no easy way of saying this, my dears,' Rosina continued. 'But Elena had been tortured and raped.'

Horror twisted in my stomach. 'Poor darling Gran…' I struggled to speak around the lump of horror in my throat.

'She was nothing but a shell. Her wonderful spirit completely crushed. I barely recognised her. Her face was terribly swollen and battered, her body covered in cuts and bruises.'

I listened to Alex translate, his voice shaking. I couldn't find words. Breathe, Lottie, breathe, I told myself.

Alex's eyes met mine, and they were filled with concern. He mouthed, 'Are you alright?'

I nodded and asked Rosina, 'Did Leonessa stay at the villa until liberation?' I couldn't imagine Gran wanting to live with the man who'd betrayed her.

'When she was released, she was made to promise that she would desist from any further involvement with the partisans. She was too ashamed of what the Fascists had done to her to want to join up with the Allies. Instead, she was adamant that she wanted to go back to Venice.'

'Is that what she did?' I tilted my head towards Rosina.

'Yes. She couldn't wait to leave. The Count provided her with a new fake I.D, and I managed to get some hydrogen peroxide from a hairdresser to bleach her hair. It was a good disguise. As soon as she'd recovered her strength, the Count arranged for her to be taken to the station and she boarded a train for Venice.'

'Did you see her again after the war ended?' I asked.

'No, my dear. She never came back to Sant'Illaria and I needed to look after my parents, so I couldn't go and see her.' Rosina waited for Alex to convey the meaning of her words, then added, 'You should visit Marta in Venice. She'll be able to tell you the rest of your grandmother's story.'

'Who is Marta?' I gasped.

'Your grandmother's dearest friend. She wasn't supposed to talk to us about her life before she came to the village, but she did tell me about Marta. And it was to Marta she went after being released.'

'How will I find this lady? I mean, she might not still be alive…'

'That I do not know. I met her once at a reunion of the Veneto partisans in Treviso. She gave me her address in case I ever came to Venice.' Rosina reached into her pocket and pulled out a crumpled piece of paper. 'You could try and go there.'

'Thank you, I'll definitely do that.' I slipped the address into the outside flap of my handbag.

'Are you sure I can't offer you anything to drink?' Michela asked.

I took that as a subtle hint that Alex and I should leave. I wanted to ask Rosina how she'd obtained Grandad's address, but that could wait until the next time I talked to her. The old dear was looking tired, and I didn't want to outstay my welcome.

Alex took his hand from the steering wheel of his Alfa and squeezed mine briefly as we headed back to the villa. 'I'm so sorry about my grandfather betraying your gran,' he said, almost choking on the words. 'I had no idea.'

'I'm sorry too. As a historian, I know what happened in the past. But this is the first time that past events have affected me so personally.'

'You're not upset with me, I hope?' He sent me a worried glance.

I shook my head. 'Of course, not. You aren't your grandfather. From what I've gathered, you're nothing like him…'

'He met my grandmother after the war. She was a widow whose husband had been killed fighting in Africa. Thankfully, my father inherited her personality and passed it on to Francesca and me.'

'He did, indeed,' I said.

'Would you like me to come to Venice with you?' Alex asked, changing the subject. 'It's my day off tomorrow.'

'Oh, Alex. I was hoping you would offer. I don't think I can face it on my own. The disappointment at not finding Marta would be unbearable.'

He kept my hand in his while changing gears. 'As long as you don't get your hopes up too much you will cope fine.'

After he'd parked the car, we walked hand in hand to the annex. He leaned against the doorjamb while I let myself in. Then he shut the door behind us, backed me up to the wall, and brought his mouth down on mine. His lips were hard, yet soft, demanding, yet giving. His tongue sought mine in an age-old dance.

'You're driving me insane, Lottie.' His breath stirred my hair. 'I've tried to go slow, believe me.'

'You've been…extraordinary…'

'It has taken every atom of my self-control,' he groaned. 'I don't want to push you, but I need more.'

I pressed my mouth to his throat, pulling at his skin with my teeth. My lips grazed the pulse that throbbed below his ear. I made the choice at that moment; I would risk my heart for Alex. 'Please, take me to bed,' I said.

'Are you sure?'

'I'm sure. And I'm on the pill,' I blurted. 'My doctor prescribed it to control period pain.' My heart pounding, I took his hand and led him up to the bedroom.

Our eyes locked as we tore off our clothes. Our breaths came fast, and we tumbled onto the mattress.

We rolled and rubbed against each other, our hands everywhere. Heat coiled in my belly, burning away my fear of getting hurt. I knew Alex, I realised. Incredible to know someone so well in such a short time. Perhaps it was my quest for the truth about Gran that had dispelled my reservations? Her tragic story had made my reticence seem trivial in comparison.

Alex kissed his way down my body, his tongue exploring my most intimate parts. And I melted. My heart. My soul. My everything became his. I didn't speak the words, it was too soon, but I loved him. Loved him so very much.

Our kisses deepened—mouths slow, lips unhurried, tongues tangling only to unravel and reunite.

Then he was rocking into me, rolling and retreating

until I no longer knew where he began and I ended. His breath became my breath. His heart became my heart. His name formed on my lips and mine on his.

He stroked my hair as our bodies stilled. I gazed with wonder into his eyes, and he gazed back at me. He brushed kisses down the sides of my face, whispering, 'I love you, Lottie. *Ti voglio tanto tanto bene.*'

'I love you too,' I breathed. 'It's totally crazy, but I do.'

He kissed me on the lips. 'Then we are both crazy, *amore mio.*'

Chapter 26

Lidia, April 1945

Lidia was helping Angelo, Stefano, Giovanna, and Marisa in the clandestine printing press room hidden at the back of a bar in Dorsoduro when Marta burst into the room. 'The Allies will soon be here,' she announced in a jubilant tone. 'They've broken through German lines and are about to take Bologna at last.'

Everyone cheered and hugged each other, except Lidia shrank back. After what Quinto and his men had done to her, she couldn't bear being touched.

She thought back to her return to Venice in early January—battered, bruised and still bleeding from her miscarriage. Marta had taken her straight to a doctor and had cared for her during the long weeks of her recovery, secreted in the Pivettas' attic.

It had been terribly lonely there. She'd seen no one

except Marta, who brought her food twice a day and sneaked her to the bathroom. Those short periods away from the safety of the loft had made Lidia break out in a cold sweat. She'd become so fearful she found it hard to consume the meals Marta pleaded with her to eat.

In that attic, huddled in blankets, her nightmares had been the worst. Every night, before she went to sleep with Mamma's prayer book clasped to her chest, she'd said a prayer for Papa. Praying for David, that he might be alive and well, was painful for her. She'd been ruined for him. But she couldn't help picturing his smiling face as she fell into slumber, and a final prayer that she might dream of him. Except it was always Quinto that had her screaming awake. Quinto laughing as he raped her. Quinto laughing as, in the bizarreness of her nightmare, he beat Papa.

'I want to kill him,' she'd told Marta one day, after she'd finally described to her friend what that Fascist pig had done to her.

'Then make it your mission,' Marta had said. 'Think of those Germans you gunned down and put him in their place. You must get better soon, bella.'

Lidia *had* put Quinto in the place of those Germans.

Bang-bang-bang, the shots echoed in her mind before she'd gone to sleep that night. She hadn't dreamt of Quinto. She'd dreamt of herself and David, chatting by the campfire, his arm on her shoulder, her head on his chest. When she'd woken up, she'd cried hot tears of regret for what might have been. She couldn't allow herself and David to be together again. The shame would be unbearable.

Waking from a good sleep, however, was something Lidia had forgotten was possible. Quinto was still there, though. A flash of his image, grinning, leering, roving his eyes over her, laughing as he…

She hadn't told Marta of Quinto's visitations. Instead she'd found the determination, to get better, to be brave, and to kill the bastard or someone like him.

In February, Lidia had emerged from the attic for the last time, prepared to carry on fighting. She hated the Fascists with a hate so intense that she felt she needed to come out of hiding and re-join the Resistance. The fake I.D they gave her was like a time bomb, though, and she knew she would have to defend herself if it "exploded". So, she carried a Steyr pistol in her inside coat pocket; she'd learnt how to undo the safety catch unobtrusively, with a flick, as if she were busy looking for extra documents or something if she happened to be stopped by a guard who scrutinised her papers too thoroughly. The necessity of perhaps having to shoot with her left hand made her somewhat uneasy. But she could hardly parade around Venice with her Sten; she kept it hidden with her prayer book under the bed in her latest digs, always cleaned and ready for action.

When she'd walked through the city in the beginning, with her forged papers and bleached blonde hair, life in Venice had seemed so alien. People were going about their own business, ignoring the guttural German voices calling out, '*Achtung, Achtung*,' in the calli. Lidia had felt she was still a *partigiana*, however. She'd looked for machine guns in the hands of milkmen, of women at newsstands, of food vendors on their boats. The first time she'd entered a café, all the men sitting at the tables appeared like Black Brigade *squadristi* in her imagination and had made her flesh crawl.

The memories would come when she'd least expect them. She might see a man who looked like Quinto and would have to stop herself from pulling the pistol from her inside pocket. And she only had to hear a man laughing like him and her heart would start to pound. Everywhere she went she looked at faces. Looked for that evil bastard.

She kept herself busy to keep the evocations at bay, dedicating herself to working for the National Liberation Committee. Her duties were to liaise between the various factions in the city. Endless meetings about liberation— how to organise it, how to handle relations with the Allies, how to make certain that the partisans in the mountains were properly armed and ready to descend to the plains. As the snows had melted, the numbers of active fighters had begun to rise sharply again, from around 60,000 after General Alexander's message in November, to almost 100,000 by late January, and they had continued to increase.

The Committee had eventually reached an agreement about strategy and the partisans had pledged to slow down the German retreat and to get information to the Allies about targets for them to bomb. Urgent circulars, orders, drafts and memoranda flooded out of the secret headquarters, carried by women on bicycles to the patriots, who were finally fighting under a single, unified command. Lidia noticed them from time to time in the dark shadows of the city. They wore a battledress uniform these days, and their emblem consisted of a tricolour flag with a five-pointed star.

She relished hearing the new songs being composed and circulated, extolling victory and freedom. The clandestine broadsheet she wrote with her friends took on an excited tone. *'The decisive moment is about to come, when the world will be delivered from the incubus of an oppressor that has no equal in history.'*

Lidia couldn't wait for this to happen. Every so often, she needed to change her identity and her address to escape discovery. The anti-fascists of the city gave her hospitality and fed her; she would forever be grateful to them.

All through the long cold winter months, she'd forced herself to remain focused on her Resistance work to avoid thinking about the past. Now the war was ending, could she allow herself to hope for an imminent reunion with Papa? It was what kept her going, the thought of being reunited with him. She never allowed herself to think about David. To go down that road would lead to despair. If David found out what those evil Fascists had done to her, she wouldn't be able to bear it. They'd tarnished her. Hers and David's love for each other had been so pure and beautiful. It could never be like that again.

'I think we should print an edition about the Allies breaking through to Bologna,' Marta suggested to the others, jolting Lidia back to the moment. 'But let us also remind Venetians that Italy is filled with new men and women, and that we are preparing to prove ourselves.'

Her skin tingling with anticipation, Lidia went to help her friends. Oh, how she prayed victory really was in sight.

Spring had come to Venice, bringing squalls of rain interspersed with bright rays of sunshine. Something of the sapphire blue sky, the soft air and the snow sparkling on the distant Dolomites played into the general mood of euphoria felt by Lidia as she realised the Fascists' days were numbered. It was all she could think about. They would soon know they could expect no mercy. The hunters would become the hunted.

In mid-April, the National Liberation Committee called for widespread insurrection. Lidia learnt that the partisans had openly attacked the *nazifascisti* in Bologna, liberating the city within forty-eight hours. Her heart sang with jubilation when she found out that the northern cities of Turin and Milan had been liberated by their inhabitants after popular uprisings. Could she allow herself to believe it would be Venice's turn next?

Early in the morning of April 27th, she was in the back room of the bar in Dorsoduro with her friend, Giovanna, filling her satchel with recently printed papers, hidden underneath dirty linen in case she was stopped for a spot check. She and Giovanna were the last to leave; the others had set off already, their bags bulging. After checking to make sure her pistol was in her coat pocket, she slung her satchel over her shoulder and readied herself to go.

With a sudden crash, the door flew open, and a young man burst into the room. He was dressed in the partisans' uniform of black trousers and a waistcoat and had a Bren machine gun slung across his chest. Lidia did a double take. It was young Vitas, one of her *lupetti* wolf cubs from Campo Croce.

'H.Q sent me,' he said, running a hand through his curly brown hair. 'They want you to print a special edition to inform Venetians that the insurrection has started. We took control of the Santa Maria Maggiore prison last night. Its strategic position near the port and the station will be a huge advantage to us. And we've liberated the political prisoners so the Germans can't use them as hostages.'

Lidia's heartbeat raced. She spoke in the Venetian dialect, 'Take me with you. I want to fight too.'

Vitas stared at her, open-mouthed. 'Who are you?'

'I'm Leonessa. Don't you recognise me? I bleached my hair…'

'*Dio mio*, of course.' He pulled her in for a bear hug, but she stiffened and squirmed away. 'I didn't know you were from Venice,' he said. 'You changed your accent up on the Grappa…'

Her mouth twisted. 'I didn't know you were Venetian either.'

'We need all the fighters we can get. There are only about a thousand of us in total against at least ten times as many *nazifascisti*. The stafette are all busy running between the different groups, which is why H.Q sent me.' Vitas gave Lidia a questioning look. 'Are you armed?'

She pulled the Steyr from her pocket and showed it to him. 'My Sten is at my digs.'

'Good.'

Lidia turned to Giovanna. 'Can you spare me?'

'Go! We'll manage. But take care. I'll tell the others when I catch up with them.'

Lidia's room was near the Accademia. She quickly fetched her gun while Vitas waited outside, his Bren levelled. 'I don't need to remind you that, if we see any Black Fascists or Germans, we must shoot first,' he muttered as they ran down the calle.

No, I don't need reminding, Lidia thought. *Bang-bang-bang!*

Rain sheeted across the water as their feet pounded up

then down the fifty slippery steps of the high wooden bridge spanning the Grand Canal. The narrow calli leading to Saint Mark's were eerily empty. Vitas's Commander, a brawny man with a black moustache, was waiting with a group of partisans, standing behind the columns of the long arcade, machine guns on their shoulders. Nazi headquarters were close, but they weren't the target today. 'We'll get the Fascists first,' Vitas hissed before introducing Lidia and telling his leader she was Leonessa from the Monte Grappa campaign.

'I've heard about you. That you risked your life for the cause,' the Commander told her, handing her an ammunition belt which she slung across her chest.

Lidia swallowed hard. She couldn't bear to think that the Commander might have heard about her being tortured. She shook her head. 'I just want to fight the Fascists,' she said.

'And so you shall,' he grunted before giving the order to his men to depart.

Stealthily, they made their way under cover of the porticoes in the direction of the piazzetta in front of the Doge's Palace. Lidia glanced with a shudder at the German gunboats in the lagoon, her eyes drawn towards Giudecca, to her old home on the waterfront. She hadn't been to the apartment since returning to the city; she didn't want to put Signor and Signora Rossi at risk. The war would end in a matter of days. Papa would return and they'd live there together again, she hoped.

'Come, Leonessa,' Vitas indicated with his hand. They crossed the Ponte della Paglia, hot footed it along Riva degli Shiavoni past the luxury Hotel Danieli, turned left up Campo San Zaccaria to arrive at the National Repubblican

Guard headquarters, an imposing stone building opposite the church.

Other groups of partisans had arrived before them. Everyone cocked their guns. A signal was given and the heavy wooden doors were opened by an insider.

Lidia's heart thudded. Her hands turned sweaty, and she wiped them on her coat before gripping the barrel of her weapon again.

The partisans erupted into the building on masse, taking the Fascists guarding the headquarters completely by surprise.

Shouts rang out.

Guns roared.

Bullets flew.

A Republican guard drew his pistol and aimed it at Lidia.

She saw Quinto. She knew it wasn't really him, but it could have been. She levelled her Sten, took aim and fired. *Bang-bang-bang!* The guard keeled over sideways, blood spurting from the holes she'd made in his torso.

With steely calm, she stepped over him and carried on firing.

Finally, the ricochet of bullets fell silent. Lidia could only hear the groans of the wounded. Enemy wounded, thank God.

'Stay here and keep your guns trained on them,' the Commander barked at Lidia and Vitas. 'The rest of us will get on with apprehending those Fascist *maledetti* in their offices, releasing political prisoners from the cells, and seizing arms and ammunition.'

'*Si, Signore*,' Lidia and Vitas saluted.

Lidia barely remembered how she got back to Dorsoduro after the Republican Guards headquarters had been secured. She was carried along with a throng of partisans who were intent on rounding up as many Fascists as they could.

She'd been tasked with organising yet another special edition of the paper. The Venetians were to go on general strike. The National Liberation Committee would assume all political and administrative powers.

Marta rounded on Lidia as soon as she stepped into the room behind the bar. '*Dio buono,* I was so worried about you.'

'I'm fine,' Lidia said, putting down her Sten and removing the ammunition belt from around her chest. Her fingers trembled, and her knees started to give way.

Marta grabbed her and led her to a chair. 'Here, sit. I'll get you a glass of water.'

Lidia spent the remainder of the afternoon helping with writing and printing the special edition. Then, after a short rest on a camp bed in the corner of the room, and food provided by the owner of the bar, she went out with her friends to help distribute the paper. It was important for the whole of Venice to know what had happened and what was going to happen.

The next day, Lidia was up early again. She'd arranged to meet Marta by the Rialto, and they would proceed from there to continue handing out their broadsheet. Lidia sighed to herself; she'd wanted to be with the partisans, her Sten levelled. She'd been disappointed when a member of the National Liberation Committee had dropped by last night to tell her that they had more than enough men now, after freeing the last of the political prisoners, and that her services would be more valued printing and distributing information to the people of Venice instead.

Today, it was evident that the uprising had gained strength. All the partisans they met told them that the Fascists were surrendering without a fight, their tails between their legs. Obviously, the black-shirted bastards knew the game was up, given that the other big cities of the north had already been liberated. Ca' Littoria, the Republic's headquarters and one of the notorious *ville tristi*, as the torture centres were known, had been occupied without a single shot being fired.

The Germans, however, continued to resist. All through the morning the echoes of heavy fighting reverberated around the city. At midday, silence reigned. Had the enemy requested a truce?

When Lidia and Marta returned to the bar in Dorsoduro in the evening, they learnt from their friends that two Allied special ops missions were billeted in the Danieli, negotiating a surrender from the Nazis, who were threatening to bombard the city from the mainland and destroy the historic centre if they weren't allowed to evacuate and take all their weapons with them. They had even mined the causeway leading to Venice.

'*O, Dio,*' Lidia groaned. 'I won't be able to sleep until I know we are safe.'

She and her friends waited through the night for news. The partisans were refusing to let the Germans leave the city until they'd handed over a chart of the minefields. Finally, news came via a *stafetta* that the Nazis had relented and were about to depart.

Bleary-eyed, Lidia and Marta went with the others to Piazza San Marco, their hearts overflowing with joy and relief as they watched the *partigiani* escort the shame-faced Germans from their headquarters and onto the barges that would take them to Mestre, from where they would begin their retreat.

'Do you realise you no longer have to hide?' Marta said to Lidia as they sauntered arm in arm on their way back to Dorsoduro.

Lidia laughed as the realisation sank in. 'I wonder if there's a salon open. I would like to get my hair dyed to its natural colour.'

'It's Sunday, but I have a friend who lives in the next calle. She works as a hairdresser but also has private clients. We'll stop there, then we'll fetch your belongings from your digs. You're staying with me tonight.'

Later, news came that the people of Venice were gathering in Saint Mark's to celebrate their liberation. Lidia and her friends rushed out to join them.

Everywhere, there was a carnival atmosphere. Partisans were marching through the calli, guns on their shoulders, women waving and cheering at them from their upstairs windows. In the piazza, improvised processions and corteges had started to arrive. People wearing tricolour armbands were running, walking, marching and singing patriotic songs. They tore down the Swastika flags on the sides of the buildings and replaced them with flags bearing the vertical planes of green, white and red—the national colours of Italy. The bells of the basilica rang out from the tall tower overlooking the city.

'Mussolini is dead!' someone shouted. 'Killed by a partisan near Lake Como.'

'*O, Dio*, can it be true?' Lidia gasped.

Marta grabbed her and whirled her in a dance of sheer joy. 'Look,' she pointed. 'There's a photographer. Let's get him to take a picture of us with the others. Today is a special day. It will be good to have a souvenir.'

'The Allies are here,' Marta's mother exclaimed at breakfast the next morning. 'They're billeted at the Danieli. And there's a strange vehicle called a "jeep" in Piazza San Marco. The whole of Venice is talking about it.'

Marta laughed. 'How did they drive a vehicle up the Grand Canal?'

'It came on a boat, silly,' Signora Pivetta chuckled, pouring coffee. 'What are you girls planning to do today?'

'I have work,' Marta huffed. 'The general strike is over.'

'I'll go and see Signor and Signora Rossi,' Lidia announced. 'Perhaps I can move back into the apartment.'

Marta and her mother protested that she was welcome to stay with them for as long as she liked, but she was eager to resume her old life. *As best as possible.* Just the mention of the Allies had made her heart weep. She allowed herself a brief thought of David, wondering where and how he was, but it was too painful to dwell on and she focussed on Papa's return instead.

Marta left for work, and Lidia was about to go to the Rossis' when a knock sounded at the door.

Signora Pivetta ushered Fazio, Lidia's contact at the National Liberation Committee, into the entrance hall.

'I came to see you,' he said to Lidia after greeting the signora. 'Is there somewhere we can talk?'

'You can go through to the lounge,' Signora Pivetta said. 'Can I get you something to drink?'

Fazio thanked her but declined. 'I won't stay long…'

There was something in Fazio's doleful expression that set Lidia's heart pounding. *Something's happened to David.* Her mouth went dry.

She perched on a chair opposite Fazio, the coffee table between them.

He leaned towards her. 'I'm sorry, Lidia. But I'm the bearer of sad news.'

Her hand flew to her breast. '*O, Dio,*' she whimpered.

'It's your papa, I'm afraid.'

'Papa? What's happened to him?'

'There's no easy way to say this. We've been worried about the fate of the Venetian Jews after receiving reports of what was happening in the Nazi concentration camps. News was published in British and American newspapers some time ago, but not here in Italy. The Fascist censors kept the information from the public, but we've known about it for a while. Our worst fears have been confirmed now the camps are being liberated, and terrible things have come to light.'

'Terrible things? What terrible things?' Lidia shook her head, not wanting to know the truth.

'Let me start again,' Fazio said on a sigh. 'Our Jews were taken to Auschwitz in Poland. The camp was liberated by the Soviets last January. They were shocked at what they found. There were gas chambers and crematoria. Most of the inmates had been murdered.' He paused, his voice choking. 'Some did survive, and we've been trying to find out if any of those were from Venice.'

'I still don't understand,' Lidia murmured, dread spreading through her. 'What are you trying to tell me?'

Fazio leaned forward and took her hand. 'There is no record of your papa in any of the transit camps. I'm so sorry, but he has not survived.'

Chapter 27

Lidia, June 1945

'Stop! Get off me!' Lidia shouted. But the foul breath of the Fascist pig reeked in her nostrils. She struggled against the fat hand clamped over her mouth.

'Shush, calm yourself, signorina,' a female voice said.

Lidia opened her eyes, and a bright light made her blink. She was strapped to a bed. *O, Dio!* What would those bastards do to her next?

'You are in the hospital, my dear,' the voice said.

Lidia turned her head. A nurse in a white peaked cap was standing next to her. 'You were taken ill a week ago.'

Lidia glanced down at her hands. Hands tied to the sides of a hospital cot. Was this some bizarre game on the part of her captors? She closed her eyes and spiralled into a cocoon of darkness.

They were hitting her.

Hard slaps landed on her face and punches to her belly. Leather stung her flesh, over and over.

Quinto moved in close, spraying spittle in her face as he laughed and thrust into her.

She screamed in agony.

'There, there,' came the soothing voice.

She felt the prick of a needle in her arm. And soon a calmness took over. She was grateful for it. Grateful to slip into oblivion once more.

Later, she woke to the whisper of her name and a dear face loomed into her field of vision. Marta's face. Her friend's expression was filled with concern. Lidia's mind was in turmoil and she couldn't collect her thoughts.

'Oh, bella,' Marta said. 'You gave us such a fright. Fazio was distraught when you fainted. You hit your head on the marble floor. Mamma called for the ambulance boat and they brought you here, to the Lido hospital.'

'I don't understand.' Lidia heard the panic in her voice and then she remembered.

Papa is dead. Murdered by the Nazis.

A keening sound came from deep within her. Like a wounded animal.

Marta smoothed her hair back from her face. 'Cry, my dearest. Cry out your pain.'

Lidia did so and felt her friend's tears splash onto her face and mingle with her own.

Time passed. Her days slipped into a rhythm of sleeping, waking, walking to the bathroom, taking medication given to her by the nurses and being examined by men who told her they were doctors and that she was suffering from psychiatric distress. She shrank every time they touched her.

The nurses would bring her hearty three course meals of pasta, followed by meat and vegetables, then fruit and cheese. She hadn't felt worthy of eating them; she'd nibble on the crusty pieces of bread provided, all the while thinking of Papa. Had he been beaten and abused like she had? Or worse? How he must have suffered—

Marta would visit every evening after she'd finished work; she talked Lidia through the horrific events of recent months, helped her breathe through her anxiety, and pleaded with her to eat. 'You need to keep up your strength,' she'd said.

Today, Lidia was sitting up in her bed. The windows of the ward were open, allowing the sweet soft breezes of early summer to mix with the bitter odour of hospital anti-septic. Lidia felt as if she were in limbo, suspended between the harshness of the past and an uncertain future. There was an empty feeling inside her; she had no desire to return to her old life. The prayer book was in the bottom of her rucksack in the cupboard next to her bed. She couldn't face looking at it. The pain would have broken her heart. For once, she allowed herself to think about David. Where was he? How was he?

She heard his gentle voice, so clearly in her mind, then gasped when she realised it wasn't in her mind at all.

He was speaking with the nurse at the entrance to the ward. Though she couldn't see him for the curtains pulled partway around her bed, it was definitely him.

David.

Her heart raced.

How did he know she was here?

She closed her eyes and summoned up all her resolve. She would tell him to go away. That she'd been ruined for him.

'My darling girl,' he said, reaching for her hand as she opened her eyes. He kissed her gently, as if she were in danger of falling apart. His lips were soft, but so familiar. And she didn't shrink from them. 'I've found you at last.' His gaze travelled over her face, searchingly. 'I thought I'd lost you.'

She gazed at him, and all it took was one look. The love she felt for him swelled in her heart and vibrated through her soul. 'I'm sorry I didn't come to the Cansiglio...' she gave a sob.

David kissed the tears from her cheeks. 'No need for explanations. When the *stafetta* returned without you, she said you were at the villa. I went to look for you there as soon as I could. That bastard Guido told me everything. God, he made my blood boil. I punched him in the face, I'm afraid. He fucking betrayed you...'

Lidia had never heard David use such language before. The force of his anger resonated with her. 'He tried to excuse himself, but I think he was a coward. He told the Fascists about me because he was afraid of being tortured. Did he tell you I was here?'

'He gave me Marta's address. She brought me to the Lido in her father's boat. She's waiting downstairs.'

David pulled up a chair and sat with his face level to Lidia's. 'I love you. I love you so much. I've never been prouder to love you than at this moment.' Tears rolled down his face. 'I'm so sorry, sweetheart. Sorry this has happened to you.'

She reached across the space between them and brushed away his tears. 'Tell me what you have been doing these past six months. How did the war end for you?'

And so he told her about his time in the Cansiglio. Told her he'd organised three separate dropping grounds and had kept himself busy coordinating the construction of an airstrip and learning to speak some Italian.

'The partisans I was helping were incredibly fierce. They mined the road leading to their hideouts and, almost every night, they carried out sabotage actions against the highways and railways on the plains.'

David added that he'd got on with them famously and was convinced there couldn't be a finer body of men anywhere. So much so, he'd regretted having to leave them when his services had been required farther north.

'What happened there?' she asked, still marvelling that he was here with her and that she hadn't found it within herself to push him away.

'By the end of April, all enemy garrisons south of the Piave had withdrawn or surrendered, he said. 'But Belluno remained occupied by Jerry. The partisans either had to kill or imprison the lot of them before they conceded defeat.

'I waited for weeks while the camps of armed and arrogant *tedeschi*, with their looted Italian vehicles, horses, and food, were broken up. At last, the partisans attended their final parade. They stood down and handed the city over to the Allies—who've set up a Military Government. I requested and was granted leave "on compassionate grounds", after I explained I needed to find my fiancée.'

She caught her lip between her teeth. 'Are you sure you still want to marry me? It's just, well...I wasn't only tortured.' She paused, struggling to put the horror into words. 'Those men, David. They raped me. I feel so spoiled now...'

He was out of his chair and cradling her in his arms before she could utter another word. 'You're my girl,' he said. 'I love YOU. Those bastards haven't sullied you. Not your force, not your spirit, not your essence. They haven't robbed those from you.'

She let him hold her close while she sobbed. 'I had a miscarriage. They killed our baby,' she wept. 'And after Venice was liberated, I found out my papa had died in Poland.'

He rocked her tenderly. 'I wish it had been me who'd broken that news to you, my love. I've long known what the Nazis were doing to the Jews in their vile concentration camps, but I purposely didn't say anything to you until there was a right moment—not that there would have ever been a "right moment" to speak of such evil.' He stroked her cheek and looked deep into her eyes. 'I wanted to soften the blow.'

Lidia snuggled against David's chest. She felt safe. This was where she was destined to be. With David. But not here. Not in Venice. Nor Italy. There were too many memories.

'If you are sure that you still want to marry me, then take me to England, please, *amore mio*. I don't want to live here anymore. Venice isn't my home without Papa. I want to make a fresh start somewhere else.'

'Ready to go, darling girl? David held out his hand.

'I am,' Lidia smiled, placing her hand in his as they stepped out of the hospital.

A month after he'd found her, he was back in Venice. He'd had to return the car he'd borrowed from someone in Belluno and then arrange for a fast-track demobilisation as well as passage on a ship to Southampton. During that time, she'd focussed on getting better, deliberately avoiding thinking about the past and making every effort to look forward to the future. She would make the best of things, she'd decided. Life wouldn't be easy in a strange country with different traditions. But David would be her rock and she would lean on him until she had the confidence to stand proudly on her own.

David slung her rucksack over his shoulder. She was carrying so little away with her, and she wanted it to be like that. Her apartment could remain in the Rossis' name; she had no desire to ever set foot in it again.

Marta was waiting for them on the hospital steps, her face wreathed in smiles. Giorgio had turned up out of the blue last week, having managed to get a transfer to the naval base in Venice. He'd proposed to her and they would get married next month. 'I wish you could be my bridesmaid,' she'd said to Lidia yesterday when she'd visited.

'I'm sorry,' Lidia had sighed. 'David has arranged everything already.'

'Here, have this.' Marta had pressed a photograph into Lidia's hand. 'It's the picture taken of us on liberation day.'

Lidia had stared at the picture and her heart panged with a sharp pain. She would miss Marta and her friends so much.

'*Grazie*,' she'd said, slipping the photo into her ruck-sack. 'I will write to you from England.'

Except, she knew then that she wouldn't do any such thing. The only way she'd be able to cope with the future would be to sever all ties with the past. Her illness hadn't been cured. She hadn't told anyone, but she still suffered from those nightmares and had made herculean efforts to control her reactions to them. As a medical student, she knew full well what the next steps in her therapy would have been otherwise; she'd be in a mental asylum under-going electric shock treatment instead of setting out for England.

They walked across the narrow Lido island to the jetty where Marta had moored her babbo's boat. Lidia's throat tightened with nostalgia as she allowed herself to take in the beauty of her city for the last time. The pearly palaces along the opposite shore shimmered in the tangerine colours of the afternoon sunshine, the high peaks of the Dolomites towering in the distance, their jagged outlines no longer softened by snow.

David put his arm around her, and she rested her head on his shoulder. 'I love you so much,' she said to him. 'Please, let's go.'

Chapter 28

Charlotte, 2010

I turned over in my bed and gazed at Alex sleeping next to me. My pulse raced as I savoured the sight of him. His dark eyelashes fanned the tops of his chiselled cheekbones, and his chestnut-brown hair was gloriously messy.

It was the morning after Rosina had told us about the Count's betrayal of Gran. Alex had stayed the night and our lovemaking had been beyond incredible. He'd lifted me onto him, his beautiful green eyes burning with love as he'd eased himself into me. Our bodies had moved in perfect rhythm, and I'd orgasmed with an intensity that took my breath and a whole lot more.

My feelings for him almost overwhelmed me. His friendship, his goodness and his loyalty had swept me away; I'd lost every vestige of my fear. Learning the devastating truth about Gran had taught me that I, too, could be brave and take risks. I hoped that, by going to Venice today, I would find the final pieces of the puzzle of her past and that, by doing so, I could move on into a brighter future for myself.

I kissed Alex awake, whispering, '*Buongiorno.*'

'*Buongiorno, tesoro,*' his smile dimpled.

'What does *tesoro* mean?' I threaded my fingers through his hair.

'Literally, treasure, but we use it like the English word darling.'

'I like it, *tesoro,*' I said to him, snuggling into his chest.

He kissed the top of my head. 'We'd better get a move on if we are to arrive in Venice mid-morning.' He grabbed my hand, pulled me from the bed, and we were giggling like teenagers as he dragged me into the shower.

Warm water rained down on us while he reached for the sponge, squirted bodywash onto it, then soaped me all over.

I released a sigh of pure pleasure and squirted some bodywash into the cup of my hand before smoothing it along his chest, his flat stomach, and lower still.

He turned me around and placed my palms against the tiles, then nudged my legs apart.

I gasped, and my toes curled as he started to take me from behind.

'*Tesoro, amore mio,*' he whispered into my ear, holding me in place.

I closed my eyes and rocked myself up and down, the pleasure building.

He took me so deep my feet came off the floor, and he kept on taking me until a shuddering climax overtook us both.

We remained coupled together and breathing heavily, the water sluicing down our bodies. I angled my head and caught his lips with mine. His tongue danced and tangled with *my* tongue as we lapped each other up.

On an exhale of breath, he withdrew. 'I love you so much, Lottie,' he said.

'I love you too, Alex. So very much.'

Tenderly, he wrapped me in a fluffy white towel and patted me dry. I stared at his handsome face. I'd fallen so hard, so fast, so completely for him, I no longer knew myself.

After a quick breakfast of a cappuccino and a croissant, I phoned Mum and told her about Rosina's revelations yesterday.

'I'm stunned,' Mum's shocked voice came down the line. 'Poor Mother. No wonder she never wanted to go back to Italy…'

'I'll let you know if we find out anything more in Venice,' I promised. 'Alex is taking me.' I'd mentioned him to her before, but as far as she knew we were just friends.

I disconnected the call and went to fetch my handbag and sunglasses. Alex had already gone to check all was well in the Corradini before we set off.

'I've booked a motorboat to be at our disposal when we arrive,' he said as he drove us out of the village.

'Please, let me pay for that,' I said. 'It'll be expensive.'

'I arranged it through our sister hotel on the Lido. Got a special deal so no need to worry.'

'You have a sister hotel?'

'A family-run place like ours. We send each other clients, which is mutually beneficial.'

We lapsed into silence, listening to CDs on the car stereo. Nerves jangled through me as I fretted about finding Marta. I so wanted to learn how Gran had spent the last months of the war, and I also hoped that her dearest friend would be able to tell me about Gran's family. For all I knew, I had relatives in Venice—

Alex took the motorway from Treviso and three quarters of an hour later he was pulling into our assigned spot in one of the multi-storey car parks at the end of the causeway. We went down the flight of stairs to the ground floor and made our way to the pier, where our motorboat was waiting. The address Rosina had given me was on the island of Giudecca. I showed our boatman the crumpled piece of paper and he nodded.

I sat next to Alex on the plush seat at the stern of the gently rocking vessel. He took my hand and brushed a kiss to my wrist. 'All will be well,' he said. 'Try not to worry, *tesoro.*'

I wished I could be so confident. Marta would be at least as old as Rosina. If she was still alive. And, given the two ladies' great age, Marta might not be up to talking to me. That's if I even found her.

With a rumble of the engines, Vittorio, our driver, steered the motorboat out into the middle of the waterway, then headed past the ferry port and cruise ship terminal into the top end of the Giudecca Canal.

Before too long, we'd turned into a narrow channel lined with houses. Vittorio manoeuvred us into a space by some steps.

'Venetians number their addresses according to how many there are in a neighbourhood, or *sestiere*,' Alex explained, helping me ashore, 'but happily nowadays they also put the name of the calle or fondamenta.' He checked Rosina's piece of paper against the figure written on the wall of a building. 'I think the place we are searching for is farther along.'

We walked hand in hand until we came to a two-storey house with red geraniums in window boxes on the ground floor. Alex rang the doorbell, and a blonde girl answered.

'*Buongiorno,*' she said, glancing at the name Alex showed her. 'You're looking for my grandmother. Whom should I say is calling?'

'You mean she's here?' Excitement bubbled in my chest. 'Please tell her I am Leonessa's granddaughter.'

Within minutes, the girl had returned, leading an old lady by the arm. Marta was so small and frail-looking she reminded me of a tiny bird. The bones of her face were covered by parchment-thin wrinkled skin, her wispy white hair pulled back in a bun. But her eyes were bright and fully lucid. 'I'm so pleased to meet you,' she said to me, after Alex and I had told her who we were. 'Please, come through to the lounge. I can't leave my husband for long... he has dementia.'

Marta's granddaughter introduced herself. '*Sono* Giorgia,' she said.

'Giorgia is named after her grandpa,' Marta clarified. Alex translated as we walked across the marble floor to where an extremely old man sprawled on a lazy-boy armchair, fast asleep. 'He came back from the war and we had five children. Our twelve grandchildren take it in turns to stay with us so we don't need to go to a care home.'

'How wonderful.' A smile tugged at my lips. 'Do they all live in Venice?'

'Of course. We are Venetians. As was your grandmother.' With Giorgia's help, Marta lowered herself onto the sofa. 'Please, sit, and I will tell you what you've obviously come here to find out.'

We did as she'd requested. Alex recounted what we knew about Elena's past. Then Marta filled us in on how Gran had suffered a miscarriage after being tortured and raped but had wanted to fight on with the Resistance. She'd taken part in the liberation of Venice, shooting and killing Fascists. It was only after learning the fate of her poor father in Auschwitz that she could no longer cope with everything that had happened to her.

Shock reeled through me at her words. *Gran had a miscarriage. My great grandfather suffered the Shoah. Gran shot people dead.* 'I looked for the name, Moretti, on the monument in the Ghetto,' I said in a trembling voice, 'but it wasn't there.'

'Elena's real name was Lidia De Angelis and her father was Samuele,' Marta told us. 'She needed to change her identity when she fled Venice.'

I listened, my heart breaking, while Marta told us about Gran's mum passing away when she was barely fourteen, how she'd been torn from her childhood sweetheart, forced to give up her medical studies by the racial laws, and how her dad, who was a doctor, had become the centre of her life.

'She didn't want to live in Venice without him.' A tear slid down Marta's cheek. 'I begged her to stay, but she'd made up her mind.' Marta released a sob. 'I visited her in the hospital before she left for England. I gave her the photograph we had taken with our friends after the city was liberated. She told me that she'd decided to put the past behind her so she could focus on the future with David. And then…and then,' Marta's sobs grew louder, 'she promised she would write to me but she never did.'

Giorgia had rushed up to put her arms around her grandmother, but Marta shrugged her off.

I took out my phone and showed her the photograph. Marta gasped and her face lit up as she pointed herself out in the image. 'We were so happy that day,' she smiled through her tears.

'I found the photo in Gran's drawer. It shows she didn't forget you.' I paused to collect my thoughts. 'I believe she was probably suffering from Post-Traumatic Stress and worried that if she raked up the past, she might have a relapse.'

Marta nodded. 'You look so like her…'

'She lived a good life,' I reassured the old lady. 'Both she and my grandad finished their studies at Cambridge. Gran became a paediatrician and Grandad a lawyer. They worked with the deprived in the East End of London.'

'What about children?' Marta asked.

'Only my mother.' I decided to keep Mum's estrangement from Gran to myself. And the fact that I'd only just had it confirmed, when Marta had mentioned the name, David, that my grandparents had met in Italy, not in Cambridge as they'd told their daughter. 'Did my gran have any siblings?'

'No. She was an only child, as were her parents.'

Having only children seemed to run in the family, I thought to myself.

'Now you are here. You must go to the *apartamento*,' Marta said, out of the blue.

'Apartment? What apartment?' I stared at her. *What did she mean?*

'Dottor De Angelis signed his *apartamento* over to his neighbour, Signor Rossi, in 1943, so the Fascists wouldn't confiscate it like they were doing to all the Jews' properties. And Signor Rossi informed his nephew, who was his heir, that the *apartamento* belonged to your grandmother. I made it my business to keep an eye on things, always hoping Lidia would change her mind and visit Venice one day.'

'My grandmother left all her assets to my mother and me,' I murmured, my head reeling. 'So the flat could be ours…'

'Signor Rossi's nephew still lives next door. He and his wife have looked after your *apartamento* beautifully. There will be some bills and taxes to reimburse, but he has always assured me that if Lidia's family wanted it, he would hand it over.'

'Can you give us the address, please?' I asked in a trembling voice.

'Of course.' Marta's eyes twinkled. 'And I will phone and tell them you're on your way.'

She insisted on accompanying us to the door, with the help of Giorgia. 'Don't be strangers,' she pleaded. 'Especially if you decide to keep the apartment and live in Venice.'

I swapped email addresses and telephone numbers with Giorgia, my head in a spin,

An apartment in Venice? The place where Gran had grown up. Had I found my roots, at last? Marta's suggestion that I could live in Venice had given me an adrenaline rush. Too much, too soon, I told myself.

Alex put his arm around me as we walked to the motor-boat. 'Are you alright?' he asked.

'I'm gobsmacked.'

He lifted a brow. 'Gobsmacked? I don't know that word.'

'It means astonished.' I ticked the list off on my fingers. 'I've had it confirmed that Grandad was the Englishman Gran met on Monte Grappa. That she suffered a miscarriage after she was raped. That she shot at and even killed Fascists during the battle for the liberation of Venice. That my great-grandfather died in Auschwitz. That Gran suffered from PTSD. Oh, and that I might have inherited an apartment in Venice.' I gave a hysterical sounding laugh.

'Momentous revelations, indeed,' Alex said, helping me onto the boat.

His calmness reassured me. Oh, how I loved him.

Vittorio took us down Rio Croce into the Giudecca Canal and motored along the shoreline until we'd reached a pier near the Zitelle vaporetto station.

Alex and I alighted and he checked the address Marta had given us, reading the number on the wall of a beautiful marble-clad palazzo.

'We've arrived,' he said.

We pressed the bell on the front door intercom and explained who we were. A male voice answered, buzzed us in and we climbed the stairs to the first floor.

A tall man with greying hair was waiting for us on the landing. 'I'm Edoardo Rossi,' he said in good English. 'I always hoped the rightful owner of this apartment would turn up one day.'

'Thank you for your integrity,' I told him. 'It means a lot.' The words sounded inadequate to my ears. I wanted to give him a hug, but that would have been inappropriate.

'I'm a mathematics professor at the University. Your great grandmother's name is still remembered. She taught English at Ca' Foscari, you know. How could I hold on to something that isn't mine?'

My eyes welled up I was so moved by his words. I couldn't speak. All I could do was smile.

He reached into his pocket and pulled out a set of keys. 'These are yours,' he said. 'We will need to get a Notary to make it official. But that can wait.' He handed over his card. 'Call me when you are ready. The code for the intercom is on the back.'

'I'm honoured you trust me so much,' I managed to say.

'We'll be sure to keep in touch,' Alex added. 'In the meantime, though, can I prevail upon you to keep an eye on the apartment for Lottie and her mother?'

'I will take the spare key, then,' Edoardo Rossi said. 'And I'll be glad to do that for you.'

We gave him back the extra key, promising to call as soon as possible.

My fingers shook as I unlocked the door.

We stepped into a dark corridor. Alex flicked a switch, and I made out six doors leading off it.

I pushed open the one in front of me and let out a gasp. The room was luminous. No other word could describe it.

A floor to ceiling window with columns at the sides, an arch above and a white marble balustrade opened onto a breath-taking view of the lagoon. I strode across the marble floor to fling wide the windows and gaze in awe across the water towards the Doge's Palace and the hazy outline of the Dolomites beyond. For a moment, I was Gran–*Lidia*–opening those windows wide and soaking in the incredible panorama. I wondered how many times she had done just that.

I felt her then, in my heart. Her courage. It bolstered me. Made me so proud.

For the second time in a week, I fell in love. Fell in love with Gran's apartment. And I knew at that moment this was where I belonged.

Chapter 29

Charlotte, 2010

'This room is perfect,' I said to Alex, enthusiasm bubbling through me as I took his hand.

I stared in wonderment at the Art Deco style lamps and lampshades, the walnut wood side tables with their richly carved details, and the comfortable-looking high-backed beige leather sofa and armchairs.

Alex pointed to the ivory and grey-white floor. 'You'd pay a fortune for something like that these days. Looks like authentic Carrara marble to me.'

'Let's explore the rest of the flat,' I suggested.

We went out of the living room into the corridor. I dragged Alex along with me to a door at the far end. The room was in darkness as the shutters had been closed. I flicked the light switch to reveal a kitchen. Apart from cleaning and dusting, it appeared nothing had been touched for nearly seventy years. The wall-mounted sink had dishes stacked to the side and an empty space under it; I couldn't see any countertops. A free-standing stove stood in front of a white tiled wall, with what looked like an ice box next to it. I loved the rectangular oak table and chairs, though, and could picture Gran sitting having breakfast here with her dad. How devastated she must have been when she'd learnt he'd died in Auschwitz.

Alex put his arm around me. 'Come, let's see what's in the next room.'

Again, the shutters were closed. This time, I stepped across the floor to open them. 'Wow. The back of the flat overlooks a garden.' I admired the green space below. A wide lawn, flower borders and umbrella pine trees. Gorgeous.

'The island of Giudecca historically housed some sizable palazzi with gardens,' Alex informed me. 'My guess is you would be able to enjoy these as part of the facilities of this condominium.'

'Amazing.'

The room itself was clearly a dining room, with heavy dark furniture that wasn't to my taste. I grabbed Alex's hand and pulled him back into the corridor. We opened the door to the room opposite. Sparsely furnished with a single bed, bedside table, chest of drawers and a wardrobe. I stared at the empty bookshelves and wondered what had happened to the books that would have been in them. Great-grandfather wouldn't have been allowed to take any with him to the camp. I needed to read up more on the deportation of the Jews from Venice, I thought. *When I can face it.*

There was only one bathroom in the flat. Old-fash-

ioned. A vestige from the past with a solid porcelain tub. I
flicked on the light switch in the final room we entered, the
second bedroom, which must have been Gran's. Tears
filled my eyes as I pulled open the lovely antique Venet-
ian-style wardrobe. 1940s dresses with their puffed sleeves
were hanging in a neat row. I shut the door and went to
draw back the curtains and open the shutters. My eyes
popped—the view was just as incredible as the panorama
from the living room.

A sultry breeze blew in from the lagoon, caressing my
face. I smoothed my hands over the cool marble
windowsill and gazed out across the water. Boats were
buzzing to and fro, weaving between the poles that seemed
to define some sort of shipping lane stretching from an
enormous white church with a rounded dome on the left, to
the more pedestrian buildings of the Lido on the extreme
right.

Again, I felt Gran's presence, as if her warm fingers
were soothing me instead of the breeze from the lagoon,
and I heard her voice in my head, urging me to make the
decision that I knew would change my life.

'I want to live here,' I said to Alex. 'Do you think I'm
crazy?'

A slow smile spread across his face. 'Didn't we agree
we were both crazy?' He pulled me in for a hug. 'What
about your job and your life in London?'

'I will need to give half a term's notice at the school.
Probate should come through on my inheritance from Gran
soon, and, once her house in Islington has been sold, I will
have enough money to reimburse Signor Rossi for his
expenses, modernise this apartment and keep going until I
find a job in Venice, I hope.'

'Sounds like you've worked it out already,' he chuckled, looking me in the eye. 'Don't you want to give it more thought?'

I shook my head. 'It feels right. Somewhat impetuous, I grant you that,' I allowed myself a wry laugh. 'Of course, I must arrange everything with my mum as well. I mean, she'll have some say in what happens, won't she?'

The thought set my pulse racing. What if Mum insisted on selling this beautiful flat? It would break my heart.

Alex invited me to have lunch in a little osteria he knew, near the Palanca vaporetto stop. Vittorio took us there, and, as we sat over coffee after a delicious seafood salad, I said to Alex, 'Before we head back to Sant'Illaria, would you mind if we visited the Holocaust memorial in the Ghetto?'

'I think it's a good idea, *tesoro*.' He leant towards me and brushed a kiss to my cheek. 'It will help give you some closure.'

Half an hour or so later, we were walking hand in hand in the direction of the monument on the red brick wall I'd visited when I'd arrived in Venice a couple of weeks ago.

The image of a train spilling out its cargo of doomed human beings made my eyes sting. I searched for Great-grandfather's name and found it carved into the plaque: Samuele De Angelis, forty-eight years old. Hot tears rolled down my cheeks.

Alex put his arms around me. I buried my face in his chest while he held me close. 'It's so sad.' I wept for a life cut short in its prime. I wept for Gran, whose father was taken from her so tragically. And I wept for all the other victims of the concentration camps, who'd suffered such evil.

'Come, Lottie, let's go home,' Alex said after I'd eventually stopped crying and we'd sat for a while on a bench in the middle of the square.

'Okay,' I said. 'I need to phone my mother. But I'll wait until we get back.'

We walked from the Ghetto to Piazzale Roma, as Alex had instructed Vittorio to return with the motorboat to the Lido. Throngs of tourists filled the calli, so different to Giudecca which had been so much quieter and inhabited by locals. What would it be like to become a part of that community? Don't get your hopes up, Lottie, I told myself.

We hit heavy traffic on the road from Venice and didn't arrive in Sant'Illaria until the early evening. Too late to phone Hong Kong—I would do so first thing tomorrow morning.

Alex went to check on things in the hotel and to fetch Gabriel, who'd been dropped off by Simonetta to spend a few days with his papa.

An idea occurred to me. I logged on to Google and researched British Special Ops in northern Italy during the war. I scrolled down and gave a gasp. There, on the screen, was a photo of a group of Englishmen, taken in Belluno in May 1945. Names appeared below the image. My jaw dropped. Standing third to the right, was Captain David Roden. Tall. Fair-haired. In uniform. I couldn't wait to tell Mum.

I mulled over what I would say to her. If she wanted to sell the flat in Venice, I'd buy her out with the proceeds of my share from the sale of Gran's house. I would have used the money anyway to purchase a place in London.

I woke early the next day. Alex had slept in his own bed. We'd agreed beforehand that it was too soon to reveal our relationship to Gabriel. I'd spent a lovely evening with the two of them. Alex had made an enormous bowl of spaghetti alla carbonara and afterwards we'd watched the *Finding Nemo* DVD. When Gabriel had gone to sleep, Alex and I sat on the portico sipping prosecco and chatting about our day in Venice. 'I'm determined to live there,' I'd said to him. 'But I won't make any plans until after I've spoken to my parents.'

I rolled out of bed now, showered, put on a pair of shorts and a t-shirt, then grabbed a cup of coffee and my phone.

Mum answered my call straight way. 'How did you get on in Venice?' she asked.

My heart in my mouth, I described Marta's revelations, that Gran's real name had been Lidia De Angelis and that she'd fought with the partisans through the liberation of Venice. Then I went on to recount Grandad's involvement in the story.

'I can't believe my father was in Italy during the war,' Mum's surprised voice came down the line. 'He always said he'd been stationed in the Middle East.'

'He was being supportive of Gran,' I said. 'Helping her not to relapse into PTSD.'

'Are you sure all those things happened to her?' Mum seemed dubious. And with good reason. The story I'd just told her was like something out of a movie. Except, it *had* happened. Not just to Gran but to so many others.

I took a deep breath. 'And that's not all.' I went on to tell Mum about the apartment. 'I want to keep it,' I added.

'Are you serious, Lottie?' She sounded incredulous. 'What about your teaching job?' Her voice rose. 'And what would you do in Venice?'

'I'd like to take a break from work. Learn Italian. Then find work. It's an international city. I'm sure there are lots of opportunities.' I went on to explain about my idea of buying her share of the flat once Gran's house had sold.

'I don't know, darling. I'll need to speak with your father. I'll give you a ring later, after he gets home from the office and we've had a chat.'

'Okay,' I released a breath. 'I'll wait for your call.'

By my calculations, Dad should be home in about three hours. I'd be on tenterhooks until then.

Alex dropped by and asked how I'd got on. I gave him a break-down of my conversation with Mum, then, to keep myself occupied, I offered to babysit Gabriel by the pool.

Alex agreed and Gabriel squealed with delight, waving his dad off without protest when Alex had fetched his swim shorts. Gabriel and I spent the morning swimming, playing with his beach ball, and sunbathing. Shortly before midday, I took him to his dad. All the while, Gabriel had chatted nonstop in Italian and I'd talked to him in English. Somehow, using sign language, we'd communicated. He was a great kid and I was looking forward to getting to know him better.

Later, I sat in the cool of my sitting room and waited, every nerve in my body on edge. Come on, Mum. Ring, I repeated over and over in my head. I took Gran's prayer book from my suitcase and held it to my chest, willing her spirit to help me.

At last, when I was about to give up waiting and call Mum myself, my ringtone sounded.

Dad's voice came on first. He told me he'd put the call on loudspeaker. 'Are you sure about this, Lottie? I know you're an adult and can make your own decisions, but have you really thought this through?'

'I've always felt like a fish out of water in England,' I said. 'Growing up in Hong Kong has made me feel a foreigner much of the time.' I took a quick breath. 'Somehow, that's not the case in Italy. People here are so warm and welcoming. I've made friends. Good friends.'

'What about this Alex chap? Is he more than "just a friend"?' Mum butted in. 'Is he the real reason why you want to live in Venice?'

'He's part of it,' I admitted. 'It's early days. We've fallen for each other, yes, but we haven't made any plans for the future.'

'I don't want you to get hurt again,' Mum said, her tone worried.

I only just realised I hadn't thought about Gary for some time. Hadn't heard from him either, thank God.

'Mum, Alex is the complete opposite to Gary. He would never hurt me.' Of that, I was sure.

'Well, if you're certain. Your father and I have discussed it, and the last thing we need is the hassle of an apartment in Venice. Nor do we want you to buy us out.'

My heart sank. *She wanted to sell Gran's flat.*

'So,' Mum said. 'We've decided to let you have it outright.'

I couldn't believe what I was hearing. 'You mean, the apartment is mine?'

'You'll be responsible for paying back Signor Rossi all

the expenses he and his uncle have incurred over the years, mind you,' Dad said. 'But hopefully you'll have enough left from your share of the sale of your grandmother's house in London to tide you over until you're settled.'

I couldn't stop smiling. 'Thank you both so, so much. This means the world to me.'

'I rather gathered that,' Mum laughed. 'Right, your father and I are going out to dinner. Call me when you're back in London. In the meantime, I'll get in touch with our solicitor and find out how much progress he's made with probate of your grandmother's estate.'

I said goodbye and shut down my phone, so thrilled I couldn't resist letting out a whoop. Then, I took a deep, calming breath and sauntered over to the hotel to tell Alex.

A week later, Alex took me to Marco Polo airport to see me off for my flight to Heathrow. After I'd checked in my luggage, he walked with me to the departure gate. We looped our arms around each other's waist, hugging as if our lives depended upon it.

Yesterday he'd gone with me to visit Rosina, and I'd finally asked her how she'd obtained Grandad's address.

'I bumped into Captain Roden when he'd called at the villa in search of Leonessa after the war had ended,' she'd said. 'It was Signora Bernardi's day off and I served the Count and David, as we all knew him, with coffee.' She paused. 'I'd barely left the room when he came storming out. I realised Count Corradini had told him what had happened to Elena. I asked David for his address and he gave it to me. I had no idea that your grandmother would move to England. I simply asked on a whim, and he was such a gentleman he gave it to me.' Rosina gazed warmly at Alex and me. 'Seeing you before me now, it cheers my old heart. Elena suffered so much but she found love.' Rosina sighed deeply. 'I met my husband on Monte Grappa, too. His battle name was Falcon. We celebrated sixty years of marriage before he passed away.' Alex and I had expressed our sympathy and thanked her for her revelations before taking our leave. 'Please, keep in touch,' she'd said, and we promised we would do so.

Simonetta had already picked up Gabriel in the morning, and Alex and I spent last night together, our bodies entwined, loving each other until we were satiated.

He held me against him now, his face buried in my hair, and he squeezed me so tightly I felt every breath. I memorised the scrape of his cheeks, the press of his lips, the taste of his mouth, and the salt of his tears. He kissed me like he'd kissed me the first time and every time after that, pouring himself out, holding nothing back. But this kiss was flavoured with the bitterness of saying goodbye mixed with the sweetness of a new hope.

He looked deep into my eyes. 'Come back to me soon, *amore mio.*'

'I will. I promise, *tesoro*,' I said.

Epilogue

Charlotte, Venice, 2011

My mobile pings with a message from Alex. *I'm on the vaporetto.* Our signal that I should go and meet him at the Zitelle stop.

A year has gone by since the first time I saw this apartment, and what a year it has been. A roller-coaster ride of resigning from my job at Tower High, selling Gran's place, then moving to Venice and going through a ton of bureaucratic paperwork to get her flat transferred to my name.

Before I left London, after I'd finished at the school and was waiting for the sale of the Islington house to complete, I took a "Teaching English as a Foreign Language" course, thinking it might come in handy, and it has. Edoardo Rossi put out word at the university, and I now have more than enough pupils who come to me for private lessons to improve their speaking skills. The money I'm earning means I don't need to dig into what's left of my inheritance in order to get by.

Nearly seven decades of bills and property taxes ate into a big chunk of my funds, and I spent another substantial sum on a new kitchen, bathroom, decorating and other modernisation work. But I don't regret it for one second. I'm completely at home here and I love it. When I'm not teaching English, I'm involved in a research project. I also study Italian online then go out and about in the community to practise what I've learnt, picking up a fair amount of the Venetian dialect at the same time.

Edoardo and his wife, Ada, have been beyond brilliant. They've become like adoptive parents to me and have taken me under their wings, introducing me to their son and daughter, both married and living on Giudecca, and they, in turn, have introduced me to their friends. They've all been incredibly friendly and I don't feel alone at all, although I'm lonely for Alex and miss him when he isn't here and when I'm not in Sant'Illaria on a short visit.

He's been amazing, respecting my wish to live apart from him for the time being, while I adapt to my new life. He's even started calling me his "girl from Venice", after leaning from Rosina that's what David used to call Leonessa.

I feel Gran's presence all the time, her courage infusing me and helping me become more like her, I hope. She was such a wonderful woman. I respect the fact that she needed to cut herself off from her past, and I think Mum has come to terms with it too. Everyone has their coping mechanisms.

Leonessa's story has inspired me to research Italian women Resistance fighters, with the aim of writing about them one day. I might even study for a history master's degree at Ca' Foscari, but my Italian will need to become a whole lot better first. So many plans reel in my head that I'm buzzing with them.

The past is never far from my mind, however. I keep Gran's prayer book in my bedside table drawer with Rosina's letters, which I've now learnt enough Italian to read. And I've framed a print of the photograph taken at the Doge's Palace, which I've hung on my bedroom wall next to a photo of Gran and her parents, found tucked away in her chest of drawers. She must have been in her early teens and my great-grandparents in their early forties, posing formally in front of a potted palm, stern expressions on their faces as befitted the period in which they lived. My heart goes out to them every time I look at the print, and I gave a copy to Mum when she visited with Dad last month.

Mum and I talked at length about Gran, and Mum said she felt better about herself now she knew more of her mother's past. Mum and Dad loved the apartment and promised to visit often.

That's when Alex and I told them we're engaged to be married and will tie the knot at the Sant'Eufemia church in Giudecca next year, followed by a reception at the luxury Cipriani Hotel. It's the earliest we could book it, but we don't mind. We're fully committed to each other and the wedding will only be to show our commitment to the world. We just hope Rosina and Marta will live long enough to attend. Giorgio passed away in January; he'd been unwell for some time. Gran's two formidable friends, however, are made of sterner stuff like she was; I see them regularly and admire them so much.

I sigh to myself as I think about Gary. He contacted me after I'd returned to London, suggesting once more that we meet up. It was a relief to finally give him the push, telling him I'd met someone else. The last I heard, Gary and Mel had got back together again. I hope they'll be happy. As George Sand said, 'There is only one happiness in life. To love and be loved.' And I've found that happiness with Alex; he's all I want and need.

As for the future, I'll probably live full-time in Sant'Illaria eventually, keeping the apartment in Venice for holidays when Alex and I decide to try for a baby. But we aren't in any rush; I'm only twenty-five and Alex seven years older. He has Gabriel and I've grown to love the boy as if he were my own—just like I've grown to love my new Italian family. Francesca is like a sister to me, and Lorenzo the brother I never had.

When I think back to the old Lottie, to how miserable she was, it's hard to recognise myself I'm so happy. Not simply happy, but confident. Nothing fazes me or holds me back anymore. All I do is remember Gran and her courage and anything in my way feels so insignificant.

I hold on to my new life and treasure it, not taking it for granted. It might be clichéd but it's true. Life is full of ups and downs, but with Alex I'll ride the storms of the future, and I pray he'll be by my side for all the years to come.

I pick up my keys from the table by the front door and let myself out of the apartment, skipping down the stairs and onto the fondamenta below. It's a short walk to the Zitelle waterbus station, and there he is, looking as handsome as ever in his trademark open-neck white shirt and black jeans.

'How is my girl from Venice?' he asks, sweeping me into his arms.

'Loving my life,' I reply, lifting my face to receive his kiss.

I hope you enjoyed *The Girl from Venice* and if you did, I'd be hugely grateful if you'd take the time to write a short review. I'd love to hear what you think, and it will help new readers decide whether to take the plunge and discover this and others of my books.

The Girl from Portofino, my next novel about a World War II Italian woman partisan, will release in January 2022.

AUTHOR'S NOTE

The first time I visited Venice, I was a child of ten. I still have the black and white photos I took with my Brownie camera of my brother and sister feeding the pigeons in Saint Mark's Square and of our gondola ride up the Grand Canal. The city captivated me then and it still enchants me now.

I was born and brought up in Hong Kong, the child of expatriate parents like Charlotte in *The Girl from Venice.* Mum and Dad bought a property near Asolo in the Veneto in the mid-sixties and it became our second home.

I'll never forget my initial impression of the Avenue of Martyrs in nearby Bassano del Grappa. The shock and the horror when I saw those trees. But it was the farmers next door whose story impressed me most. They'd hidden a Jewish couple during the war, and I based Rosina's family on them.

My fictional village of Sant'Illaria is inspired and founded upon the villages at the foothills of Monte Grappa, all of which lost young men in horrific circumstances in 1944. The events of *The Girl from Venice* are all built upon on what happened in Venice and the Veneto during that dark period of Italian history. Any mistakes or embellishments to the actual record, where I've filled in the historical gaps or furthered the story, are well intentioned and completely my own. Names of real people have been changed, out of respect for their memory. Lidia is a fictional character, as are all the main protagonists in this story.

I have read the following books for inspiration and information:

Maria de Blasio Wilhelm, The Other Italy, The Italian Resistance in World War II

Lorenzo Capovilla, Federico Maistrello, Assalto al Monte Grappa

Paolo Maggetto, Roberto Zonta, I massacri nazifascisti a sud del Monte Grappa

Luigi Meneghello, The Outlaws

Caroline Moorehead, A House in the Mountains, The Women Who Liberated Italy from Fascism

Sonia Residori, Filippo Simioni, Partigiani del Grappa

Maria Teresa Sega, Voci di Partigiane Venete

David Stafford, Mission Accomplished, SOE and Italy 1943-1945

Maria Teresa Tomada, Volti abbronzati e fucili arrugginiti, il diario di Filomena Dalla Palma, Gina, partigiana sul Grappa

H. W. Tilman, When Men & Mountains Meet

ACKNOWLEDGMENTS

I have so many people to thank for help in writing this book.

Firstly, *grazie mille* to my chief editor, John Hudspith, truly "a doctor of words, a surgeon of writing". Also thanks to Trenda Lundin, my content editor, for her comments on the final draft.

Huge thanks to my beta readers: Ann, Fiona, Joy, Luisa and Nico for their helpful feedback on my chapters.

I owe an enormous debt of gratitude to my cover designer, Jane Dixon Smith, for her patience during various changes, and for being able to incorporate the painting of Venice by my wonderfully talented sister, Clodagh Norton, into her fabulous design.

And last, but not least, I'd like to thank Ellie Yarde of The Coffee Pot Book Club for taking on the promotion of *The Girl from Venice.*

ABOUT THE AUTHOR

Siobhan Daiko is a British romantic historical fiction author. A lover of all things Italian, she lives in the Veneto region of northern Italy with her husband, a Havanese dog and two rescued cats. After a life of romance and adventure in Hong Kong, Australia and the UK, Siobhan now spends her time, when she isn't writing, enjoying the *dolce vita* near Venice. You can find out more about her books at https://siobhandaiko.org/

BOOKS BY SIOBHAN DAIKO

The Orchid Tree

Lady of Venezia

Veronica COURTESAN

Printed in Great Britain
by Amazon